Visions of Love

2nd Edition

Kezia Davis

Visions of Love

2nd Edition

Queen E Publication

www.keziadavis.com

Visions of Love 2nd Edition
Copyright © 2013 by Kezia Davis

Cover Designer: AMB Branding Design
Cover Designer Editor: Ibadullah Sadfar
Book Interior Designer: Anca Popescu
Distributed by: CreateSpace, a DBA of On-Demand Publishing, LLC

Library of Congress Control Number: 2013920762
ISBN-13: 978-0615919485
ISBN-10: 0615919480

Printed in the United States of America

10 9 8 7 6 5 4 3 2 1

This is a work of fiction. Any references or similarities to actual events, real people, living or dead, or to real locales are intended to give the novel a sense of reality. Any similarity in other names, characters, places, and incidents is entirely coincidental.

This book is dedicated to everyone who is lost in love, seeking love, and needing to be loved.

"For God so loved the World… That He gave His ONLY Begotten Son…" John 3:16

Contents

Acknowledgments

What can I say about Him… He is the love of my life… He loved me before I knew what love was… He loved me before I was created in the womb of my mother… It is, He… **The LORD GOD ALMIGHTY!** *What can I say about a Creator filled with glory and magnificence… A God that can be in one place but at another place all at the same time… He is the manifestation of Christ in the flesh… What can I say about a love so strong, that He is willing to come down from the throne of Heaven and sacrifice Himself for me… There's are no words… there are no letters… so I'll just say Thank You Lord and I Love You!*

There's something magical… something unexplainable about having someone in your life that has literally been so close to the heart, that they know exactly how loud the heart beats… She knows the strength of my love because she has been in the inner depth of my womb… To the one who inspired me to keep living, to keep pushing, to keep striving, and to remain strong, **ALLANAH,** *you are truly a gift, wrapped up and presented to me with a bow, from God Himself. I love you and over the course of my life, I realized that I needed you more than you need me. It is because of you that I made the choice to change my life, and allowed God to save my life.*

I can go on and on about my Guardian Angel… everyone has or has had someone in their life that has been a light in their lives, if not, then I feel sorry for you… My grandmother, no… my mother, **QUEEN ESTER,** *reminds me everyday of how blessed my childhood was. Her compassion, her sacrificial love, her strength, and her courage reminds me so much of the "Virtuous Woman" that is spoken of in Proverbs… she is the exact representation of who Maya Angelou speaks about in her poem "Phenomenal Woman". I thank God for sharing her with me, for loving me enough to bless me with her. Sing with the Angels! Rest Peacefully!*

To my sisters, **AUDRIANNA & FAITH,** *we have our own lives, our own personal struggles, our own personalities, and our own views, yet we compliment each other. You can choose your friends, but you can't choose your sisters, I'm blessed to have a two-for-one special I love the both of you!*

You can't make up for all the lost times, but you have done a heck of a job *trying. To my father, **GUYRE**, thanks for your love, your support, and your much needed advice. I'm grateful to call you "daddy"…*

*To my adopted parents, **BRENDA & TONY SR.**, you are as close to me as any parents should be. Thanks for your open arm, your love, and your support.*

*To my second mom, **HELEN**, if it had not been for your positive influence in my life, no telling where I would be. You will never know how much your time, your love, and your presence in my life impacted me. God has been truly looking out for me… Because I was not only blessed with one angel… but two…*

*To my adopted brothers, **DALONTAY, TONY JR, & LIONEL**, each of us have our own special bond. Thank you for accepting me into the flock, thanks for your love, and for caring enough about me as if I came from the same womb as you. I love y'all!*

***JAMES**, we may not always see the eye-to-eye on many things, but when it comes to our daughter we're both on one accord. I thank you for being the best father you can be and for having my back even when you didn't have to. I'm sincerely grateful for you!*

*Some people aren't blessed to have someone in their life that is willing to remain loyal to you in spite of your weaknesses and flaws…. I'm lucky to have someone like that in this lifetime. **COURTNEY**, it's been a long journey and the path is still long. But I thank you for your love, your patience, your faith and for believing in me. You're still holding on, with me in mind. I love you!*

*Never thought I'd have a girlfriend that I could call a sister, let alone bestfriend… **LATOYA**, over the years, we have created a beautiful bond. We've been through it all together… the test, the trials, and the triumphs. Thank you for the ear, for the advice, and for the love. Thank you for being loyal, for being real, and for being true… I love you girlie!*

*I would also like to thank the **WHOLE DAVIS FAMILY!** Family is everything and I love you all and all my **FRIENDS** and everyone else who has touched my life in their own special way.*

I hope that the message in this book, motivate you, uplift you, and bless you to be a blessing!

Kezia Davis

Prologue

There are an array of assumptions, perspectives, and philosophies of how one defines love. Each person may have their own idea of what love is, what it does, and what it looks like. I often hear many people say "love hurts" or "love can make you do some crazy things". It is not love that hurts, but it is rejection that stings you. It's loneliness that shatters emotions, it is uncertainty that pulls you back into a slumber of fear and doubt. It is the people who you choose to give access to your internal house that can wreck havoc on the heart. Healthy love is not crazy love, but it is one's actions or choices that they make in "the name of love" that defines the craziness. Real, pure, and natural love is so mind boggling that one may not be able to explain it. It massages the heart, give comfort to the soul, and fill empty and broken spaces. It's a mystery to me, but I thank God that I can identify it. From the world's view, love means to have strong feelings to feel affection for. However, from the Biblical view, love is patient, it is kind, and it does not envy or boast. God is love…

Love covers a multitude of sin. For "love bears all things, believes all things hopes all thing and endures all things" (1 Corinthians 13:7). Love covers any pain, any loneliness, any fear, and any doubt. For God is love… When pain sets in, God is there to give you peace, He will lighten your burdens and comfort you. But even through the pain He will give you strength. Pain is there to teach you, to build you, and to press you into the arms of the One who loves you most… When you're lonely, He says, "I am with you always, to the very end of the age" (Matthew 28:20). When you're in fear, He says "Fear not, for I am with you; be not dismayed, for I am your God, I will help you, I will uphold you with My righteous right hand" (Isaiah 41:10). When in doubt, God encourages you not to lose heart. For all things are possible and know that if you have faith in God, He will lead you.

God never intends to bring pain, disruption, or confusion to no one. His love intends to build, rejuvenate, revive, and liberate.

It is safe to say that one's perception of love is based on their own experiences influenced by what they learned along the or their ideas of what love ought to be, what it should look like, and what they've viewed love to be by others around them. It is unfeasible for anyone to know authentic love if they've never experienced the Creator of love. Yes, everyone have their own makings and dissimilar definitions of love… Yet, some will never take the time to explore and understand the true meaning or it's true source.

I've discovered that many people have a comical way of how they perceive love to be. There are some characters that will do a lot of crazy things for "love" (and I say that loosely).

For example:

There are some women who will promiscuously dishonor their temple (their body). Allowing any man to sexually use and abuse the most delicate and sacred part of their body. Some females often gravitate towards this behavior because they think that they can find fulfillment in the one who they entrusted themselves to. Sex can easily be confused as love. Females are emotional beings, and feel the need to express all of themselves to show how they feel. Often time's intimacy is confused with sexual gratification and lust is confused for love. And most men are not as "emotionally expressive" as women. Sex is a hobby, a goal, and a mission for some men. Some men do not have intentions to caress the heart, but to caress the flesh. They work their charm and pretty soon you caught up in the magic of their sweet, persuasive, and tantalizing words and your legs end up wrapped around their waist. But then you are mad because he doesn't live you a little note on your pillow the next morning or doesn't call you anymore. Instead of getting treated, you get tricked.

Fiona… Fiona… Fionnnaaa… why expect a knight in shining armor to slay the dragon (which can be the need inside of you that needs love that you missed from your daddy or the feelings of self-doubt, low self-esteem, low self-worth) and grant you "true loves first kiss", when you're constantly waking up with Shrek? Shrek may have intentions on getting in, getting out, and keep on moving. But then, you have some women have that "act like woman, and think like a man" attitude. There is no shame in their game... they're not looking for a ride in the sunset, only for a roll in the hay. Ignorance proceeds itself. And you wonder why your price tag label says "discount". One of the greatest loves of all is to love yourself. Live in integrity and embrace the value in you. It is okay to wait. It is okay to clink, clink... lock it down (in my Madea voice). I mean, why just stop with dinner and a movie, aim towards, cars, houses, and his last name. If you don't respect yourself, then why expect respect from someone else...

Since women like to play in character (based off their media outlets) I must speak in their language.

Okay... *Let's start with Miss Ring around the Rosie . . . You go looking for love in all the wrong places and faces, trying to find a love of your own. A love that you can't give to yourself, a love you didn't get from daddy, or just to be in the company of a man. It doesn't matter; you'd rather have a piece of a man, then no man at all.*

If you can't be by yourself and enjoy your own company, then something is wrong with that. I can't fathom how someone is not able to be by themselves and think that being with somebody else will make a difference. Alone does not mean lonely. Man cannot complete anything that was already completed by God. If anything, fulfilling completeness is found in God. Then when you get the man, you find out that you're still empty. And on top of that you're miserable too because he wasn't what you thought and being with him is worse then being alone. Learn how to live with yourself, love yourself and enjoy being in your company. I'd rather be by myself and do GOOD by myself instead of being with a man that I'm not sure whether he loves me or not.

*And you Miss Destiny's Child, who wants to cater to her man... You'll move him in, feed him, clothed him, put money in his pockets, let him lie around all day in **your** house and ride around all night in **your** car while you work like a dog trying to support his sorry behind. You'll accept all of his ways because you think maybe if you love him a little harder than he'll change.*

Listen, with **acceptance comes continuance**... If you continue to accept what he does than he'll continue to do what he's doing. A man won't change unless he wants to change or feel he has to. If he loved you then he wouldn't need to change because he wouldn't do anything that needs to be changed. For the record, there is nothing wrong with showing your man how much you appreciate him, but he must equally show his appreciation. I have seen many women put up with a lot of things just to be please their man. They are so fearful of competition that they feel that they have to lose themselves. Listen… if the man wants to leave, then he is going to go. If he had canine tendencies when you met him, then rest assured doggie treats will not keep him from straying. We often ask why men cheat, but we failed to answer as women, why do we allow them the permission, the ability, and the access to become cheaters…

Then there is Miss Ghetto Fabulous… You'll trade in your food stamps and spend your whole welfare check (your kids money) lacin' your man while you parade around like a clown in polyester and pleather; while he's stylin' and profilin' in the latest gear with another woman.

See this goes back to ignorance, mental instability, and the lack of knowledge. I solely believe in the notion "if a man doesn't work he doesn't eat". I've never been the type to put my needs and my child's needs on hold to focus on the needs of a man. The government provides financial support to those who are in need of financial support to help families, but you have so many people who abuse the system and then rebel when the system starts noticing. If you are with a man and still need financial assistance from the government, then it is time for you to do some spring cleaning.

Need I go on? Yes, I must go on, I don't want to leave nobody out.

And you Miss 007 (double-o-seven)… these are the type of women who will stalk a man to try to keep him. You'll slash his tires, put sugar in his tank, break into his house to destroy his stuff, and then throw a brick into his window. You just have to make sure you're known. You'll prank call or even harass his wife or other woman; all in the name of love.

Never allow anyone to take you out of character. You are doing too much... If it takes all of that then, maybe it's time for you to find a new hobby.

And you Miss Night Prowler . . . You'll drive around all night trying to spot his ride, and sit out there until sunrise and wait until he come out. Just to see who he comes out with. And even when you see it with your own eyes you'll still let him talk your dress up and your panties down.

Surely he can't be that good... I don't like the idea of sharing. It is not like you can enjoy it by yourself because he's sharing it with somebody else. It makes it so easy for him to keep doing what he is doing, and it makes it so unhealthy for you because he can end up bring you home a sexually transmitted disease (STD). And when that happens, you want to have a temper tantrum over something you accepted. You sealed the deal and made it acceptable when you kept taking him back. You have to love you above anything else, rest assured, he loves him and anything else that "pleases" him.

And let's not forget Miss Inspector Gadget . . . You'll drive yourself crazy checking his pockets, wallet, cell phone, credit cards, checking account, collars for lip stick stains, smelling his clothes for unknown perfume, and even look in his underwear for sex stains.

You have worked yourself up an appetite. "Seek and you shall find". So why are you mad once you find what you seek?

And last but not least. Miss Lonely on the Holidays . . . You don't mind having someone that does not belong to you. You like them married. You have hopes that one day he will leave his wife and that you will no longer be #2. You get mad when he has to go home or when he is not with you on the holidays. But what in the world you thought he would be?

I believe women often date married men not because they are intrigued by the idea of having something that belongs to someone else, but having a man that they assume is "ready made"... Ready for commitment, ready for a family-- already groomed to be a husband. They often times are attracted by the idea that all the good men are taken and so they just have to have that good man. Wow... he's good, yet he's cheating on his wife. It is quite interesting to me how God created a woman. They are created to be suitable and to be the company of a man.

They already have it in them to be a wife. There are so many factors that play apart in what a woman expects or wants from a man. T.D. Jakes is such an inspiration to me. I was listening to one of his sermons and this is what I took from his message based on how I understood the message: Women were first girls, before they reached womanhood. During this time they grew up on the "hoopla" around them—soap operas, romance novels, movies, and love music. So they often aim to seek out men that can match up with what they have seen in the movies, what they have read about, and what they have heard in songs.

They are oblivious to the fact that movies, books, and songs are built up on fictitious elements to create a story. Here is a reality check for those of you with your drawn out, impracticable lists (you know that list)… THAT MAN DOESN'T EXIST.

You want perfection when there is no such thing as a perfect human being. There is nothing wrong with high expectations, but you must be able to accept the humanness of man. You want a man to become just like you imagined and no matter how hard u pray, wish, dream, search, fast, and put drops of "holy" oil in his collard greens, he still want be exactly how you imagined. You have to be able to understand the architect in order to understand any man (rather man or woman). You see, man, neither male nor female, is created to be what we (as humans) imagined, but what GOD imagined. He has a purpose, a gift, and a help mate for each individual. See, your imagination may be influenced by media material. Your imagination is no more real than the books you read, the movies you see, and the songs you hear.

Then, you sit back disappointed, disgusted, and angry with your boyfriend or husband because they didn't meet up to your unrealistic expectations. So you keep looking, trying on men like you try on panties, searching for something you'll never obtain. Until you let go of the childhood imagination; that formulated dream... you'll continue searching. It is important to know your architect (God) in order to discover what He has imagined for you. Make a decision with Him in mind. Want what God wants for you. He has to delete that hard drive that you have, which has all kinds of downloaded information that will not be essential to your processor. It is wise to ask Him to be your teacher, your guide, your movie, your song, and your soap opera. You need a new way of thinking that doesn't leave you playing the leading role in *Day's of Our Lives*, a Disney movie, the main character in a romance novel, or as the leading lady in a music video.

Ladies teach your children that the fairy tale books they read is fiction, the songs they listen to is for entertainment, the movies they watch is a form of acting, and Barbie and Ken are *just* dolls.

"Beyond the Infatuation Phase"

1

MAMA SAID there would be days like this. She told me marriage was not as easy as saying "I do" and not as simple as jumping a broom. There is more to a marriage then instant attraction, the bliss during the honeymoon, and the butterflies you feel as newly weds. There's not always days of sunshine, waterfalls, and rainbows, but there will be some days when the sun do not shine, when the clouds gets dark, and the forecast predicts that a hurricane is nearby. But what about the unpredicted storms, the one's that just sneak up on you that you don't have your umbrella for or a safe place to go and find shelter? Then there are times when you can see signs that a storm is coming, but you never know exactly when the rain is going to fall.

I felt a storm a brewing when Trevor started changing on me. The warning signs were there, standing right in front of me, but I ignored them and decided to proceed anyway. The late nights, early meetings, and secret phone calls had my antennas standing straight up. But I told myself that my husband wouldn't have the audacity to be that stupid, that crazy, and that low-down. But that feeling inside of me… you know the feeling we women get, that woman's intuition, was screaming "Wake up girl! He's cheating. Never think that he's incapable of it. Yes, you have the ring, the kid, and the house, but that doesn't mean you can control his choices."

The Holy Spirit was guiding me, pushing me to pray for my husband and for our marriage. I didn't get in it to quit. I promised myself that I if I ever got married that it would definitely be with a man that I was head over-hills in love with, because I would never get a divorce. I strongly believe in the sanctity of marriage and divorce has never been my style. Call me a little old fashion, but I believe that divorce is a sin and that if a person does not have the strength to deal with the bad and the good parts of marriage, then it is wise that they never marry. However, I also believe that a man ought to respect, properly love, and reverence their wife, just as the wife ought to with the husband.

Marriage is about two people coming together, unifying as one. I AM (God) took a rib out of the side of Adam. This means that Eve was intended to be by his side, not behind him. One is not superior over the other, but a helpmate to each other. Yes, the husband is the head over his wife, but God is the head over the husband. Divorce is the shattering of the dreams, of hope, and of the future of two people who stood before God and vowed that they would become one flesh in unity. It is the breaking of a filament that opens up a wound that can not easily be healed. That's why the Bible says a man must cling to his wife and wife to their husband, because there is a sense of oneness that occurs that compliments both of them beyond human comprehension.

See, marriage was not designed by what man *wanted* it to be, but what God *intended* for it be. Somehow, people have found a way of eliminating what God intended for marriage to be and instead, they have created their own rules, guidelines, and principles on what they think marriage ought to be. What God put together, let no man put asunder. But the mistake is when we chose to put something together that was never in God's planning in the first place, and then we question God about why things didn't work out. When we realize that the man/woman is not what we imagined or what we initially wanted we throw in the towel.

You see as girls, we grow up playing house with our little play kitchen sets and our Barbie dolls, waiting for Ken to come home so that we can bake him something in our EasyBake ovens. But little boys don't. They are taught to play with race cars, big trucks, and action figures. So we find ourselves eager to play house without building a foundation to place the house on. See some men don't mind playing house as long as they are not writing the check for the mortgage. The mistake is when we give men too much access, allowing them to have too many opportunities, and too many choices to choose from.

Nowadays, young girls, young ladies, and women do not have enough integrity to wait for someone who is worthy of their sacred place. Some are even bold enough to invade into a space that is already taken. I never understood women who wanted another woman's husband. I never understood why they never could understand that what they thought they had was never theirs in the first place. See, the man is entitled to his wife, not his mistress. Then women get all hung up and hung over, because the man devastates her with the already revealing news that he wants to stay with his wife.

Adultery is something that definitely does not sit well with me. There's nothing worst then a cheating husband, but there is something so disconcerting about those who choose to cheat with a married man. Many people say that often times men cheat because of what they are missing at home. But what is the excuse for some who are getting everything they ever could need at home? It's not always about the lack of what the wife does not give, but it is about the flesh that rises up in the man that convinces them that what they have at home isn't enough.

Some men cheat because it is in their nature to cheat. They are selfish, driven by lustful desires and lack of self-control. It is easy for them to say no to the one who holds the palace all together, but find it irresistible to turn down a woman that doesn't hold the key. Some men (and women) say "I do" without knowing what they are saying "I do" to. Indeed, the concept of marriage is perfect, but it is when damaged material is chosen that we end up with risky disappointing results. You see, once you have been with a man for a long time, you know their patterns and their habits. They are predictable creatures.

They are so predictable, that the slightest change can be noticed. What really started the alarms in my head to ring out of control was when he all of a sudden started making up excuses as to why he didn't feel like having sex. It would have not been so unsettling if Trevor didn't have such a high sex drive. Of course I didn't want to believe that my husband was cheating. I fought tooth and nails trying to get myself to think of other solutions. But that intuition or was it the Holy Spirit, was screaming truths at me that I closed my ears to. I didn't want to hear what neither one had to say.

I rather not know, because to know would kill me, but not knowing is driving me crazy. So instead of focusing on what Trevor wasn't doing, I was focusing on what I was doing to keep him from coming home to me at a decent hour. I told myself that maybe it was my attitude lately. No man likes a nagging wife. Then I looked in the mirror to examine myself. I did gain a few extra pounds; my goal was to work on that. Then I looked through my drawers and in my closet and examined my clothes. Maybe I needed to change the way I dressed. I made a reminder to go get a few pieces of lingerie. Maybe that's what it is… I'm too boring in the bedroom, which explains why he doesn't want to have sex with me.

"Yes, that's it." I said to myself as if a light bulb came on.

I bet that is why Trevor has changed. I am not doing anything to make things exciting for him. Instead of waiting, I decided to go to Vikki and let her know all my secrets. I was going to find something that will make me blush and make him realize what he's been missing. I parked into nearest parking space at the mall and walked inside of Victoria's Secret on a mission to find something that would ignite a spark in my husband. As I was browsing the isles, looking from one piece of revealing article to the next, I find myself confused. Obviously the clerk must have sense my uncertainty.

"Hey Miss, can I help you find something?" She said, with a welcoming smile on her face.

"That obvious, huh." I said, a little embarrassed.

"Oh, don't worry about it, you'd be surprised how many come in here with the same look you have, but I'm going to help you find something that will make your boo want to take a bite." She implied, winking at me.

She had me try on several pieces and after trying on countless of items, I settled for a cream and light beige stain and lace cami set and sexy ruby red pleated stain and lace gown. The items were classy and revealed enough that would make him wonder. When I got home, I made a candle-lit dinner, lit some candles around the Jacuzzi, and poured some vanilla-scented bubble bath as the steamy running water caused bubbles to form. I put in a mix CD that had songs by Kenny G, Patti Labelle, Teddy Pendergrass, and many other artists that is appropriated for this night of bliss. I decided to put on the ruby red stain lace gown.

As I was walking down stairs, I heard Trevor's keys unlock the door. I was filled with excitement and couldn't wait until he saw me. I stood at the stairs in a sexy pose waiting for him to open the door. When he opened the door a look of shock and then what seem to have changed into displeasure, yes, I was sure of it, displeasure that appeared a cross his face. He looked me up and down and all of a sudden I felt a bit exposed, embarrassed even. My own husband was making me feel uncomfortable. After looking at the perfectly set dinner table, he took off his tie and walked up the stairs.

He didn't say a word to me. Next thing I heard was the door shutting. My heart melted in my chest. Tears begin to stream down my face as I blew out every candle, put the food that I'd just prepared in the fridge, and let out the water that was in the Jacuzzi. I looked in the mirror and the mascara was running down my cheeks. My eyes were puffy from crying and my face was flushed. I scrubbed the makeup off my face, took my hair down and put it in a pony tail. Then I slipped of the beautiful gown and changed into a comfortable pair of cotton pajamas.

Trevor was sound a sleep as if he didn't have a care in the world. I got in the bed beside him, trying not to wake him up. I laid beside him and cried silently and there was that voice again… tormenting me… telling me what I didn't want to hear. Pain turned into anger and I surprised myself when I suddenly turned around, took my feet and pushed Trevor out of the bed.

"Whaa…" He yelped, alarmed by the sudden impact.

I just looked at him, as tears ran down my face, but I was seething. I could feel the heat rising up in me.

"What is wrong with you woman?" He looked at me like I was crazy.

"We need to talk." I motioned, ignoring his facial expression.

"It's almost 2 o'clock in the morning, we'll talk later." He said, picking his self up off the floor and getting back into bed.

"I don't want to talk later; I want to do it now." I demanded.

"And I said later now leave me." He said dismissively, as he rolled over.

I got out of the bed and went into what I called my "secret closet", which was a small room across the hall from our bedroom. I read a few Psalms and singed a few hymns. Tears began to fall down my cheeks as I kneeled down to share my pain with my Father.

Lord, let not my anger cause me to sin. Lord please give me Your peace that surpasses all understanding... Let Your warmth fall upon me. Hold me tonight because Lord I need to feel Your loving embrace around me. My heart is breaking and my husband doesn't even care. Forgive him Father. Help mim Lord. Help him be a husband and a friend to me. I know that You will strengthen this marriage. You will fix whatever is broken. I believe that You will work things out for my good. I love You Father, and even now, I give You praise. Weeping may endure for a night but joy is coming in the morning, and Lord I speak it that my joy is coming. Set my mind at ease so that I can sleep peacefully. Amen.

After I prayed, I felt a sense of calmness sweep over me. All I could do was just lay in the center of the floor, close my eyes and let the calmness of the Lord rock me to sleep.

2

THE SUN PEAKED IN from the curtain and invaded my sleep. I squinted and look beside me… Trevor side of the bed was already made up. I looked at the time; I jumped out of our king-sized cherry wood sleigh bed, put on my robe and headed towards the kitchen to make some breakfast. Alana, our fourteen-year-old daughter, decided to stay overnight with her best friend since she was studying for an upcoming test. Since she didn't have any clothes there, she promised she'd be home early in the morning to get ready for school. I walked down the hall towards her room, peaked inside to see if she was ready.

"Good morning mom." She smiled up at me and looked back at the vanity mirror in front of her.

"Sweetheart, hurry up or you're going to be late." I told her.

"Yes mom." She said, as she quickly applied lip gloss on her lips.

She had a combination of me and her father in her. Her light brown complexion comes from her father, he is mixed with black and German, but she gets her long hair and looks from her mother. No offense to her father because he's a very handsome man.

"What you want for breakfast?" I asked her.

"Ummmm . . . . Just surprise me."

"Okkaaaayyy, don't get mad if I just make toast." I said jokingly.

She looked at me as if she knew better.

"You're right." I laughed and headed towards the kitchen.

My little girl is growing up and I am a tad bit scared considering that she'll be interested in boys soon, but in a way I'm looking forward to her becoming a beautiful and respectable young lady. I have a feeling that it'll be a long time before she started paying attention to boys. I overheard her telling one of her friends the other day that liking boys are not her main focus. She stated that her school work was more important. At that moment all I could do was smile and I was relieved because I know I wouldn't have to worry about her at the moment. She's very smart just like her father.

He's always been smart scoring higher than the whole class on his SAT scores and he graduated from Harvard with a 4.0 grade point average. He was accepted as partner at one of the top criminal law firms in Atlanta, by age 28, he opened up his own firm, representing celebrities, athletes, and businessmen. Not only does he handle criminal cases, but he helps with their legal contracts, etcetera. His career began to sky rocket after he won a case involving some popular football player, who played for the Atlanta Falcons that was on trial for allegedly killing his pregnant girlfriend. Now we live in a million dollar home, with over seven acres of land.

I have a few credentials of my own. I too went to Harvard, so that Trevor and I could be close to one another. After getting my Doctorate Degree in Psychotherapy, I decided to open up my own private practice. Trevor and I initially met in the fifth grade and he would always ask me for a pencil. I already knew he had a pencil because he'd always have one sticking out the side of his ear. Every girl in school liked him and boys were jealous over the fact he was getting so much attention and the girls envied me because all his attention was on me and not them. Even though he was the best player on the basketball team he never let that interfere with his work.

He studied hard and worked hard during practice. I too secretly liked him, but I grew up in a strict Christian home. Boys were out of the question. However, things began to change as I tried to break free from the strict rules of my parents, and made an attempt to branch out and be the me who I wanted to be. I was tired of my parents trying to mold me into who they wanted me to be, I was ready to reconstruct myself while holding on to Jesus all at the same time. I loved the Lord, but I really didn't understand how to fully walk in the righteousness of God. All I knew is what my parents taught me and what the preacher said in the pulpit.

If you are interested in someone, then he would have to be prepared to marry you if he was ready to take it to the next step. So, kissing, touching, feeling, and rubbing was an act of sin, at least that's the way my father put it. My father told me if I'm good enough to sleep with, then I'm good enough to marry. He said I should honor my temple and not just let any somebody dwell up in it. I was excited about going to the 7th grade; I thought I was all grown up— a different school, a new atmosphere, and a new me. All eyes turned towards the door when he walked in the door.

He'd gotten taller over the summer and an yes, cuter. He had an aura that called for attention. He was about 5'9, athletic built, Colgate white teeth, light brown eyes, smooth hazelnut skin with just a hint of milk, and a low-cut fade with deep waves rippling through his soft jet black hair. He reminded me so much of the actor Boris Kodjoe. It was clearly obvious why girls were so into him. I watched as he glided, yes glided, across the room. Maybe it was my imagination, but I could have sworn he was walking in slow motion, in my direction. I was silently praying that he wouldn't come talk to me, but God must was too busy at the time to answer because there he was standing in my face. He was even cuter up close.

"Celeste Morris, you are still the prettiest girl in the school." He said, flashing that smile of his. He had the type of smile that held you captive. But of course, I couldn't let him cast me under his spell.

"Trevor Daniels, you are still full of it. Save the drama and tell me what you want." I said, slamming my locker close.

I may have looked like I did not want to be bothered with him but I was really feeling him. If he wasn't walking behind me he would have seen the huge smile on my face.

"Here we go again; he said catching up with me. Why are you always giving me a hard time?"

"Why are you always in my space?" I said with attitude.

"Because I like you and you know it, but you keep playing hard to get. What have I ever done to you?"

"Nothing, I just don't have time for all the games and you know Trevor Daniels knows how to play those games." I said, arching one of my eye brows.

I knew the type of attention Trevor had and I knew that he most likely had a list of girls that he checked off of it. My father warned me about boys like Trevor. You know the pretty ones with a cute smile and tempting words. He said they weren't interested in but one thing.

"The only game I play is basketball sweetie. If I wanted to play games I'll just go on the court." He said, putting up his hands as if he was shooting a ball.

"Yeah right, like I'm supposed to believe I'm the only girl that interests you." I said, not even entertaining the thought.

"Believe it. You know you look good but it isn't about that. You smart too. I've wanted to talk to you since fifth grade." He said.

"I hear you." I said, but I was beginning to warm up to him.

"I thought you'd be more interested in Brittany. Why me and not her? The captain of the cheerleading squad would look good on your arm." I wanted to know.

"Because Brittany is not Celeste and besides she has a bad attitude that makes you want to slap the mess out of her." He frowned.

I smiled at him and decided to give him a chance, after all, he has been chasing me for some time now it wouldn't hurt to give him a chance. Even though I could hear the chastising voice of my father in my ear, I made every effort of shoving it out.

"Okay." I said giving in.

"Okay what?" He said confused.

"Okay, I'll be your girlfriend, but under one condition… keep those females out of my face. Don't think because I am a church girl that I am weak." I frowned.

Celeste was a natural beauty. She wasn't allowed to wear makeup, but she didn't need it. Her personality screamed beauty. She was a sight to look at on the outside, but that was because the beauty inside shined brightly on the outside. She was about 5'3, slim built, and black mixed with Cherokee Indian. She had a dark tan complexion, long silky dark black curly hair that cascaded down her shoulders, dark brown eyes, and long lashes that naturally curled up. Although many boys tried to talk to her, she didn't give them the time of day. She actually made every effort not to attract too much attention. She never wore revealing clothes and she spent most of her time at the library studying or reading.

Her father always told her education is the key to opening many doors in the future. She and her brother could not bring home anything lesser than a B+, so they excelled in school. It was no surprise when her brother graduated top of his class in medical school. He was now one of the most prestigious medical research scientists in Georgia. Even though she kept to herself, she had two best friends who were very different from her, yet they seem to come together perfectly. Rachael was always told that she could be Reese Witherspoon's little sister and she really could.

Christie was African American, with short brown hair, dark brown eyes, with a caramel complexion. She had a figure like Tyra Banks and a face as beautiful as Naomi Campbell but truth is, they couldn't hold a match to Celeste. Celeste and Christie had been friends since kindergarten and they'd later befriended Rachael in the third grade. The only difference out of the three was both Christie and Rachael was more into boys but their parents was uprooted in their Christianity, strict, and posed a higher standard for education just like Celeste's parents. As a matter of fact, their parents were all friends and went to the same church.

"Deal. You want have to worry about that anyway because you're the only one that'll have my attention." He promised.

I blushed. He took my books out of my hands and walked me to class. From that day on, he'd walk me to each class and later on down the isle. We'd gotten married after we both finished college. Two years later came our beautiful daughter Alana. Its funny how time flies and you find yourself trying to hold on to those memorable moments. Those memorable moments that leave you wondering about the good old days and afraid to discover what the future may hold. The smell of Trevor's cologne distracted me from my thoughts as he brushed against me at the dining room table. He looked GQ smooth in his black Italian suite, olive green dress shirt, black Bell Air's, and on his wrist he sported a platinum Cartier watch incrusted in diamonds.

"Hi pumpkin." He said to Alana, kissing her forehead.

"Hey daddy, did you sleep well?" She asked.

"Barely." He said glaring at me.

I don't know what his problem is all I did was ask him if we could talk, sure I kicked him out of the bed, but he ignored me and went back to sleep. I dared not expressed what I truly wanted to say in front of my child. We agreed that we would never argue around her. I noticed how he intentionally avoided making conversation with me. He decided to make conversation with Alana instead. I sat quietly, listening to their conversation, while I barely ate anything on my plate. If a person could look in our dining room window right now and witnessed what was going on inside, they would of thought we were a perfect family, sitting together having a perfect breakfast.

3

AFTER I TOOK Alana to school, I decided to go pick up a hot cup of coffee from Starbucks. I couldn't start my day without it and I had a long day ahead of me. I couldn't get my mind off of Trevor and his behavior towards me lately. There was a time when he used to call me at least six times a day to see what I was doing. When he used to surprise me with gifts just because and bring me lunch at the office and sit with me discussing his present cases. But now, I can barely get one phone call and when I do it's only when he's calling in to tell me not to wait up because he's "working late", quote on quote. Before I could pick up my cell phone to dial his number a call came in.

"Hello, this is Celeste Daniels speaking." I said professionally.

"Hi, Dr. Daniels, I'm sorry to call you so early." Wilson said apologetically.

Wilson was a client of mine who lost his wife and daughter in a fire two years ago. He's been battling with guilt, blaming himself for the death of his family. He was a successful real estate agent before he began to drown all his sorrows by taking antidepressant medication and eventually put his papers in. Even after seeing me for over a year he still continues to have nightmares about the day of the fire.

"Oh its fine Wilson, I am already out, what can I do for you?" I asked.

"Well, if it's not too much to ask I was wondering if I could come in ten minutes early instead of at eight?"

"Yes, that'll be fine. Is everything okay?" I asked concerned.

"As a matter of fact everything is fine. I didn't have a nightmare last night. This is why I wanted to come early so I can tell you about the dream I had." I could sense a burst of happiness in his voice.

"That's so good to hear and I will be looking forward to hearing it." I said looking at my clock noticing that it was about seven twenty.

When I got in my office I set everything up for my session with Wilson. When he came in he smiled at me and took a seat wearing a pair of khaki Dockers' with a white dress shirt. Wilson put me in the mind of the guy that starred on the TV show "Law & Order: SVU" which plays as a detective that spends more time with his partner than at home, except Wilson looked a bit thinner, considering that he spends more time drinking and less time eating.

"So, it's exciting to hear that you didn't have a nightmare last night." I said, as I wrote the time and date on a pad.

"No, thank God." He smiled, and I could tell he was desperately ready to tell me about the dream.

"And may I ask you what your dream was about?" He sat down on the loveseat beside me and looked at the wall as if he was in deep thought.

"Mariska and Molly were sitting in a field of beautiful flowers, white lilies I believe, but anyway, they were looking at me like they wanted me to join them. It was like we were in a meadow with the most breathtaking scenery I had ever seen. The sky was clear and blue and the sun felt just right." He answered closing his eyes as if he was reliving the moment.

Mariska was his wife and Molly was his daughter. At the time Molly was only five years old when she died and Mariska was thirty-two.

"Molly ran into my arms and held me as tight as she could. And when Mariska kissed me it felt so real and I asked her if it was really her. She smiled at me and told me it was. She grabbed my hand and pulled me towards where they were sitting and we all sat down and talked."

On my pad I jotted down, white lilies, clear sky, and green pasture. When I looked up at him I saw a tear trickle down his cheek. But I didn't say anything I just let him finished what he was saying. As I listened I took the time to scribble down the *breakthrough* in my pad.

"They both kept looking at me and my sweet little girl stared into my eyes and told me that she loved me and that it wasn't my fault. She said she was happy so very happy. And all I could do was hug her and I refused to let her go. And it was like they both vanished into thin air and I woke up holding myself." He said, opening his tear-filled eyes.

"Everything will be okay." I assured him, while giving him a tissue.

"I didn't want to let her go." He looked into my eyes and at that moment I thought I was going to need a tissue as well. The look on his face broke my heart.

"I understand but didn't it feel good to hear your daughter say that it wasn't your fault and that she's happy. Aren't those the words your soul and heart has wanted to hear for so long? Your daughter wants you to be happy and to stop blaming yourself for something you couldn't prevent. Now it's time for you to be at peace and let them rest peacefully." I told him, trying to comfort him.

"I know but how do I begin? I mean, I believe that Jesus will give me rest if I ask, but what if it's me that is afraid to enter into His rest?" He said between tears.

"You have a strong belief in God so you need to allow that same strength to be the driving force in your life. If you're going to believe in Him then you must believe in what He is able to do. Jesus said, "come to me who is heavy laden, and I will give you rest." Don't hinder yourself from walking into your resting place; it is there where you will find the solutions to every problem." I replied.

"How can I get over this?" He said looking at me, hoping that I had the answer.

"What you went through was horrible, but have you ever read the story of Job--. How he lost his family and everything he owned, yet he still trusted God. He still held on to his faith, and to his knowledge about the God he served. That's what you must do. You may have to take things one step at a time, but you have to take those steps in order to walk into the purpose that God has for you. God will not put anything on you that you are not able to bear. And I believe that God has allowed this dream to manifest so that you can get the closure, the peace, and the rest that you so desire to have." I said, placing my hand on top of is.

"I sense that. It's so hard you know. I have prayed and prayed and prayed, asking God to bring my family back, but what I failed to do was ask Him to give me understanding, give me the strength to accept this, and the courage to move forward. I often asked Him why, but like you said Job had a similar story and he still trusted God. Now I ask myself, why not me?" He said smiling at me.

"Yes. Often times we get so caught up in the good things, that when bad things happen, we find ourselves getting out of sync, and out of focus. But God is still the same God, who brought Job out and He is bringing you out, right now. You mentioned that in the dream you saw white lilies, a clear sky, and a green field, right?" I asked for confirmation.

"Yes, yes." He whispered, shaking his head in agreement.

"To dream about lilies is said to mean that it is time to act upon a long-thought upon plan. Further, it indicates that you are coming into a fuller integration of yourself and developing personal balance. It is also a sign that a person is seeking rest, peace and tranquility. White lilies symbolize hope, growth, freedom, process, and development." I was telling him.

"I understand where you are going. It is making sense to me. God is helping me with the help of my family." He said with a bright smile on his face.

"Yes. Think of the clear blue sky and the perfect weather... this represents hope, possibilities, and peace. You know back in ancient times, the Israelites thought of green pastures as a symbol of trusting in God for their daily sustenance. You were in your valley and in the wilderness for so long, that He is trying to remind you that although you have wandered in the desert and have swam in the deepest valley, He is there to sustain you, but you have to trust him."

"The Lord is my Shepherd; I shall not want. He maketh me to lie down in green pastures; He leadeth me beside the still waters. He restoreth my soul, He leadeth me in the paths of righteousness for His name' sake. Yea, though I walk through the valley of the shadow of death, I will fear no evil: For thou art with me." He prayed the 23rd Psalm.

I grabbed his hands, close my eyes, and silently prayed for Him to finally accept the peace that God is trying to give him.

"For God is with me.... My God is with me... Thank you Lord, for being with me." He said over and over again.

And I could have sworn I heard a loud clanking noise as he kept repeating these words over and over again. I could hear the chains falling off of him. He was finally breaking free. He was finally allowing God to set Him free *indeed*. I was praying and crying out to the Lord. I know I may have come off unprofessional, but I was and still is a servant of the Lord way before I took on this profession. Many psychotherapists may have their opinions about how I integrate therapeutic approaches, but if God is not in it, then it wouldn't make sense to me. I believe that prayer is the best therapy to a profound breakthrough. I am just a vessel, who leads people to Jesus. Yes, I may start the process, but He finishes it. After we gave God the praise, hugged, and wiped away our tears, it was now time for me to end the session.

"You have now entered the place of your breakthrough. You have allowed God to do what He set out to do. How do you feel?" I asked Him, still overjoyed in the spirit.

"I couldn't explain it to you if I tried. My soul feels freer, my mind is clearer, and my heart is singing praises to God. You know I miss this. I miss the feeling of being wrapped up into the arms of God. I knew He was around me, but I…" He couldn't even finish, from singing praises to God.

"Yes. You have now reached the resting place. Now let's go to the next step. Here is what I want you to do—sit down when you get home and write a list of all the things that your wife did to make you happy and then on another sheet write about some of the things she's told you in case something happened to her."

"What do you mean?" He asked confused.

"What I mean is that everyone has to come to the realization that one day their time to die will come. Some people have the opportunity to tell their loved ones what they didn't or did want after their demise. Like my husband told me that if he dies he wanted me to move on with my life and be happy." I explained.

"Oh, I understand what you're trying to say. When should I bring it back to you?" He said, looking at me.

"At our next session." I told him.

We talked for another ten minutes and he left. I was still praising God and filled up with joy when my next client came in. After my twelfth client left, I was tired and ready to go pick up Alana from my in-laws. Luckily, Alana was on the porch waiting for me. I love my in-laws but I was too tired to talk and a hot shower and my bed were calling my name.

4

WHEN I LOOKED at the clock and looked over on Trevor's side of the bed I felt like a single woman, who just happened to be married. I turned on my lamp and opened my Bible to Psalm 119. The book of Psalms was my favorite book and I always found gratification in each psalm that I read. David didn't know that he was saying prayers that can help the human heart, even in the new century. It was three in the morning when I lifted myself off the floor from praying and Trevor was still not home. So, I went down stairs, made me a cup of chamomile tea, and waited for him in the living room.

"W-why are you still up?" He stuttered, when he noticed me. You could have sworn he'd just got caught for sticking his cookie in the forbidden cookie jar.

"I was waiting on you to come home so that we could talk." I answered, calmly sipping on my tea.

"Celeste, I've had a long day and I don't feel like talking." He said, heading up the stairs.

"Yes, of course, I'd figured you'd say that. I had a long day too, but when I woke up a couple hours ago, I found myself sleeping alone, wondering, now where is my husband at such an hour as this... Huh? Now, I don't know what's going on, but I know it's something. Be aware, that God not only knows all things, but He can see all things as well. But I know you know all this." I said, sipping on my tea again, the hot liquid warmed the coldness that just had rose up inside of me.

He stopped in his tracks and turned and looked at me. He was about to come back down the stairs but instead he stopped.

"Good night Celeste." Was all he said while he made his way to our bedroom and slammed the door.

Now, the flesh in me told me to run up the stairs and let him have it because I wanted some answers, but the Holy Spirit shouted for me to be still. But although the Spirit is willing, the flesh was weak, and even when I try to do good, evil is always present, and I wanted to stick it to the enemy, who happened to be in the form of my husband. So, when I walked in our bedroom I heard the shower running. I walked in the bathroom and pulled the shower door open.

"What the hell is wrong with you?" He yelled.

"Don't you dare curse at me or in this house." I yelled back.

"Girl, what do you want? Can't this wait until I get out the shower?" He said, trying to close the shower door.

"I have a lot of things on my mind and I'm tired of putting my thoughts on hold just because you don't feel like hearing what I have to say. So, what I need you to do is dry off and come sit down and listen to what I have to say. As a matter of fact you don't even have to do all that we can talk right now." His eyes widened a little surprised at my tone of voice. I've never spoken to him like that so I know that had gotten his attention.

"You want to talk Celeste? Well let's talk." He said quickly wrapping the towel around his waist and heading to the bedroom.

"Now you have my attention, talk." He said clearly annoyed.

"Look, I need to know why you've been acting the way you have? You haven't touched me in weeks and I know something is wrong. So, give it to me straight, after all you owe me that much." I said giving him the evil eye.

"What?" He asked sucking his teeth.

"If you can say what, then you can hear. Are you having an affair, Trevor?" I spat it out.

"Awww, here we go with this." He blow out a breath as he shook his head.

"Well I guess there we went. Now answer the question." I asked, not even sure if I wanted to know the answer, but I needed to know. He rubbed his hands across his face, and he really did look exhausted.

"Like I told you I've been too busy to be thinking about sex right now. I have a job that has to be done and it takes a lot of time to do it. You think it takes a day to complete something? Just because you sit around in your office all day doing what you do, doesn't mean I have the luxury of sitting around. I am a business man and I am out working, making sure these bills get paid."

I like his nerve, he act like my job is not work. I work my behind off just like he do. What makes my job less tedious than his? I wanted to know. He acts like I don't bring money in to help around here. Now he is trying to push a nerve and I won't give him the satisfaction.

"Trevor I get just as busy and exhausted as you do. You don't think my job is tiring? I have to build clientele, just like you do. I have a business to run daily, just like you do. I work hours on end, just like you do. So please don't belittle my work. I made a choice in my career to help others with their problems and my salary is enough to pay the bills." I told him.

"I hear you." He said snidely.

"You know what you are un-be-lieve-able."

"Am I? You're the one acting like a school girl." He stood.

"Baby, it's too much woman in me, to act like a girl. I'm not going to say what you're acting like, because Lord knows I'll give the devil something to be proud of, but you act like you don't have a wife at home. What happened to the man I married?" I said, so angry I could cry.

"Well, I'm older now and things change and I've changed." He said, pulling the cover back on the bed.

"This conversation isn't over." I said looking at him.

"It's up to you whether you want to sit up all night and talk to yourself but I'm going to bed because as of this moment, the session has ended." He said sarcastically.

He got in the bed and pulled the covers over his head and didn't say a word. I've known Trevor long enough to know, that when he is done talking he is done. So, I took a pillow off the bed and headed towards my daughter's room.

"Is everything okay mom?" Alana said groggily.

"Everything is fine honey; I just wanted to sleep with my favorite daughter in the world." I said putting on a smile so big, I could win an Oscar for that performance.

"Yeah right, I'm your only daughter." She said scooting over so I could get in the bed.

My baby wrapped her arms around me and I allowed the love of my child to be my blanket. Alana's alarm clock went off. I was so tired I could barely open my eyes. Thank God it was the weekend, so I didn't have to take Alana to school this morning or she would have just had to be late. Alana mentioned something about going to her best friends to eat breakfast before I drifted back off to sleep. When I woke up three hours later, I felt rejuvenated. So, I decided to do what I do best and go to Starbuck's to pick up a cup of coffee and maybe grab a bite to eat.

I walked in my massive walk-in closet in search of something comfortable to wear. I decided to put on a knee-length white Prada dress. I chose to wear a pair of gold Versace sandals, grabbed my white and gold Versace purse, and slipped on my gold Versace shades. As soon as I sat down at Starbuck's Tiffany came right up to my table to take my order.

"Girl you are always looking sharp." She complimented, pleased with my attire.

"Thank you so much. I would like to get the usual, a cup of coffee light and sweet." I told her.

I was so busy thinking about Trevor that I didn't realize this Morris Chestnut look alike standing above me.

"Can I help you?" I asked, wondering if there was a problem.

"I'm sorry I didn't mean to disturb you like this, but I was just wondering why a fine lady like yourself was sitting here all alone." He spoke. His voice reminded me of something but I just didn't know what it was. His voice was as smooth as chocolate frosting and I had to catch myself. After all I am a married woman— a *saved* married woman.

"Well, I didn't know I needed a man with me to enjoy a cup of coffee." I said picking up the Styrofoam cup.

"No, I wouldn't suppose you would but if I had a pretty lady like yourself to come home to I'd never let you go." He said, uninvitedly sitting down.

"Well, I wish my husband had the same mind as you." I put that out there just to let him know that I was married.

"Well, he better know what he's got before a brother like me picks you up." He laughed but I knew he wasn't joking.

Tiffany came back with the croissant I ordered and sat it on the table. When she walked off I looked towards her direction and she winked at me. She didn't know I was married because I always came in here alone and I was relieved too.

"So you're that type huh? It's typical." I shrugged, biting into my croissant.

"What do you mean that type? I'm just telling the truth."

"The type that thinks just because he has a nice face and a couple of smooth lines, that he could have any woman he wants." I answered, leaning to close to him.

He just looked at me and smiled.

"Ha! You don't seem to care whether I'm married or not, do you?" I said, rolling my eyes.

He just stared at me smiling.

"Why are you smiling at me like that for?"

"You are a beautiful woman especially when you get feisty. I like that." He smiled, displaying the sexiest smile that I'd ever seen.

"Is that so?" I said flirting, just a little tiny bit.

"Indeed." He said.

Am I sitting here flirting with this man? I better put my flesh under subjection. The fire was blazing hot and I was not going to play with fire. I didn't even finish my croissant. I quickly gathered my things.

"I don't mean to be rude but I have to go." I said, getting my keys out of my purse.

"Oh, I understand here's my card and when you have the time to call do so. And maybe we could have lunch or something and I promise I'll choose a place that's comfortable for you so that you want have to worry about your husband running in on us." He said.

"Excuse me? Any man that doesn't care about talking to another's man's wife has nothing to say to me." I said, with attitude.

"Whoa, calm down I was just saying. Obviously something is bothering you?" He said cautiously.

"And why you say that?" I snapped.

"It took you a while to notice me standing at the table earlier. I noticed the long face and clearly you were in deep thought. I don't know what you were thinking about, but whatever it was it must have been something deep, since you weren't aware that I was standing at your table for at least two minutes before you even noticed. " He said with a sincere look of concern on his face.

"Whatever."

"If you just want to talk, please give me a call." He insisted, handing me his card.

"And what makes you think I want to talk to you?" I replied, with a look of disdain on my face.

"Well, pretty lady, you wouldn't have put that card in your purse if you weren't at least considering it." He said, as he excused himself from the table, and walked out the door.

I stood there staring at the door for a while, wondering why I accepted his card. I couldn't call it, but there was something about him that wanted me to know more. I don't know if the devil was tempting me or God was testing me, but I had a strong feeling that I was going to find out.

5

NOW, ALL I could think about was the mystery man that I met two weeks ago in Starbuck's. When I looked at his business card it had his cell and work number on the front and I'd noticed that he'd written his home phone number on the back. I read the name Dennis Frasier. I sat in my office debating on whether I should call or not. I was so nervous; you'd have thought I'd stolen something. I kept picking up the phone and hanging it up. Even though I should have been consulting God for a solution, I decided to call Christie instead.

"Hey girl." She answered, after picking up at the second ring.

"Wow, let me find out you were waiting by the phone looking for a phone call from me." I joked.

"Child boo… get your life." Christie sucked her teeth, letting the ghetto and the Tamar Braxton come out of her all at once.

All of that… coming out of a college professor-- an English college professor at that. Christie had the courage of a lion. She refused to let anyone or anything hold her down or to define who she is. Yeah, she kept up her grades and went to Sunday school like her parents expected of her, but when she turned sixteen things changed. When her father found out that she'd gotten pregnant he blew a gasket. He kicked her out and told her that she could never come back to his house again. Christie was hurt by her father's words, but she did not let her circumstances get to her.

She moved in with her grandmother and when she had Naomi, she went to school, got a part-time job, and still graduated with honors. She lived in public housing until she finished college and found her first teaching job at one of the local colleges in town. Now she is an English-college professor at Morehouse. She inspired me and reminded me that your circumstances do not define you.

What have Trevor done this time?" She asked, knowing that it had to be something about Trevor.

"Not enough that's for sure, but I'm not calling you about him." I paused, wondering if I should tell her or not.

"So if it's not Trevor then what could it possibly be about?" She gasped dramatically.

I laughed at her exaggeration. I am always calling every time Trevor and I are having our outs which are a lot lately so it's a breath of fresh air for me to not be talking about Trevor this time. As a matter of fact Trevor isn't even on my mind right now.

"I met this guy in Starbuck's a few days ago and he gave me his card but I'm little skeptical about calling him." I blurted out.

"Oh, my goodness, what does he look like girl?" She asked excited.

"Calm down, did you forget that I am ma…rieed…" I stretched the word for emphasis.

"Girl please… if that's what you want to call it." She spoke, dismissing my statement.

"Anyways, I said ignoring her, he gave me his card with his numbers and . . ."

"Hold up! She said cutting me off. What do you mean numbers as in more than one?" She asked. I could tell she was smiling from ear to ear and I caught myself smiling back.

"Yes, it has his home, cell, and work number on it." I said, trying to sound like it was no big deal.

"Well, any man that gives you all his numbers, especially his home phone, must be really feeling you. Go head girlfriend! I know you're married and all of that but I think you should give that man a call. Trevor isn't doing what he's supposed to do and knowing him he's probably doing him anyway. Now before you get all "jesusfied" on me… I'm not saying that you should jump in the haystack and roll with the man, but call him and see what he's talking about." She said.

"Trevor is not cheating." I said half-heartedly, because I've been thinking the same thing as well.

"Okay, whatever you say to make yourself feel better." She replied.

"What do you think I should do, Christie?" I asked a second time.

"You know Celeste, sometimes I forget that you went to Harvard. Goodness, get off the phone from with me and dial one of his numbers and talk to the man." She said, as if I'd asked the dumbest question ever.

"Okay." I said, not knowing whether to be offended by her statement.

Click.

She hung up on me.

I hesitated a little while longer and decided to follow Christie's advice. I picked up the phone again and dialed his house phone just to see if a woman would pick up and if so I would hang up and never have to call him again. The phone rang and I sat on the side of my bed, nervously chewing on my bottom lip.

"Hello?" He answered, with that smooth chocolate tone of his.

"Hello?" He asked again.

"Hello." I finally said nervously.

"Yes." He asked confused.

"May I speak to Dennis please?" I knew it was him, but I was nervous.

"Speaking." He responded.

"Hi Dennis, this is Celeste, you met me at Starbuck's the other day. I know it's a little late—" I rambled on. I always over talk myself when I'm nervous.

"I remember who you are. How could I forget a pretty face like that?" He said, putting my rambling at a halt.

I blushed. "If it is too late, I can call you another time."

"No, as a matter of fact you can call me anytime-- day or night. If I am sleep I'll wake up for you." He said in a serious tone.

"Oh, stop it." I was smiling and blushing like crazy. I leaned back on my bed and relaxed.

"I wouldn't play with you, baby." He said.

He called me baby. I squirmed. I was acting like a school girl talking to the most popular boy in school *again*.

"I was wondering if we could meet up some time." I suggested.

"Like a date?"

"I wouldn't get that deep, but I would like to see you again." I laughed.

"It sounds like a date to me and of course I will. What time is best for you?" He asked.

"Friday night let's say, at seven?" I said quickly.

"Friday at seven it is." He said.

We talked to the wee hours of the night. I don't know when we called it a night but when my alarm clock went off it felt like I hadn't slept that long, but for some reason I was energized. The phone was off the hook and on Trevor side of the bed. He must have not come home last night and surprisingly I didn't care. If I wanted to be honest with myself, I would admit that I was actually glad he didn't. I turned the alarm off, hung up the phone and went back to sleep.

Friday Night @ 7

Dennis made reservations at an Italian restaurant called "Dolce Enoteca" which is considered to be the most popular and expensive restaurant in Atlanta Georgia. I tried to keep it classy and Christian so I wore my black Chanel pants suit, with a turquoise silk blouse, with my turquoise Gucci pumps. To dress my neck and arms, I wore my white gold necklace with a cross pendant adorned in diamonds with a turquoise stone in the middle, with the matching earrings, and bracelet. My phenomenal stylist Kathy worked miracles on my head at the last minute. I could tell Dennis was a man of style, he wore a black Italian suit, with a light pink Calvin Klein dress shirt, with a stripped pink, white, black, and purple tie, and a black pair of Bel Air's, similar to Trevor's.

"This is all so wonderful." I said looking at the menu, trying not to reveal my nervousness. This is my first time ever going out with a man, besides my husband. I was feeling a mixture of glee, guilt, and my nerves were all over the place. My throat was so dry and even though I kept sipping on the water in front of me, it wasn't working.

"Yeah, I love this place, are you okay?" He said looking up at me with a look of concern on his face.

"Are you guys ready to order?" The waitress asked stepping to our table, before I could respond.

"Excuse me for a moment while I go to the ladies room." I said as I quickly headed to the restroom, without giving anyone a chance to respond.

"Girl calm down." I said to myself as I looked in the mirror. I turned on the faucet and ran some water over my hands. Then I filled my hands with water and splashed it on my face. The cool water was calming as it hit my face. I quickly dabbed the water off my face, careful not to ruin my mascara, took a long breath in and exhaled, and walked back to the table.

"I hope everything is okay." He questioned, as soon as I sat down.

"Yes I am so sorry, everything is fine." I grabbed the menu again and scanned over it.

"Good. This place is great. I didn't want to order without you, so I told the waitress to come back." He said.

"Ah, there she is." I said as I watched her come towards our table.

"Are you guys ready to order?" She asked, looking at me for assurance.

"Yes, I would like the Chicken Marsala, with a glass of white wine." I answered.

"And I'd have the Penne with Vodka Sauce and Capicola with white wine as well." Dennis said smiling at the waitress.

"Would you guys care for an appetizer?" She asked, while she gathered the menus.

We both agreed to order cheese sticks with marinara sauce. I was enjoying his company so much that I didn't even realize the waitress coming with our food. The Chicken Marsala melted in my mouth and I was tempted to order some to take home, but I didn't want Trevor to know that I came here. He knows what kind of restaurant this is and he knew I wouldn't come to a place like this by myself.

"So, how is your daughter?" He asked, cutting off my train of thought.

"Oh, she's doing just fine, thanks so much for asking." I smiled.

He asked me about my favorite hobbies, food, clothing, color, and all sorts of questions. He'd told me all about him without me having to ask and I wasn't going to. With him everything felt natural. He was so easy to talk to and for a minute it felt like there was no one else in the room but just him and me. Time just slipped away and before

I knew it we were headed to my car.

"Well, I enjoyed this lovely night with you." He spoke, looking into my eyes.

His eyes was so alluring that I could have stood there all night wrapped in those beautiful deep brown eyes. I don't know what came over me but it felt like I had a swarm of butterflies flying around in my belly. Those eyes... there was something about those eyes, or was it something about him? He was so attentive, so patient, and so kind. I wondered whether all men were like this, but I thought about Trevor and tossed that thought out to the wind. Trevor has always been a helpless romantic, but he has never been the communicative type. That's probably what got me so drawn to Dennis, because he liked to talk, he listened, and he seems to care about my thoughts. He seemed so promising so perfect.

"Celeste, are you okay?" He asked, looking at me skeptically.

Hearing his voice caused me to tare my eyes away from his.

"Yeah, I'm fine." I said blushing.

"I was saying that I enjoyed your company and would like to do this again."

"Of course, that would be nice." I suddenly got nervous. I was ready to get out of that parking lot as fast as I could. I knew I'd made a fool out of myself. The man must have thought I was losing my mind.

"Are you nervous?" He sensed, as he noticed my hands where shaking.

"A little, I admitted. I've never done this before and I must admit I feel a little guilty for even being here with you."

"Don't be." He said walking towards me. We were about a half of an inch away from me. The Calvin Klein cologne filled my nostrils and I caught myself drinking up his scent. I walked up closer to him, again, hypnotized in those brown eyes. He leaned closer and kissed me so softly I almost melted. My legs felt like Jell-O and if he hadn't of wrapped his arms around me; I would have fallen right into him.

Bonk!

Bonk!

The car horn caused us to break away from the trance we were in.

"Sorry, sir." He said, holding up his hand, still not taking his eyes off of me.

"Ummm . . . ." I paused, still lost for words.

"I know. You have a good night Celeste." He smiled and walked away. I couldn't move. I stood there for at least three minutes before I decided to get in my car. I felt so jittery and full of excitement that I didn't even notice Trevor sitting at the dining room table.

6

"HAD FUN?" He said.

The smile, the excitement, and the butterflies that were dancing in my stomach ran for cover. Nervousness swept all over me and I could feel myself sweating. I knew I looked like a deer caught in the head lights. Oh Lord, he knows. I said to myself, getting paranoid.

"What?" I asked, as if I didn't hear him.

"I asked if you had fun." He stood up, heading towards me.

"Yes, I did." I said, making a bee-line for the stairs. I had to get my mind together.

He didn't know anything and if I could just calm down everything will be just fine. Thank God he didn't follow me. I closed the door behind me, closed my eyes, and allowed the oxygen that I was holding escape from my lungs. I thought I was caught.

"Don't let him steal your joy. You had fun tonight. If he paid enough attention to you, then you wouldn't have had to worry about getting it from nobody else. Enjoy this time. He doesn't care anyway, he didn't even follow you. Have your fun, because he's probably having his."

I heard the voice loud and clear and instead of testing the spirit like I knew to do, I took its advice. I refused to let Trevor steal the joy that I was feeling. He comes home all time of the night, don't call or nothing, and all of sudden tonight he decided to come home like he's suppose to. Unacceptable! If he was going to have his fun, so was I.

"Right is never wrong and wrong is never right. Never let your anger causes you to sin. For love, covers a multitude of sins."

That small still voice has spoken. I knew that voice, but I didn't want to hear it. I was tired of having to be the one to fix things; tired of trying to meet Trevor half way. Trevor doesn't care, so why should I. I am going to stay wrapped up in this joy that was given to me tonight. I felt that I deserve to be happy and I was so tired of wondering, worrying, and drenching my pillows with tears because my husband was nowhere to be found. I was not alone, yet I was still lonely. About an hour later Trevor came in our bedroom and looked at me.

"Problem?" I asked, as I applied lotion on my arms.

"No, there's no problem, you looked good tonight." He said looking me over.

"Thanks for noticing." I said tactlessly.

"So, where did you go looking like that? He questioned.

"I just felt like treating myself for a night out." I shrugged.

"So, what was it that you wanted to talk about?" He asked.

The nerve of this man… I told him six weeks ago that we needed to talk so now he wants to come up in here and talk.

"You know, that's been so long ago, it must have slipped my mind." I said facetiously.

"Well, don't say I didn't try." He said, walking towards the closet.

"When have you ever tried to talk to me?" I said with a look of disgust.

"Just now." He said nonchalantly.

"Okay, let's talk." I said wanting to get a few things off my chest. I was heated and ready to fire.

"I'm all ears." He said sitting up.

"Let's talk about how you come up in here all times of the night and not even have the decency to even ask how my day was or anything. You don't call, you don't spend time with me, and you act like it disgusts you to have sex with me."

"I've been busy." He said, sticking to that lame excuse.

"Yeah, I bet you have." I threw up my hands.

"What are you trying to say? You're the one who's coming up in here looking like you just had a hot date. You the one should be answering to me." He said flipping the script.

I thought about Dennis and the kiss we shared and I was beginning to feel a little guilty. I couldn't answer I just sat there in looked at him.

"Yeah, like I thought." He said.

"I told you I wanted to go out and enjoy myself tonight alone." I lied.

"Whatever." He said unbelievingly.

All the guilt quickly flew out the window. "You know... it's funny how someone will accuse you of the very thing that they are doing." I found it laughable.

"Like I said, I'm working late all the time. I don't have time to cheat on you and if I did I would tell you." He beckoned.

"To hell you will." I yelled.

We both stopped right there, with a look of shock on our faces. I've never said a curse word a day in my life. I would never even give entertain an argument. Instead of arguing I'd be the first to walk away and go off and pray. But I was so tired of being the one to walk away. I was so tired of holding my feelings in while he let his out. I wanted him to know how I felt. I wanted to be heard and I decided that I was going to tonight.

"Celeste, you need to check yourself."

"Check myself . . . you the one who need to be checked." I yelled, poking my finger in his chest.

"I didn't come up here to argue with you, but I see that's all you want to do so I'll go sleep in the guest room." He grabbed some pillows and got up out of the bed.

"That's not nothing new and the way I'm feeling right now that's your best bet." I lowered my voice, throwing a pillow at him.

He left out the door as I was throwing another one at him. It missed him and landed on the floor. I sat in the dark and shed a few tears not even knowing why.

Thanks a lot for ruining my night.

Two Weeks Later

Trevor and I have been avoiding each other since the argument. I've been so wrapped up in Dennis that I didn't even care enough to address it. Dennis and I have been spending our lunch time together everyday. At first I was feeling guilty, but as the days went by guilt began to dwindle away from my conscience. We talk, we laugh, and we just enjoy the company of each other. We understand each other and what I like about him the most is that he has not asked me to be intimate with him. It felt great. I soon learned that he was a heart surgeon and owned his own practice, but he also worked on call at the hospital when he was needed. He didn't strike me as the doctor type and I asked him why he had decided to work in that field.

"My mother died of heart disease when I graduated from high school and since I couldn't help her I vowed that I would be of help to someone else." He said sadly.

"I'm so sorry to hear that."

"I believe that. I marvel over how many lives God saves through me. You know Celeste, there is something about the way the heart functions that interest me. It's a small organ, yet it is so strong and so vital to the human body; if it stops beating, then, the whole body stops functioning." He said.

"Yes you are so right."

"People die inside every day because of the maltreatment of the heart. It becomes hardened, broken even; because it has not been treated fairly."

"I definitely know what you mean." I said knowing all too well.

"If you let me, I wouldn't mine doctoring on you. I'm good at what I do. No lie." He motioned, crossing his heart.

I laughed, "Doctor on me? I don't need a doctor."

"Quite the contrary. I can see past the doubt. I see you, Celeste. I see the pain in your eyes, the quiver in your lips, and I hear the breaking of your heart. Your heart needs to be stitched back together, it needs to be massaged and feel the warmth of my hands, because it is growing cold. You can't fool heart a expert." He laughed.

I know he noticed the look of pain and shock on my face. Was I that transparent? He'd blown me away by revealing inner truths that only God and I knew.

"Can you remember... do you remember when you had a heart blossoming with love and strength. Do you? You had a heart that had a beat for love, for hope, for life, but its getting weak. Who are you allowing personal assess to your heart? Whoever it is, is interfering with your heart. Your heart no longer beats the same beat. You no longer feel the love, you're beginning to feel a sense of hopelessness, your joy is diminishing, and if you don't be careful the life will be sucked out of you and pretty soon the heart want have enough electricity in it to keep it beating." He finished. I couldn't speak. I couldn't stop the tears from flowing. He knew all about my situation without me having to say a word. God why are you telling this man all of my business?

"Do you understand what I am saying to you, Celeste?" He soften, as he put my hands in his.

"No matter what you do. Don't let him take the most greatest element that you can have. Don't let him take your love away. Because if you don't have love then you don't have anything. Remember... God is love."

"To God be the glory. You just don't know how much you've blessed my Spirit. It's been hard, but--"

"But you cannot let the valleys in your life overtake you. You stay prayed up and you believe in God, because He is your strength. There isn't anything that you can ever go through that is too hard for Him to solve." He said.

"You sound like you're speaking from experience." I said, shocked. We never talked about his religious beliefs.

"Yes. Although I am not perfect and I'm far from saved, I do know Jesus and I know the Word. My mother was a true woman of God. Even through her battle with her disease she did not question God, get angry, or none of that. She died believing that God will heal her and He did, just not in the way I imagined." He said, dejectedly.

"I can tell you loved your mother." I replied, almost in tears.

"Yeah, yeah, go ahead and say it... I'm a mama's boy." He laughed.

"Oh no, nothing funny about that. I love a man who loves his mother, because if he love his mother, then that indicates how much respect and love he would have for his woman." I told him.

We looked at each other, transfixed in each other's eyes. I was so close to him, I inhaled the minty scent from his breath.

"So, how's your day going so far?" He said, suddenly dropping our stare, and changing the subject.

"So, how's your day going so far at work?" He said, breaking our stare, and changing the subject.

"Ummm... I said, clearing my throat, it's going okay. Wilson decided to terminate his session and I am so proud because he has came a long ways." I said, with a look of pride on my face.

"So whose going to help you?" He asked, looking at me.

"I'm sorry... I don't understand your question?"

"As a mental health professional, you're trained to know all the right answers. You are capable of helping everyone else with their problems, but is unable to recognize that you are in need of therapy yourself."

"That may be true for some, but I've got Jesus to help me along the way." I assured him.

"That sounds really good, but even those who were once strong in their faith, can become faithless." He replied.

That hit me hard. I have been ignoring that small still voice in my head. I haven't been praying as much as I used to and I haven't read the Bible in a while. For the rest of the day, I wondered whether I was losing my faith.

7

"CHRISTIE TOLD ME about your date with what's his face." Rachael said, with a look on her face that I couldn't place.

Rachael and I decided to have brunch at the country club. It wasn't surprising because I knew as soon as I spilled the beans to Christie she'd call Rachael soon after, but what surprised me is that she waited a while to mention it to me.

"His name is Dennis and he's such a wonderful guy." I smiled, trying not to make it more than what it was.

"Tell me more." She insisted, as she scooted up beside me.

I told her about all the time we've been spending together and how I really felt about him.

"He's overall, an amazing guy. I never laughed so much until I met him. He is like a breath of fresh air. You know what I mean... I can't place these new found feelings that I have. I miss him when he's not around and can't wait to see him when the clock strikes twelve for lunch. I'm falling for him and hard too. I know it's wrong because I am a married woman, but Rachel, I can't help these feelings that I'm feeling." I said balling my hands against my chest.

"Have you prayed, sis?" She asked me.

"Huh?" I said, knowing I know what she said.

"Have you prayed about this?" She repeated.

"Yeah, I prayed." I lied.

"Hah... Did you stay down there long enough to get an answer?" She said, knowing better. Rachael was what the type of Christian that really tried to live by the Bible word-for-word. God reveals things to her and if she says something is about to happen you can bet your last dollar that it will come to past. She reminded me of David. She was a woman after God's on heart. I wish I had the tenacity that she has.

"Rachael... please." I said, not wanting to hear it.

"Okay, I'm not going to discuss this right now, but rest assured my sister, we will discuss it later. I just want you to really think about what you are doing. You're still another man's wife, don't forget that. God don't like ugly, no matter how pretty it looks." She reminded me, as if I forgot.

"Yeah, I know."

Rachael can come off a little self-righteous at times, but if I wanted to be honest, she have lived up to it. I know that if you walk in righteousness then you are righteous. She is the level headed one out of the group, and I was glad to have her in my life to put me back in place when I've fallen off the bandwagon.

"Listen, I know Trevor could be jerk sometimes but that doesn't mean that you should be out catching feelings for another man. I know things are not the way they should be at home, but you have to keep praying, believe in Jesus, and know that there is nothing too hard for God. He's going to fix your marriage, but you can't go out there trying to find comfort in the arms of another man. Just because it seems right doesn't make it right, it's still wrong. Now, if you and your husband are having problems, go to him, talk to him, and if he does not listen, then leave it in the hands of our Savior." She said squeezing my hand.

I knew she was right whether I wanted to admit it or not. I enjoy all the time that I spend with Dennis but I know that some good things must come to an end. I have to try to restore my marriage and go back and re-introduce myself to Jesus, because the way I've been acting, I'd be surprised if He still knew my name.

"I know… that's why I am going to tell Dennis that I can't see him anymore." I said, trying to stop the tears.

"I know that it can be hard sis, but you have to do what is right." She said, handing me a napkin.

"I know sis… Thank you so much. I love you and I have enjoyed our little heart-to-heart. I will talk to you lady. There's something that I have to do." I told her.

As I sat at the bench in the park, I silently prayed to God. Asking Him to forgive me for being disobedient, for trying to take matters into my own hands, and for not trusting Him enough to make things right in my life. I asked Him to restore me, renew my mind, and

Kezia Davis

cleanse my heart. I prayed that He let the Holy Spirit flow within me and that the Holy Spirit speak into my words, think into my thoughts, and work in my deeds today and from this day forward. I asked Him to give me strength, give me the words, and give me the courage to walk away from here today.

"Hello, gorgeous." He stood and gave me a light kiss. There it was that cologne that took away all my senses. But, I couldn't let the things of the flesh distract me today. Today I was operating in the Spirit.

"Dennis… you have been so wonderful, but you have been my distraction. With you, I can avoid the pain that has been going on in my house, with me and my husband. But this has to stop, because I know I have not being pleasing God with my behavior. This has all been fun, and you are a great guy, but we can't see each other anymore." I said, avoiding eye contact.

"I understand. I got caught up too. At first I was just trying to brighten your days, because I knew that you were going through something, but I've fallen in love with you. I know it's wrong, because you belong to someone else. You were never mine to have and I'm sorry. I know I played a major part in your actions, so please forgive me." He said, making me look into those brown eyes that I loved so much.

"Don't blame yourself. I knew what I was getting myself into, but I played along. I help create this. It was never my intentions to hurt you and I'm sorry." I said, wishing that I could make the situation better.

"What I told you about that word, he said lifting my head up. Don't be sorry for doing what is right. I respect you even more for it. I would be lying if I said I would like to be your friend, because we've passed that stage. So, instead I'm just going to wish you well." He said, leaning over to kiss my forehead.

"Thanks. Well I guess I'll see you around." I said.

"Yeah, but I hope not too soon." He said winking at me.

I almost ran to my car, trying to get a way from the pain that was left in the eyes of the man that I'd fallen equally in love with. Now it was time for me to fix my marriage and I was eager to get home

62

to prepare myself for when Trevor got home. Prayer with my Daddy was definitely what I had to do first, because I knew I was going to need Him to help me through this. The conversation with Dennis was already too much for me. I called my receptionist and told her to reschedule all my appointments today.

I tried to call Trevor's cell but I didn't get an answer, so I figured he was probably in court. It was Friday, so I called Alana to see if she was staying at her best friend house this weekend and she assured me that she was. I headed to the grocery store to pick up something for dinner and headed home singing, "This Place" along with Tamela Mann. I was so ready for a fresh new start and even though I know things have been rocky, I believe that God will smooth things out. I still love my husband enough to fix things with him.

Trevor car was parked in the driveway; he must have just gotten home. I quickly parked beside him, grabbed the grocery bags and headed towards the door. I quietly placed the groceries in the fridge and treaded upstairs. I passed by Trevor's office downstairs, so I figured he would be in the bedroom. A funny feeling came over me but I quickly dismissed it. As I got to the top of the stairs, I heard a strange noise outside my bedroom door. Without hesitation, I opened the door and almost dropped to my knees. I wasn't prepared for the hard blow that hit me in my chest.

8

MY EYES had to be deceiving me. Clearly I am caught up in a nightmare that I am trying hard to wake up from. The blood in my heart seemed as if it was being squeezed out of me. I couldn't breathe, the tears in my eyes where making it hard for me to see. Who was this stranger with my husband's face? His face was twisted, not in anger, but in pleasure. This stranger with my husband's face was in my bed with another woman, soiling my sheets. Defiling my bed and doing explicit things to another woman that he was supposed to be doing with his wife.

Yes, this man with my husbands face was making sounds that rattled my mind and shook me to my core. He was moaning in pleasure, as if it was the best he'd ever had. My heart was breaking, because I knew he'd never been that gentle, that passionate, and that turned on with me. Not since our honeymoon.

"Am I hurting you, baby?" He moaned to her, as he softly thrust himself inside her.

"Mmm… don't stop." She replied in sheer pleasure, as she dug her nails into his sweaty back.

It couldn't be… not my husband… not the one who I gave my life to, my heart to, and who help me bare a child. It can't be the same man who I met in high school, the one who stood with me down the isle and promised I would be his forever. Not the one vowed that he would stay true to me for the rest of his life. No, not the one that I just stood up for, the one that I chose over someone who I knew could love me better. An anger that I never felt before brewed up inside of me and I was suddenly afraid of what I might do.

"Oh, my… Celeste…baby…what you doing here?" Trevor said, leaping out of the bed.

Yes, that man with my husband's face had just confirmed that he was, indeed, my husband. I just stood there stuck in my own rage. Fear swept across the young girls faced as she crawled up in the corner of the bed, gripping the sheets up to her chin. Trevor grabbed the end of the comforter that had fallen on the floor and covered himself. He was trying to hide his sins, he'd lied to me too many times and now he couldn't deny it. He couldn't just say that he was working and brush me off and go to bed. No, the truth was there, hitting me hard in my face. I never felt so stupid, so humiliated, so disgusted, and so hurt in all the days of my life.

Yes, I was falling for Dennis, but I'd never had it in me to sleep with him. That would break the code and that will ultimately break the vows that I'd taken with my husband. Looking at him standing there, covering himself from me fueled the fire even more. I was seeing red. Without hesitation I went to my closet, tossing everything that was in my way to get to the safe that was hidden in the back of the closet.

"22...11...3..." I said to myself, furiously turning the dial on the lock. I'd made several mistakes before I head the lock finally click. The safe was open, and I grabbed the .38 chrome revolver that my father gave to me when I was 18, for protection. He said that he didn't want me going so far from him without protection. When I told him that I had Trevor to protect me he quickly dismissed the notion and told me to not be so silly. My father must have known something that I didn't and I regretted missing the message.

"Celeste, baby, please…What are you going to do with that, baby please." He begged looking at the gun in my hand. He looked like he was about to urinate on himself. I opened the clip and took out all six bullets, totally ignoring him.

"I have taken out all six bullets out and now I am putting in two." I conferred, as I put two bullets in two of the empty holes. I close the clip and watched it spin.

"I remember when I was 8 years old. My father took me to an open field, and there lie a row of cans sitting on the table. He took this same .38 and shot a can right off the table. He said to me, 'Celeste, I am going to teach you how to shoot.' After about six tries, I finally was able to shoot the remaining three cans off the table with my eyes closed. So, you see, it would be nothing for me to visualize your heads as those cans." I said looking at them with a look that made Trevor shiver.

"Oh, Lord." I heard the girl cry out. Her face had turned ash white. She had bone-straight blond hair, blue eyes, heart shaped lips, and wore about a buck ten. If it wasn't for her voice I wouldn't have even recognized her. It was Trevor's new assistant, who I hadn't had the pleasure of meeting… until now.

"Lord— I said to her disgusted. How dare you use the Lord's name in vain? Just a few minutes ago you weren't praying and crying out to the Lord… No, you were praying that my husband wouldn't stop and crying out in ecstasy. Tell me— what do you get out of sleeping with people's husbands?" I asked her, ignoring the terror in her eyes.

"Baby, I know what this looks like. I'm sorry." He said, cutting me off. He was shaking like a leaf, but he dared not move.

"You're right about that. You are very sorry. I'm sorry I didn't notice just how sorry before I married you." I said shaking my head in complete repugnance.

"Baby—" He said taking a step towards me.

"Don't you move and don't you ever call me baby again. I don't won't to hear that word come out of your mouth, while referring to me never no' more. Because it seems like to me you use that word loosely. Weren't you just referring to your "boo" over here as your baby? So, Trevor I am confused, who exactly is your baby." I said not really posing a question.

"Celeste, I'm sorry, you have to believe me. I never meant for this to happen, I never meant to hurt you, I swear."

"Believe you? Man, I don't even know you. You say you never meant for this happen… humph, I bet you didn't. What you really meant to say is that you never intended on getting caught. You didn't care about hurting me. You brought a woman into our house and into our bed. This is where I lay my head Trevor. Clearly, you've lost your mind." I said, aiming the gun at him.

"Celeste." He said trying to remain calm, but his legs where shaking uncontrollably.

"Regina, I think it's best that you leave." He said, looking at her.

I don't know what came over me, but I took the gun and fired.

"Jesus Christ." Trevor screamed.

I was shocked myself, as the debris from the ceiling showered down on me.

"Poor ceiling, it took a bullet for you. Now you and Miss Regina sit right here. I have a few questions for her." I demanded.

"I…I…think it's best that I leave." She said stammering over her words.

"Did I ask you to share what you feel is best? The best thing for you to do is to settle down, and answer my questions, then I will determine whether I should let you stay or go. Now… tell me… is this what you do… I said looking at her and then at my husband, sleep around with married men?" I waited for her to answer.

"Ma'am I don't know what you want me to say." Her voice was trembling.

"It's not about what I want you to say, it's a simple question. Only you can be the one to answer the question. I don't have an answer for the slut in you." I spoke with pure malice.

I couldn't stop the hate that I was feeling in my heart. It was hard for me to be the Christian that I desired to be. Right now, all I wanted was for somebody to suffer. And those somebodies were standing half-naked in front of me. She looked at Trevor and then at me again. She didn't know whether to answer or try to make a run for it, but the look on my face made her second guess her decisions. I felt like that girl in that Tyler Perry movie, who found out her husband, was cheating Diary of a Mad Black Woman. Yes, I was mad as hell.

"Look, could you just put down the gun." She inquired, holding her hands up in surrender.

"You're not in a position to make any suggestions. In case you forgot, this is my house, you're in my lane. You have some nerve." I said looking at her as if she'd lost her mind.

She closed her mouth and just looked at me. I know I looked crazy, demonic even, standing there with debris all over me, with a gun in my hand, and fire in my eyes.

"Regina, how long have you been sleeping with my husband?" I repeated.

"Trevor told me that you two was not together, and that he was filing for a divorce. He and I have been seeing each other for about 6 months now."

My facial expression weakened and I almost crumbled. But I wouldn't dare let either of them have the pleasure of seeing how bad that hurt me.

"Celeste, let me explain." He pleaded.

"There's nothing you can say to me that I don't already know. You said that we're not together and that you're getting a divorce, then you have sealed the deal. Your wish is my command. But let me tell you something, you're going to wish you never met me. You think you've seen the worse of me now, then just wait, you haven't seen anything yet." I seethed.

"Celeste you are my wife, I love you, I don't won't a divorce, Celeste please let me explain."

Before I knew it, the girl slapped the taste out of his mouth. I smirked. I must admit that, I wasn't really mad at her. She didn't know me. She wasn't the one who said "I do", she wasn't the one who took the vows, who made those empty promises. Yes, she's just as wrong as he is, but a sinner is too blind to care who they hurt. They are too blind to know that they are hurting themselves. She's not committed to me. I can't blame her if my husband wanted to find pleasure outside our marriage. It's not her fault that what he had at home wasn't enough for him to stay faithful.

"Let not your anger cause you to sin. Even in the midst of the storm, show yourself approved. Be a light in the midst of your darkness. I know it's hard, but you can still represent Me. I tell you vengeance is Mine."

There it was, that small still voice that has always directed me. What was I doing? Why was I losing myself like this? No matter what the situation is, I knew better. Even through the midst of this foolishness, God is correcting me, rebuking me, and reminding me that just because foolishness surrounds me doesn't mean I have to join in. I am a child of the Most High God. And no matter what is going on in front of me, I must come in alignment with the Word and hold myself accountable. Yes, I have a right to be mad, but this behavior was unacceptable. I was wrong and I knew it. I was out of line and out of character. I should have never allowed anyone or anything to take me out of my character. I closed my eyes and let the Lord caress my broken heart, and uplift my broken spirit.

"Now what? Now what are you going to do Celeste?"

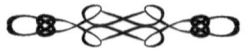

9

"Regina, sit down." I beckoned, pointing to my bed.

"Ye, ye, yes, ma'am," Regina stuttered as fear put tears in her eyes.

"How old are you?" I asked.

"I'm 24." She said.

"You're just a young girl, fresh out of college, am I right?"

"Ye, yes ma'am… I just turned 24 last month and I recently received a degree as a paralegal two weeks ago. I know I don't deserve your pity, but please let me live to see 25." She pleaded.

My heart softened. I thanked God for not allowing me to do what I really wanted to do to her and to Trevor. If I had done what my flesh told me to do, I would be at the police precinct being fingerprinted and booked right now. If I could help it, I would never allow anger to consume me like this again. For the first time I saw a scared, naïve young girl, who was just making a fresh start in her life and I glanced over at my naked, fully grown, husband. All I could do was shake my head. I couldn't resist. I went into my praying room and grabbed my Bible.

"Regina… do you know what this is?" I asked, holding it up.

"Yes ma'am it's a Bible." She sniffled.

"Have you ever read one?" I asked, sitting next to her, opening it up.

"Yes ma'am I have. I go to church." She replied.

"Knowing the Word and going to church is two separate things." I informed her.

"Yes, ma'am." She said, putting her hands in her lap.

"Read this." I said handing her the Bible.

"Let marriage be held in honor among all, and let the marriage bed be undefiled, for God will judge the sexually immoral and adulterous. Hebrews 13:4." She cited.

She held her head down in shame.

"Turn to 1 Corinthians chapter 6 and read verses 8-12." I told her.

She went to the front of the book to look for what page the book was on. When she finally found it, she read aloud, "Flee from sexual immorality. Every other sin a person commits is outside the body, but the sexually immoral person sins against his own body. Or do you not know that your body is a temple of the Holy Spirit within you, whom you have from God? You are not your own, for you were bought with a price. So glorify God in your body."

After she finished reading, she looked ashamed and embarrassed. She took the sheet that was around her and held it tighter. I took the Bible from her and read Romans 6:23 to her. She cried out and sheer agony and dropped to her knees.

"God will never forgive me for this." She said covering her face with her hands.

"God is a merciful God and He loves you so much that He has already given up His only begotten Son, so that whoever believes in Him will not perish but have eternal life. It is because of that that you are able to ask for forgiveness. First John 1:9 says, "If we confess our sins, He is faithful and just and will forgive us our sins and purify us from all unrighteousness."

"How?" She said looking up at me, helplessly.

I got on my knees with her and asked her to repeat the Sinners prayer, and then I told her to read Psalms 51.

"Did you really mean what you said?" I asked her.

"Yes. I do and I do believe that Jesus died for me and that He has forgiven me. I feel so good Mrs. Celeste. I can't explain it but this feeling feels so good." She said weeping, but this time not out of fear, but because of freedom.

"That's the kind of love God gives." I told her, as I threw my arms around the weeping young lady.

"Now cover up, since the Lord has already exposed your nakedness." I told both of them, as they quickly picked up their clothes that were sprawled on the floor.

"I'd wished I understood this long ago, maybe I wouldn't be standing here in somebody else's husband's bedroom. I thank you so much for saving my life… twice." She smiled at me.

"Don't get it twisted; it was God who saved you. You were lucky that I had God in me, holding me back. God is a forgiving God. He'd forgiven me for my sins, so it's only right that forgive you for yours. Now get dressed and go home." I told her.

I didn't have to tell her twice. She quickly put on her clothes and ran towards the door. But she quickly turned around, ran into my arms and hugged me tight.

"Thank you. I'm sorry for the pain I caused you, but if this wouldn't have happened tonight I don't know what would have become of my life." She said sincerely, looking into my eyes.

I nodded and watched her walk out the door.

"Celeste… honey…" He said with a look of panic on his face when I picked up the gun off the night stand.

"What? Oh' this? I said holding up the gun. You're not worth it." I said heading back to the closet to put it back in the safe.

He blew out a long breath, with a look of relief on his face.

"Baby I am so sorry and I promise you… on my life… I would never cheat on you again. I'll spend the rest of my life making it up to you. Just tell me, baby… Tell me what you want me to do?" He begged with his hands on his knees.

"Here's what I want you to do. Get up off the floor; pack you a couple of things, and go." I told him.

"Celeste, please, let's ta… talk about this… I don't won't to lose you…. Please. " He said, trying to hold my hand.

I quickly pushed him away. "You had so much time to talk to me. You had an ample amount of time to contemplate how your actions can result into you losing me. Maybe in time I will forgive you, but right now, I cannot say that I do. Just don't say another word, just get your things and go." I was about to crack.

He simply nodded his head in defeat. I watched him take a few items from his drawers and a few suits from his closet, looked at me again, and walked out of our bedroom. As soon as the front door closed, I collapse on the floor and let all the pain pour out on the floor. Every ounce of strength that I had was gone and I couldn't even pick myself off the floor. Lord, please, hold me... hold your child.

10

"I TOLD YOU what he was about when you first started dating him in school, then you went ahead and married his trifling behind. I knew something wasn't right with him. I knew it was too good to be true. Once a dog always a dog…He have changed from Scappy to Scooby Doo." She said angrily.

"Christie, I don't know what happened to him. That man that was in that room was not my husband. I just don't understand why he would do this to me." I said almost in tears again.

"Well if he wasn't your husband, who the hell was he? What is even harder for me to understand is why would you not think he would do it to you? What make you think that he is incapable of cheating? Huh? Girl, you're just a woman wearing a ring. I am sure the signs were there. Every woman that I've witnessed who has ever been cheated on, always tell that same tale. I know the thought of him cheating, had to have crossed your mind. Girl it doesn't matter how long you know a person, you still don't really know them. We set too many high expectations on men and we fail to realize they are just men. Men will deceive you, so why you can't believe it." She was getting worked up. You'd think she was the one who got cheated on.

"Correction... I'm more than a woman with a ring... I am a *wife*. Don't devalue my status. I understand where you are coming from, but still. And yes, the thought of him cheating has crossed my mind, I admitted. But Christie he is my husband, I didn't want to believe that he would cheat on me. I thought we were better than this. If I can't trust my husband, then who can I trust?" I was almost in tears again. All this crying was working on my nerves.

"Girl, a devoted wife is no different from a devoted girlfriend. The only difference is the ring and a piece of paper. Devoted girlfriends take the same vows that a wife takes, except she's not standing at an altar. But who can you trust? Oh my dear friend, I know you know that answer. It's quite simple... God. She said, looking at me. But you should know that, considering you know Him a lot better than I do. I'm just saying."

"No comment on the wife versus girlfriend thing. I can understand that a woman can commit to a man way before they get the ring. And oh, yes, missy, you know Him just as much as I do." I said looking at her disappointedly. I prayed that one day Christie would repent and recommit her life to God, but I know what she has to be the one to do it, but I am still hopeful.

"In the beginning of our marriage everything was fine. I could feel the love, the joy, and the happiness." I said, crying again.

"Yep, that's in the beginning but after the infatuation fades then everything changes and all the things you didn't know starts to show. But girl you are better than me because I would have laid her behind out and kicked his bony ah—"

"Watch it now." I said warning her.

A curse word or two or three will fly out her mouth when she's not careful. She tries to keep them at a minimum around Rachael and I. I knew she was just venting.

"Well, I can't be mad at the girl." I said.

"Yeah you right. Girrrl...when you told me about the girl getting delivered brought tears to my eyes. I don't see how you did it." She said, holding my hands.

"It had to be God." I assured her.

"And Trevor, Ol', slick mother—"

"Girl, shut your mouth." I said stopping her.

"I'm sorry, pray for me, I still need deliverence, but I am sorry for cursing in front of you like that. I'm just so mad. He better thank whatever god he serve that I wasn't there cause all hell would have broke lose. IF you couldn't shoot him, I would have." She said.

"And then what? Your behind would have been headed to Dekalb County Jail, then off to prison you go. I wouldn't have forgiven myself if something happened to you. You were right where you needed to be. I just can't believe he would be this stupid." I said shaking my head in disbelief.

I still loved my husband but it does not excuse the pain that he was putting me through and I don't know if I could ever forgive him for this. He hit me with the lowest blow ever and I don't think we can pick things up from here. After all we've been through he goes and does something so scandalous. I feel so betrayed and played all at the same time.

"Well, you know a lying man is a half a man and a half a man ain't no man at all." She said.

"What am I suppose to tell Alana?" I said softly.

"Alana is old enough to understand but I wouldn't tell her what's going on. Just tell her you and Trevor need some time apart for a while." She sighed.

"I'll come up with something." I said to her.

"Do you need me to call Rachael? I can tell her to bring something to drink so we can all relax and you can calm down."

"No thank you. I'll be just fine." I rejected her offer.

"Okay, we can eat some hot wings too for old time's sake." She said not letting up.

"I appreciate you just being here right now. I just need some time to sort all of this mess out, you know. I just need some time to my-self." I said, hoping that she understood.

"I get that sis. Just call me if you need me." She said, telling me to try to have a good night before she left.

After I waved her good bye and locked the door. I closed my eyes and allowed the tears to flow. I'd never felt this kind of pain before. This type of hurt can't be explained. I had so much hope into a man that didn't have enough hope in us. I had been faithful to a man who didn't deserve to be trusted. I'd put so much into this marriage and he just threw it all away. He didn't take the vows, the commitment, me, or his family seriously enough to remain true. I was having a hard time trying to keep myself together. I was trying to think back to when things was going bad. I had a feeling something was wrong, but I didn't want to believe it. I was afraid of knowing and I wished that I would have never found out. He brought her into our home... How could he have been so disrespectful...so careless... so cold? Did I not mean anything to him? Did he not care enough about my feel-ings and consider our child? What if Alana would have been here?

Did he even care? My family was falling apart and I didn't know where to start from here. I didn't think how life would be without him. I spent most of my life with that man and now I didn't know what to do without him. Since high school it's always been me and him against the world. But then again that was then and this is now. Things change and like he told me that night he's changed. He told me what it was and I was just too stupid to comprehend.

I put my back against the front door, looked around the empty foyer. I was home alone. Everything was quiet. There was no sense of life. I was there all alone to face the pain, the fear, and the truth. I slid down to the floor and just when I thought I was all cried out, I was mistaken. I felt broken; like the earth beneath me was cracking and I was falling into the darkness. I couldn't understand what I did wrong. I didn't understand how he could betray me and dishonor me so easily. Was I that bad? Was I not worthy enough? Was I not enough?. I cried for believing his lies. I cried for loving him so much. I cried for still wishing he was still around. I cried because he had not called me today to beg me to take him back. I cried for allowing him to hurt me like this. I cried for not listening to the Holy Spirit. I cried for being so weak, for not having the strength to fight. I cried for crying.

The next morning I was so drained I called my receptionist and told her to take the day off and cancel all my appointments for today. How was I supposed to speak life into my clients, when inside I'm dying? How am I supposed to tell them to keep striving and to believe in themselves, when my life was in shambles? I don't have it in me to help anyone, cause I can't even help myself.

So whose going to help you? (this should be put in italics) I heard Dennis voice in my ear.

"Father, I know you are near, but I don't know how to reach you right now. Please tell me... why is this happening to me? Why did he have to do this to me? What did I do Lord? What?" I said holding up my hands in despair. My heart felt like it was breaking into. I never felt this kind of pain in my life. It was like my body was broken into pieces, scattered on the floor, with nobody there to pick them up. A shriek came from the inner depths of me. Then I screamed until my throat was raw. I pressed my pillow to my face and a river a tears begin to flow, then my whole body shook, and then I begin to punch the pillow until I fell asleep in exhaustion. . I couldn't move and I didn't want to. If I could hide under my sheets for all eternity I would. Three days had passed and I was still in bed. I'd told Alana to stay at my parent's house for a few days; thankfully she didn't ask any questions. Trevor tried calling me several times but I didn't even think to answer the phone. He tried to explain his self over the answering machine but I ignored them too.

Apart of me felt a little better because at least he was calling… that meant that he cared. Love can be tricky sometimes. It is so easy to fall in love, but so hard to fall out of. I wondered will I ever be able to get over Trevor, my very first love. How can I pick up the pieces of my life when he holds most of the pieces to my puzzle? I haven't talked to anyone and I really feel the need to talk to my baby I know she'll make me feel better. I picked up the phone and dialed my parent's number.

"Hello." My daughter sweet voice came over the phone.

"Hi sweet pea, are you having fun?" I tried to sound cheerful.

"Yeah right mom, grandma got me over here trying on your clothes from when you were in high school."

"Did you find something you liked?" I joked.

"Yeah right, those clothes so out of style, it makes me wonder just how old you really are." She laughed.

"Oh I see you got jokes, but for your information, what we used to wear back then, is what you young ones are wearing today. You think your style is new, sorry to tell you, we were wearing those styles before you." I checked her.

"Mom…you okay?" She asked, seeing right through me.

"I'm alright sweetie, mommy just need some time to herself that's all." I said swallowing my tears.

"Mom, I'm not five years old so don't treat me like that. I know you and daddy is having problems because I overheard grandma talking to grandpa in the living room." She revealed.

"What I tell you about ease dropping on people?" I asked her, but not angrily.

"You are always trying to keep things from me. I have a right to know. You can't try to protect me forever, mom." She said, surprising me.

"Oh, baby." I said full of emotion. There was nothing else I could say.

"It is okay mom we can get through this. Just let me come home so I can keep you company. You don't need to be home alone." She said.

There was so much sincerity in her voice that I couldn't refuse. I told her to give her grandmother the phone and pack up her things. My mother tried talking me out of coming to get her but it would be better for me to have my baby around me. Alana is right, I have to stop trying to be so protective and let her know what is going on. The biggest problems with parents is that we try to shelter our kids from things that they need to be aware of and we wonder why they aren't prepared for life when they get older. I have to open up to her and tell her everything. She deserves to know the truth.

After reassuring my mom that it would be okay it only took me thirty minutes to get up and head to my parents house. It felt real good to get some fresh air. I inhaled the air and allowed the wind to blow through my hair. It was indeed a beautiful day and people were outdoors soaking up all this nice weather. After I hugged my parents and assured them that I was feeling okay, Alana and I decided to go to the mall on a little shopping spree. Thanks to Trevor Platinum American Express card we were able to get whatever we wanted. I picked up a pair of pink Jimmy Choo leather pumps that I had to have.

They cost three hundred dollars but it didn't hurt me one bit when I handed the credit card to the cashier. I was satisfied and relieved to be out of the house. After we shopped we went to Red Lobster, my daughter's favorite restaurant, and ordered some crab legs, grilled shrimp, and pilaf rice. Everything was going fine until I glanced towards the entrance and almost choked on a shrimp.

11

JUST WHEN I thought I was beginning to have some kind of stability in my life, here he comes once again stirring up feelings that I'm still trying to get over. I scooted down in my chair so that he wouldn't spot me, but I was too late there he was walking to our table.

"Hi there, I almost didn't recognize you." He starred. Those eyes still had an affect on me.

"Dennis, how have you been?" I asked, trying to be cordial.

"I've been trying to heal my broken heart." He replied, touching his chest.

"Hi there, you must be Alana?" He said smiling at Alana who was giving him that 'who are you' look. Dennis must have caught her expression.

"I am a friend of your mothers, and she's told me all about you." He spoke still smiling at her.

"Oh, okay." She said softly and went back to eating her food.

"It's good seeing you Celeste. Maybe we can grab a bite to eat sometimes for old time sakes." He said looking at me.

Those eyes… there's something about those eyes…

"Yeah, that'll be good." I confirmed, clearing my throat, trying to find my escape.

"Well, call me when the time is preeminent for you. Just in case you forgot my number here is my card." He said handing me the card and walked away.

I put the card in my purse and tried to enjoy the rest of my food. After everything I told him he still wanted to see me and whether I wanted to admit it or not I wanted to see him too. There it is again, Trevor is now far from my mind. It was almost ten-thirty when we finally made it home and I was exhausted.

"Mom, I'm about to call it a night. Will you be okay?" She asked.

"I'll be fine honey, you have a good night." I told her.

"And mom . . ." she looked back at me.

"Yes, sweetie?"

"I could tell Dennis likes you and that you like him too by the way ya'll was looking at each other. I know you're still married to daddy but I don't expect you to be with him if he's making you sad." She said.

Oh my goodness, my little girl has once again left me speechless. I couldn't say anything to her. All I could do was nod my head and smile. I was tired but I couldn't go to sleep. When I looked at the clock it was just eleven-thirty. I went downstairs to get a glass of water to quench my thirst when I spotted my purse on the kitchen counter. I took it with me to my room and pulled out the card that Dennis gave me. Here I go again with this nervousness. I thought since we've already shared so much it would be easy to talk to him.

I kept thinking about our last conversation and I sat there trying to figure out what would I say if I did call him. Then, I thought about what Trevor did to me and I quickly grabbed the phone and dialed his number. The mistake that I made two times too many is that I never thought to ask God, what he thought about it.

"Dennis, this is Celeste I was just giving you a call."

"I'm glad you did. To be honest I thought you weren't going to call. I've missed you." He said softly.

The way he said it tugged at my heart and I wished I could take back everything I said.

"Why don't you meet me at Starbuck's in the morning and have a cup of coffee with me." I said, trying to enlighten the mood.

"Gladly." He cheered up fast.

"Okay, in the morning it is. We need to talk anyway." I said.

After hanging up the phone I contemplated on what I was going to say to him. Then it hit me and I hope and pray it'll be the right choice, but then again I wasn't exactly asking God.

Starbuck's was crowded as usual and I could barely walk in there.

"Excuse me." I said, bumping into this white plump lady who was trying to keep her little girl from running around the store. I stood on my toes trying to see if I could find Dennis and spotted him by a window.

"Just when I thought you weren't going to show up." He said, lighting up the room with that smile of his.

"It's so crowded in here I could barely get threw the door." I murmured, with a roll of my eyes.

"Well you're here and that's all that matters. I hope you don't mind but I took the liberty of ordering you some coffee light and sweet." He said, letting me know that he remembered.

"Yes. Thank you." I smiled.

"You're welcome."

"How have you been?" I asked him.

"I've been doing okay, you know. How have you been?" He asked.

"Well… I've been." I said.

"Ooo…kayyy… so, you wanted to talk to me about something?"

"What do you mean?" He looked perplexed.

"I mean me and you." I said sarcastically.

"I know what you meant, but I'm trying to figure out what about us?" He said.

"I would like to give us a try." I said swallowing hard.

"Hmph… you sure you will not run back to your husband and leave me alone to deal with the tears?" He said jokingly, but I knew he was serious.

"Ouch, I winced. I deserve that."

"Will you excuse me; I have to go to the ladies room." I told him, quickly getting up from the table and heading to the bathroom.

When I got into the bathroom I took a look in the mirror and wondered what I was I doing. All I knew was how he made me feel when I was with him and I just wanted to have that feeling again. I walked out of the bathroom, and headed back to our table.

"Is everything okay?" He asked, once I sat down.

"Everything is fine."

"Was it something I said?"

"Not at all," I said taking a sip of coffee.

"Because I want you to know that I will never intentionally try to hurt your feelings."

"I'm fine, and thank you Dennis. You are so sweet." I smiled.

"So, what is it that you want to talk about?" He asked, taking my hand across the table and holding it. I held on firmly and wasn't sure if I could let go.

"Well, I'm a little nervous and I don't want you to think that I'm trying to be with you on the rebound."

"On the rebound, what are you talking about?" He asked puzzled.

"Trevor and I are getting a divorce." I blurted.

"Oh, Celeste, what happened?" He said getting out of his chair and sitting beside me.

I told him everything that happened and he ended up holding me while I cried in his arms. We walked through the park a few hours and ended up in my bed. The next morning, I woke up with the same clothes I had on that following day.

"You want some breakfast?" He stood at the door, with a tray of waffles, an omelet loaded with steak, green peppers, onions, and cheese, a hot bowl of grits, and a tall glass of orange juice.

"Let me find out you know how to burn in the kitchen." I was amazed.

"Girl, don't let this finess fool you. I can cook, clean, and do laundry. My mama taught me well."

"You're right about that. The finess, I mean." I said, taking a bite and he was right about knowing how to cook too.

12

DENNIS was doing exactly what I knew he would do— help me forget about my husband and love on me the right way. Even though I seldom listen to R&B music, I would often time listen to artists like Whitney Houston, Patti Labelle, and other soulful artists. Right now I was allowing John Legend to take me "So High". As I sat in thought about Dennis the lyrics seem to tell all my business. Dennis and I have been going strong for about four months and I warned myself to take things slow. I didn't want to jump so high that I couldn't break the fall if I came tumbling down.

Alana loves him and enjoys his company and for her birthday he took us all to a Mary Mary concert. That girl love her some Mary Mary and since then couldn't anybody tell her anything bad about dear o' Dennis. I was cleaning up and preparing some horderves for my guests. I wanted my best friends to meet my special guy tonight. I wasn't quite ready to present him to my parents, because I knew they wouldn't be pleased with me still being married and all. I know Christie would be happy about me moving on but Rachael is another story.

When I noticed that she was the last one to sit at the dinner table, I figured something was up.

"Hello, Rachael, my name is Dennis, how are you?" He motioned towards her to shake her hand.

"Celeste and Rachael, can I speak to you for minute in the kitchen please?" She asked plastering on a fake smile, while shaking his hand.

"Sure." I said, looking over at Christie who was rolling her eyes. We both knew what was coming.

"Don't you think it's a little too soon for you to be bringing him in the house? For God's sakes Celeste, you're not even divorced yet. What in the world are you thinking bringing this man around Alana like that? Have you lost your mind?" She carried on, throwing questions at me left from right.

"Rachael, you need to hush. You white girls get on my nerves. Y'all may be okay with your man cheating on you, but black women don't play that. Shut up and let that girl live her life and you worry about yours. You always got to run your mouth, like you all righteous. I know the names of all of your skeletons girlfriend. As far as I'm concerned her marriage was over when Trevor decided to be with another woman. He didn't care about her or her feelings when he brought that woman up in her house, so why should she just sit back and not move on with her life." Christie said letting her have it.

"The color of my skin has nothing to do with anything and I do not think that I'm better and you know it. I know I'm not perfect, but still. And first of all, I'm not talking to you Chris I'm talking to her." She said throwing her finger up at me.

"Look Rachel, I'm a grown woman and I don't need you coming up in here throwing judgment. You aren't God and I don't owe you any explanation. After what Trevor did to me you should be happy for me. You're supposed to be my friend and here you are sitting up here like you're mother Theresa or something. I don't need this right now I need your support." I told her.

"Brothers and sisters, if someone is caught in a sin, you who live by the Spirit should restore that person gently. But watch yourselves, or you also may be tempted." She said quoting scripture.

"My point exactly." Christie said, throwing up her hands.

"I am your friend and I only want what's best for you. The truth never needs support and you know it. Yeah, Trevor was wrong for what he did to you but I will not agree that you're doing the right thing by falling into bed with this man. Give yourself time to heal before you jump into another relationship." She said trying to make me understand.

"Falling into bed? What in the world are you talking about? Dennis and I have never had sex." I said, looking at her like she was crazy.

"Cause she's judgmental like that… Always speaking on what she doesn't know." Christie said, rolling her eyes at Rachael.

I am down for her and her devotion to God, but at times I just want to shake her. Saved people act like they get amnesia. Like they've never done anything in their life. Even I have been guilty of that. All of those times I used to back her up every time she snuck out the house with different guys during high school.

"Whatever, Celeste. Just because it works for you doesn't make what you doing right." She said.

"I don't have to explain anything to you. In case you didn't get it last time, I am a grown woman and I don't need you making decisions for me. I don't tell you what to do with your life and I'd appreciate it if you did the same for me. I'm not perfect and you aren't either. We've all made mistakes that we're not proud of." I let her know.

"I know that's right. You need me to jog your memory?" Christie said giving Rachael the eye.

"You don't need to, because I was there. You see my sister; my past does not define me. God forgave me for that a long time ago. It is funny how man finds it hard to forgive what God has already forgotten. I thank God for what I had to go through, because it made me run right into His arms. Let the redeemed of the Lord, say so… So, you want to talk about what I did in my past, I'm simply saying… so… Cause God has tossed all my past mistakes in the sea of forgetfulness. I'm not trying to run your life, I'm just trying to look out for you. You already know how I am anyway." Rachael said.

"I understand all of that and I appreciate you looking out for me. But this time Rachael, I'm going to need for you to stay out of it. Dennis makes me happy and he's been here for me through all of this. Now, you came up in here with a judgmental look before you sat down. You should go out there and apologize, but since I know it will not be genuine I'll apologize to him for you. But if you can't say something nice then don't say anything at all and if you can't help but act like a silly rabbit then you can go play tricks with your kids at home." I pointed towards the door.

"Now that's funny." Christie laughed.

I was not in the mood for Rachael tonight and I didn't have to deal with her. She looked at me and noticed how serious I was and decided to go back in the dining room to sit down. While we ate at the table we all had a nice chat and laughed but I noticed that she held back a bit but that was fine with me because she was way out of line and she knew it. I am not about to apologize to her for defending myself. For years she's been looking down on people and it was time somebody put her in her place and who better to do it then me.

The following afternoon, I stood in the doorway, frozen, as I ran my fingers across the letter addressed to me in a familiar handwriting that I knew all too well. I didn't want to know what was in the letter and I really didn't have the energy of reading it. When I first saw the letter I wanted to just throw it in the garbage but instead I left it on the kitchen table with the rest of my unwanted mail. Three days passed before I took the time out to read the contents of the letter.

Celeste,

I know that the last person you would want to hear from is me. That's why I decided to write instead of come to the house. Celeste I am sorry that I hurt you and I know you didn't deserve anything like that. I want you to know that it was nothing that you did wrong. It was me in my selfishness. All those times you've tried to make everything work out for us I pushed you away. I must have lost my mind and I've lost my family because I decided to think with the head in my pants than the head on my shoulders. I love you Celeste.

From the first time I laid eyes on you I knew you were the one for me. I know I messed up and I know by me saying I'm sorry isn't going to change the pain I've put you through. I feel like I've thrown my whole life away and I haven't slept much in days. I don't know what I was thinking because nobody can do me like you. Can make me feel the way you do . . . Who can love me like you do . . . ? Please give me a chance to plead my case and if you still don't want us to be together then I'll understand and let you be. Meet me at Isabella's tonight at 8:30pm and if you don't show up I'll then know that we are truly at the end of our journey together. I'd follow your wishes and sign those divorce papers that was served to me 2 weeks ago.

I love you,
Trevor

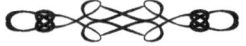

13

I TOOK MY TIME reading over the letter again as tears rolled down my cheeks. I didn't know what to make of the letter and I couldn't believe that I was really considering going to meet him until I showed up at the restaurant. I made sure I had on my best attire just so he could see what he was missing. When he stood up to pull out my chair he stood there for awhile, transfixed by what was in front of him. My make up was immaculate, my hair was hanging down my shoulders just the way he liked it, and I wore a forest green sheer dress made by Prada, with a pair of silver stilettos that matched perfectly.

"You look beautiful." He said almost speechless.

"And you look . . . terrible." I said looking at him from head to toe.

He really did look a mess. Even though he wore expensive clothing he still looked as if he hadn't shaved in days and his suit was wrinkled. He was right... things do change.

"I know. Celeste, I would first like to thank you for coming because I know you didn't have to. And secondly, I would like to say I'm sorry for hurting you the way that I did. I was so stupid and I regret all of the things I've done. I never wanted things to go the way that they did and now I've lost the most important women in my life. You and Alana . . . I know she's mad at me and I always wanted to be the man she admired. But I failed as a father and I've failed you." He sniffed, as tears fell from his eyes.

I haven't seen him cry like that since his grandfather funeral and my heart tugged at me and before I knew it I was grabbing his hand.

"Trevor, as hard as I've tried to understand why you did what you did. I spent so much time thinking about what I did to cause it, that I failed to realize that the blame was on you and not me. You failed to think about our marriage, our family, and what we had when you did what you did. You really hurt me and even though I will never understand why, I do forgive you. I forgive you because God has been too good to me, even when I didn't deserve it. You could have came to me and told me if something was wrong. All of the times I wished you would talk to me, you didn't. Your letter does not justify anything. It doesn't take away the pain, the heartache, the shame and the disappointment. Don't expect me to run into your arms and take you back." I told him.

"I know I was wrong Celeste and I'm sorry for everything that I have done to you. All I'm asking for is another chance to make things right with you and Alana. We've been together for too long to end it like this and I can't imagine life without you. Please, let's try to work thing out. I'm willing to do whatever it takes. I love you Celeste and I'll love you till the day I die. You are what I want and I will never intentionally hurt you again. I thought about what you said, you know… that night. I've asked God to forgive me and He has. The night that you told me to leave, I sat in my car all night talking to God. Cause I know that if the God you serve can make you forgive the woman that I was sleeping with, then I know He must be some kind of God." He said.

"He was some kind of God before the foundation of the world. It just took this to happen for you to realize it. My God is awesome and He is good." I told him.

"He sure is. I know for myself." He said smiling.

"What do you mean?" I asked him.

"That night, I accepted God as my Lord and Savior. I've been spending a lot of time in the Bible and going to church and now I understand a lot of stuff that you were trying to tell me."

I didn't know what to say. I just sat there and listened to him talk about the goodness of the Lord and what he has learned.

"Celeste, I never understood the seriousness of marriage and how important my vows were until I read about Adam and Eve. The Lord made a woman from the rib of Adam and brought her to him. Then Adam said to Eve, "this is now bone of my bones and flesh of my flesh. God had taken a rib from the side of Adam and created Eve out of it. That means that not only are you apart of me, but you are apart of God… I disrespected God when I disrespected you. You were designed to walk beside me, to be my helpmate, not to be treated any kind of way." He said, wiping his nose.

"You are my rib baby. When I hurt you, I was hurting myself. You are bone of my bone and flesh of my flesh. I know without a shadow of a doubt that our ribs match and that God made you just for me. Celeste if you let me in, I promise I'll honor you, love you, and take care of you the right way, this time around." He said looking into my eyes.

My mind was all over the place.

"I can't do this right now. I just… can't." I said moving my hands from his and walking out.

After the conversation I had with Trevor, it took me another week for me to clear my head and think things through. I prayed hard, read my Bible more than I have been doing lately, and allowed the Lord to speak to me. I knew what the Lord wanted me to do, but I didn't know if I could do it. I know that I have to follow God's prompting because He will never steer me wrong. It was so hard for me to make this decision because I knew that someone would end up hurt in the end, but I have to do what I have to do.

Dennis helped me put my life together. When he promised me that he was a good heart doctor he wasn't lying. He was there to help me stand through the toughest time in my life and when I thought I'd lost myself, he'd help me find me. Being with him has been the happiest ten months of my life and I wasn't ready to let him go. Trevor took something from me… His infidelity took me to a place where I've never been before. Even though I have forgiven him, I don't know if I could ever trust him like I used to. I called both Trevor and Dennis and told them to meet me at Starbuck's in about an hour.

I was there about twenty minutes early. I was so nervous and I asked God to comfort me. After praying this morning for confirmation, I knew what I had to do. Trevor was the first to show up. He didn't say a word to me; he just kept looking at me timidly. Shortly after, Dennis arrived, looking at the both of us, wondering what was going on. He didn't know what Trevor looked like; I had put all our family pictures and anything that reminded me of Trevor in the attic.

"Dennis this is my husband Trevor. Trevor this is Dennis." I said introducing them. Neither one of them spoke they just looked at me. I sat down and took a deep breath.

"I know you two are wondering why you are here and Dennis I know that you don't really know what's going on." I looked at him.

"I've been calling you for days." He said.

"I know you have, but I have been doing a lot of soul searching and I have to make some decisions that I know that will not be pleasant for one of you." I said, trying to find the words.

"Every moment I've spent with you is more than a fairy tale. You were there for me when I needed you the most and I adore you. I love you for letting me see that there are better men out there. Alana really likes you and I know you two have bonded. But my husband and I have been together for a long time and I have to be truthful to my vows and stand by him. I'm so sorry." I said dropping my head.

My heart was hurting so bad that I questioned whether I was really making the right choice.

"Why did I put myself through this with you, again." He said shaking his head. The pain on his face broke my heart.

"You are a wonderful man and I think you should—"

"It's cool." He said interrupting me. He stood from the table and headed towards the door.

"Dennis, please?" I needed him to understand where I was coming from but how did I expect him to.

"Dennis." I yelled after him. Everyone stopped talking, and looked towards us.

"Celeste, let him go. No matter what you say, he is too hurt to understand." Trevor said, putting his hands on my shoulders.

"But I—" I couldn't find the words.

I walked out Starbuck's with a heavy heart, holding the hand of my husband. Sometimes the hardest decisions can be the best decisions and as I looked up at my husband, I knew I had made the right decision. I understood that marriage was more than the teenage love we shared in high school, way beyond the infatuation we felt in college, and that the honeymoon wasn't the end, but just the beginning of something beautiful.

UNpretty

One

MANY PEOPLE SAY that I am stuck-up and can come off too conceited for their taste, maybe a little too narcissistic but what they fail to realize is that I am not seasoned for their taste buds. There's nothing wrong with a woman being sure of herself. You see, I don't need anyone to tell me how pretty I am or how fine I look, because I look in the mirror all the time. Since I was a little girl, girls have been jealous of me, so I have learned how to easily dismiss the haters and besides I walk alone. I don't need any new friends. It doesn't take much for me to get a man, and it doesn't take much effort for me to take someone else's.

There's no shame in my game. I'm not in it for love, just to get a little affection. I promise I will not keep anybody's man. I'm sure at one point or another, I have given him back. I really don't know what it is, that keep those men salivating over me. A female always wants to confront another female about their man, when they should be checking their man. Marriage is not going to keep a man faithful; it only means that they are locked down trying to be rescued, so they come to women like me, for freedom. No, I am not a prostitute. I am too classy, too rich, and my body is just too valuable to be giving it away to any ol' body.

I have the luxury of choosing who I want to sleep with. Prostitutes have to take what they can get. Oh, did I forget to mention how beautiful I am. Oh well, if I did, let me remind you. Many people tell me I look like the spitting image of the model and singer Denyce Lawton. I have a Korean mother and my father is African American. My skin tone is copper with a hint of cinnamon, which is smooth and flawless, might I add. I have an hour glass shape—long model-shaped legs, a small waist, a fully toned behind and a flat stomach.

I have dark brown eyes, long, flowing, dark brown hair, and full kissable lips. From the time I was five up until I was seventeen my mother forced me to do beauty pageants and she even had me model a little. All my life I heard people comment on how beautiful I was. Soon, I would fine that this hour-glass figure and pretty face would be a blessing and a curse. It didn't take me long to embrace the "act like a woman and think like a man" philosophy when I understood that men only wanted me either to fulfill their sexual desire or as a trophy to put on their arms for public functions, then that's when I stopped looking for Mr. Right and focused on Mr. Right Now.

There was times when I looked in the mirror and was over come with sadness, because had I not been this beautiful maybe daddy wouldn't have been so hasty to come in my bedroom every other night. He would lustfully run his hands over my body and tell me how beautiful I was. He would promise me that no other man would ever love me like he did. He'd told me that it was normal for daddy's to show how much they loved their daughters. He reassured me that intimacy was the only way. He'd sworn me to secrecy and whisper sweet nothings in my ear that has haunted me from my youth up until my adulthood.

Now, I know you may think my father is some kind of twisted son-of-a… you know the rest, and I'd say you're absolutely right. Somehow he'd convinced me that what he was doing was right, so he and I had a secret love affair up until I left for college. I loved my father, beyond how a child should love their father, and he rocked me to the core when he told me we had to end our relationship. You see, what had happen was, daddy almost had a heart attack when I was 21, and I guess that shook him up. He told me that what he was doing to me was wrong, that he was sorry, and that he lied about everything he told me. He told me that he wanted to have a "normal" relationship with me, like fathers are supposed to have with their children.

"So you are saying you don't want to be with me anymore?" I asked, confused, tears streaming down my face.

"Sweetheart, you and I, was never in a relationship. Your mother is my wife and you are my daughter. I'm sorry. I never meant to hurt you. Do you believe me, if I told you that I was in love with both you and your mother? I loved you both, I was wrong… I was wr… onnggg…" He whimpered.

I still couldn't quite understand what he was saying. In my mind he was choosing my mother over me and I hated her for it. He told me that I was the light of his life, the center of his joy, and that nobody could ever take my place. He said I was daddy's favorite little girl. Soon after he got out of the hospital, he retired from the bench as a judge, and was nominated the State Senator of California. Hatred filled me when I discovered this. It wasn't that my dear father was trying to make things right because he had a near-death experience, but he didn't want his reputation smeared.

I was so angry, so hurt, and so disgusted with him and myself. Up until now he showers me with gifts and money so that I will not air out his dirty laundry. Call it hush money, but I call it revenge. See, I don't have to work a day in my life; daddy supplies all of my needs. He bought this lavish 2 bedroom, 2 bath, split-level home over looking the beach, that ruby red *2014 Mercedes*-Benz S-Class parked inside of my garage, and he gives me a weekly allowance of $15,000 to shop. I never did go back to college to finish my broadcast journalism degree. I wanted to be a news anchor for ABC7 News.

Daddy always tries to talk me into going back to pursue my dreams, but I told him that I didn't need all that, because I had him to take care of me. I could tell by the look on his face that the demons he held hidden inside were eating him alive. He looked older, frailer, and so defeated. I could even see sadness in his eyes. Mother never did notice, because she was too busy in the malls, at the country club giggling with her fake friends, and making too many cosmetic surgery appointments to notice the silent cries that I held deep within my heart. Then I wondered whether she did know what my father was doing and just turned a deaf ear to it.

She didn't want to challenge my father, she didn't want to let go of the lavish life-style, the red-carpet events, and the prominent functions that her and my father frequently attended. This revelation made me despise her even more. What kind of a mother would allow a man to touch her daughter like that? Then, I often wondered, what type of father would touch their daughter like that? Then I asked myself, what type of daughter would want their father to touch her like that? Maybe if my mother taught me how to make men respect my mind and not my body, then maybe... just maybe... I wouldn't be this cold.

Love has never been a friend of mine. So far it has not really been working for me, so I say to hell with it. It doesn't like me, and quite frankly, I can care less about it. Now that I got that out of the way, where was I? Oh... my mom did teach me or showed me rather, that men are only good for one thing. A good lay and a great ATM machine... I've slept with a few decent guys who I would have considered fooling around with a bit longer than usual had they not been so clingy. Then there was that *L*-word that they used that turned me off, so I had to dispose of them quickly.

I've had my share of men—single, taken, separated and married, so I am not oblivious to the ways of a man. I guess you just have to take the good with the bad. I bet you wondering why I would even sleep around with a married man. I bet you think I'm some Jezebel, like the church folk call it or a floozy, like my mom calls it, or maybe some desperate little girl trying to look for love that she didn't get from her daddy, according to mental health theorists. Or is it that you think that I'm so lonely, so desperate, and so eager to have a man that I can't find one on my own. Maybe you think that I only want him because he's already taken and ready-made? Hmmm...

This may help you keep your man and keep your marriage intact. Let me help you understand why your man doesn't come home at night and why he chooses to sleep with Jezebel's and floozies like me, who is seeking for love that she didn't get from her daddy, and is sooo desperate to have a man that she can't find one of her own. Let me help you with something that could probably save your marriage from the Jezebel's and floozies in this world. Have you ever stopped to think that not every man cheat because of good sex... Sometimes men can find affection from someone else at their most vulnerable moments. Yes, men can be vulnerable too.

They may act all macho like they don't have needs, but inside every man there is a sensitive side. So while you are adding to his stress, he finds himself being emotionally carried away by someone or should I say "something" new. A man is not eager to come home to a bickering wife, who is adding more stress than comfort. Men want a woman who they can talk to, without being argued down and nagged about finances, babies, and quality time. They can't communicate with you because you can't relate to them in a way that brings on a connection that opens the outlet for communication.

So, they go to someone who doesn't judge them, that won't look down on them, and who won't bring up their weaknesses during a heated argument. They are attracted to the thrill of being with someone who will not hesitate to please them. See that's where you women mess up at. You get too comfortable. You think just because he married you that you have to stop taking care of yourself and stop taking care of him. He's not going to be attracted to the cotton pajamas and the sleeping cap on your head. I can hear some of you women now, "Well if he can't love me for who I am, then he doesn't deserve to be with me anyway."

That may be your truth, which is probably the reason why you laying there right now wondering where your husband is. Wondering why he doesn't call you beautiful or why he doesn't want to be around you. And here is another problem that women need to consider. They need to stop trying to hold on too tight and stop holding out. A man shouldn't have to run into the bed of another woman, because his wife doesn't want to give up what he thought he was entitled to. You make it so easy for us—the Jezebel's and the floozies to come in and take your position. Men are often attracted to the very thing wives hold hostage.

Then you get mad at the other woman and claim she stole your man. How is somebody going to steal something that they have the permission to take? It takes two to tangle. One can't force the willing. He chooses who he chooses because that's what he wants, not because a woman had to hold him hostage to steal his possessions. Much like the others, I worked my magic to get the attention of my sexy boss, Kirk. I knew I just had to have him the moment I first saw him.

I knew he was married before he offered me the executive assistant position at his physician's office. Of course it didn't stop me before, so why should it have made a difference to me then. But in time, I found that Kirk was different from all the rest. He wasn't like the rest of the men that I'd dismissed and sent their merry way. No... Kirk had the type of sex-appeal that made you want to fall at his mercy and surrender. I was unaware of the trouble that I would find myself getting into. I'd must have missed the signs, gotten soft, or just got stupefied from the passionate kisses, his tantalizing love-making, and his sweet promises that dripped from his lips to my heart, like sweet molasses. I was like Mariah Carey, he had me wrapped up, packed up, ribbon with a bow on it.

Two

MY MOTHER called me asking me if I could come over for a minute. I guess she called herself wanting to have some mother-daughter bonding… whatever that means. Lately, she's been making a huge effort and when I asked her why the sudden change, she just said she wanted to spend some time with her daughter and that she hoped that I didn't think that she was asking for too much. It always has to be about her. She always wants someone to move when she say move and like the subservient girl that I have always been, in spite of my detestation, I followed suit. Dad may get the short end of the stick, but my mother has always had away of making me feel like a little girl who had better do what she was told.

My mother was stern and was the disciplinarian in our household and my father was like putty in my hands. He always allowed me to do whatever I wanted, whenever I wanted. So when I would ask my mother for something and her response to me was no, I'd go and ask my father. Mother used to always argue with him about that. She would always tell him that he was teaching me how to disrespect her and not heed to her instructions.

Maybe she was right, because I did find myself always going to my father when I needed to talk or when I needed something. I never once thought to go to my mother about personal things. Not when I first scrapped my knee trying to ride a bike, not when I first got my period, not when I first started liking boys, and certainly not when my father gave me my first kiss. My mother and I were like distant strangers living up under the same roof. She didn't seem to have an interest in me and I learned not to care. Now all of a sudden she wanted to establish a relationship with me.

But it was too late; she's already missed out on the most significant stages of my life. There was several times where I wanted to run into the arms of my mother. I always knew deep down inside what my father was doing to me was not right. All the things he whispered in my ears had to have been wrong. My mind believed his every word, but my heart couldn't trust him. My father had just left my bedroom and I couldn't call it and I still can't place the feeling today, but a strong feeling of sadness and pain came over me. I couldn't stop crying. My mother must have passed my door because I heard a sudden knock.

"Konnie, are you okay in there?" I heard her voice behind the door.

"Mom." I said, whimpering helplessly.

"Konnie, what's wrong honey?" She said, after opening my door and noticing how terrified I was.

"Mom, I have something to tell you, but you have to promise not tell daddy." I told her, looking at her.

"Tell your daddy what, what is going on?" She asked with a look of confusion on her face.

"Nara?" I could hear my father yell for my mother.

"Coming."

"Your father is calling, let's talk later, eh." She said, patting the top of my head, and hurried to see what my father wanted.

So there I lay, in my tears, trapped in my fear, imprisoned by the constant secret that would ultimately shape my tomorrow. I went through my huge walk in closet and sorted through my clothes trying to find something suitable to wear for brunch. My mother loved the country club, so when she called me and told me to meet her there, I quickly changed my mind about what I had on. I enjoyed being in the comfort of my home and when I wasn't out shopping, I'd just stay at home and sit on my terrace and look out at the ocean, watching the waves crash into each other. The sound and smell of the ocean always calmed me and there... on that terrace... is where I found tranquility. Every time Terrance would come over he'd marvel at my kitchen.

He was a great cook and I would always have him come over to cook for me. Terrance has been my best friend since junior high school. I've never been too fond of having too many girlfriends. I can understand why Terrance loved to come over. I must admit, my kitchen was to die for with its stainless steel appliances, Caesar Stone countertops, veneer cherry wood cabinets and floors. My whole house was beautiful. I had high-rise ceilings, two fireplaces (one in my room and one in the living room), a gym with a sauna; a laundry room with top notch laundry units. My bathroom is sanctuary, my most favorite room in the house.

My tub is a fusion whirlpool with built in chromatherapy and in line heating. Surrounded around it was white scented candles. What also attracted me about my bathroom were the limestone countertop, the natural wood vanity, the wide mirrored cabinet, and the IPOD that was already installed. I had built in speakers and I was able to adjust the sound of my music from every room in my house. My bedroom could have been in a magazine. I had a cherry wood vanity bed with silk white sheers that hung from each post. My house could have been in any in home magazines.

My father hired a top interior-designer, my request of course, to decorate my home just the way I liked it. Settling on an rose pink cotton dress made by Prada with raw cut edges with pleats and a pair of nude Prada heels, I was headed to the country club to play the mother-daughter game with my mother. When I arrived my mom stood up and we air-kissed before we sat down. My mom has never been the affectionate type. I vaguely remember her giving me a kiss on the cheek, or giving me a hug. Some people are just not built to be mothers or maybe she just was never taught the attributes of motherhood from her own mother.

Although I love my Grammy (that's what I called my grandmother), my mother doesn't seem to care for her much. When we used to visit my grandparents in South Korea, I could always sense some tension between them. They hardly spoke to each other and I never quite understood that when my Grammy would try to hug her or show her some form of affection, she would reject it. One day I asked her about it and she just brushed it off, like she didn't know what I was talking about. My mother could never understand me, like her mother couldn't understand her I assume.

Looking at my mother you will detect a sense of grace, style, classiness, and flare. My mother looked like she was just hitting forty, but she had just celebrated her fiftieth birthday. I guess those frequent visits to the cosmetic surgeon really paid off. Another thing I learned from her —having the ability to flaunt the best designer pieces in style. She looked ravishing in a knee-length mint green silk, draped off the shoulder dress. It had petal-like folds, off the shoulder neckline; dipped v-back, front asymmetric draping that complimented her soft blushed skin.

Based on my knowledge of clothing designers, it looked like the work of Lela Rose, adorned on her feet was a pair of chocolate brown Manolo Blahnik pumps. Her make up was perfect, her short jet black her was pinned up in a bun, and I could smell the floral scent of jasmine tickle my nose as she sat down. She was wearing her favorite perfume, Ange ou Démon Le Secret by Givenchy.

"So… how have you been doing?" She asked, as she sliced a piece of chicken from her chicken salad.

"I'm well mother, thank you for asking. How have things been with you?" I asked, pretending like I actually cared.

"Ohh… it's your father dear. She said exaggeratingly, he has been getting ill to much lately and I am afraid it is something serious this time."

"You know how daddy can be; he'll bounce back sooner than you know it." I said as I watched the waitress come towards our table.

"I don't know… He hasn't been his self lately and I don't think he's well enough to keep working. I told him that he needs to consider retiring, but that stubborn man will not listen." She said with a sigh.

"Hello madam, did you find something you'd like to order on the menu?" The waiter asked me.

"I would like the chicken salad on wheat bread, with your home-made potato chips on the side, please." I answered, not even looking at the menu.

"Yes ma'am… he said jotting my order down on a pad. And to drink?" He asked, looking up from the pad.

"Yes, I'd like to have a club soda please." I smiled at him.

"Sure." He said bowing and walking off.

"Daddy can be stubborn; maybe asking him to retire is not a good idea. You know how he is about his job." I said, focusing my attention back on my mother.

"Maybe you're right. I can only imagine how your father would be if he didn't have a job to go to." She said in agreement.

"The most disturbing thing happened last night while he was sleeping... He kept calling your name and saying he was sorry. He was literally crying in his sleep." She said shaking her head in dismay.

I almost choked on my water, "Wha...what did he say it was about?" I stuttered.

She looked at me strangely, "He wouldn't say.... He just told me that he had a nightmare and for me to go back to bed."

I can only imagine what my daddy was thinking about. But I was scared that my father was on the brink of unleashing our deepest, darkest, secret and I don't think I am prepared for it. I had to have a little chat with dear o' daddy and see what's really going on. He may be having one of his death scares again.

Three

AFTER THE conversation I had with my father I was too rattled, too distracted to concentrate. He was sicker than I thought. He'd told me that he'd been diagnosed with stomach cancer and that every doctor he went to said that the cancer had spread so much that it was impossible to remove it all.

"Konnie, I'm dying." He coughed.

"Don't say that daddy, don't you ever say that." I said with tears in my eyes.

All the anger and resentment I felt towards him washed away at that moment. It was at that moment where I felt like a little girl again. I was scared for my father, and even though he'd hurt me badly, I still wanted him around. Cause deep down, I still loved him. Not like a woman who loved a man, but like a daughter who loved her father.

"Konnie… listen to me… he said grabbing my hand. I haven't told your mother about the diagnosis yet. I just can't bare it. I will tell her when I'm ready." He moaned.

"Okay." I said as tears rolled down my cheeks. His skin looked like a pasty brown, he'd lost a lot of weight, and I no longer saw the strong judge who sat on the bench in a courtroom, but a man who was frail, weakened and afraid.

"I have to tell your mother… he coughed. I have… to… ta… telll… your mother. It is eating me up inside." He said closing his eyes, as a tear slipped out his eyes.

"Please don't…" I begged.

"Kon…Konnie… I know you have hated me for a long time. You think I betrayed you and I did on so many different levels. I was supposed to be your protector, but instead I was your monster. I did some awful th…things… to you and I'm ssss….sorry." He said trying to catch his breath.

"Ssshhh… just stop talking. You need your rest." I said, pulling the blanks up to his neck.

He just shook his head, grabbed me to him with every ounce of strength he had and hugged me tight. I couldn't do this right now. I didn't want to face the music. I couldn't stand it. I wasn't ready yet. I quickly pulled from his embrace and ran out the door. I didn't even look back when my mother called my name. I ran passed my car and right out of the drive way. I allowed the burning from my loins to assault me. The wind smashed against my face, causing me to shiver, but I kept on running. I didn't want to think, I didn't want to feel, so I kept running. I didn't know where I was going or where I was headed, but I was going to keep running. I was drenched in sweat as I exhaustingly pounded on Terrance door.

"Konstance? What are you doing here and why are you so sweaty?" He asked, as he pulled me inside.

"I didn't know where else to ga...go." I shivered.

"It is almost thirty degrees outside and you don't even have on a coat." He said, running to the closet to get a blanket.

"Just sit here in front of the fireplace, while I go get you something warm to put on. You left a few items here." He said looking at me concerned.

He practically had to undress me himself. I felt warmer in the grey jogging pants and white long sleeved shirt. He tossed the clothes I had on in the washer and gave me a steamy cup of herbal tea. After we sat there in total silence for at least thirty minutes Terrance spoke.

"So, are you going to tell me what happened?" He asked breaking the awkward silence.

"My father is dying of stomach cancer." I murmured.

"Man… he said rubbing his head, I'm so sorry. I know this must be hard for you." He said sympathetically.

I just nodded my head and listen to the wood from the fire place crackle in the open fire. Terrance was unaware of my past, so he didn't know… nobody did. He motioned for me to come to him and just like I normally do when I came over, I put my head in his lap. He just rubbed my hair as I cried for dear life. My best friend in the whole wide world held me close and rocked me in his arms. Without saying much of anything, he understood, our silence spoke volumes. I woke up to the smell of bacon and the sound of clanking pots. I had to blank a couple of times in order to recognize where I was. I rubbed my eyes, yawned, and stretched. My whole body was aching, my nose was stuffy, and my throat was sore.

"Good morning sleepy head." Terrance said, coming out the kitchen, handing me a cup of tea.

"Thanks, I really need this." I could barely speak.

He looked at me with concern, touched my forehead, and asked me was I feeling okay. He went into the bathroom downstairs, grabbed a thermometer and told me to open my mouth.

"You have a temperature of over 105 degrees. I am taking you to see a doctor right now." He said, after checking my temperature.

"No, it's okay. You've already done too much… I said, sounding like Fran from The Nanny. I'll be fine. All I need to do is sleep for a few more hours and I'll feel better."

"I'm not hearing that and you know it. I'm taking you to see a doctor right now." He demanded.

He was so cute, with his Hershey chocolate skin, sexy, athletic physique, and tightly twisted dreads that ran down his back. Terrance and his family moved from Montego Bay, Jamaica when he was ten years old. We call ourselves dating in high school, but after 3 weeks we realized that we were better off friends. Terrance and I was too much alike, he wasn't looking for a long-term relationship and was just having fun, sowing his wild oats. We used to compete against each other to see who had the most dates and at the end of the week he'd win every time. He was the only man in my life who I fully trusted with my life. So why was it so hard for me to tell him about my father and me? What was I afraid of?

Terrance took me to see his personal physician.

"If Terrance here, had not have brought you in when he did you could have been in a bad state. You have pneumonia." The handsome doctor said, as he wrote my prescription.

"I am writing you a prescription for Amoxicillin and Vancocin to help you knock this thing out. Follow the instructions on the label and use as directed. If your fever does not break in 24 hours, please, feel free to call me." He said looking at Terrance.

"Okay, I will."

"You take care of yourself, okay." He said looking at me.

"Yes, Dr…" I said glancing at his lab coat to see his full name.

"I'm sorry; I'm Dr. Kirk Reynold's. I thought Terrance had already informed you." He looked over at Terrance.

"No, I got so caught up in trying to get her in here, that we missed the introductory part." Terrance obliged.

"That's quite alright. I understand." He said, smiling at me.

I know I was sick and all, but he was already making me feel better. I looked at his finger for a ring, and just as expected he was married. I was still dying to pump some information out of Terrance about the sexy doctor. Before I left, I noticed that he had a help wanted sign for an assistant and that's when a great idea popped in my head.

"No, Konnie, you are not applying for that position. I already know what you're up to." Terrance said overtly, throwing his keys on the kitchen counter.

"I have no idea what you're talking about." I responded, acting like I was oblivious to his unsaid accusation.

"Yes you do. The man is married girl." He said, looking at me like I must have missed something.

"Yeah, I saw the ring." I said nonchalantly.

"We're not going to have this conversation right now." He said, throwing his hands up and going into the kitchen to check on the homemade chicken noodle soup he was making for me.

"Okay." I said dropping the subject, but I already had a plan and if Terrance knew me as well as I thought, he knew that his demands were ignored. What Konnie wanted, Konnie got. I knew what I wanted, when I wanted, and how I wanted it and I wanted the good doctor, anywhere, anytime, any day. But since he told me that he was a friend of the family I might keep an open mind and reconsider. But I won't make no promises.

"Does he have kids?" I asked, bringing the doctor back up.

"Yes. He and his wife have 2 kids, a girl and a boy." He shared.

"Hmph… so I take it that he's happily married." Asking a question without actually saying it like a question.

"Konnie, I'm telling you… drop it. Don't go breaking up people's marriage." He said pointing at me.

"Wha…what are you talking about? I'm not trying to break up nobody's marriage." I said, acting as if I was hurt by his words.

"Ummm… hmmm… right." He said.

"What you mean by ummm…hmmm…" I rolled my eyes.

"I told you the man was married and you still going to pursue him aren't you?" He asked knowingly.

"Terrance if he is as happy as you say he is, then you have nothing to worry about." I shrugged.

"Now why you got to go there? You women are a trip." He said, with a loud sigh.

"No, it's you men who are a trip." I said, with a little attitude.

I didn't know where he was going with this, but he was already working my nerves.

"What's up with you Terrance, you run threw women all of the time." I reminded him.

"Yes, but not anybody's wife." He stabbed.

"As far as you know… you barely even know any of their names, let alone whether they are married or not." I jabbed back at him.

"Well if they were married, they sure didn't have a ring on their finger, I check for stuff like that." He told me.

"Whatever. I don't care about none of that." I said, sneezing.

"Look at you, sick and trifling." He said, shaking his head.

Oh… no he didn't just call me trifling…

"Now why would you say something like that?" I was hurt.

"I just told you the man was married. For pete's sakes and you still talking about pursing him. So yes, I call it as I see it." He replied bluntly.

"You know, you're not that much different from me, so don't be the pot that calls the kettle black. What a woman can't do what a man does? Why is it like that? Why women have to be wrong when they play the same games? A woman is labeled as a hoe if she have sex with more than one man or get in where she fit in but a man is labeled as a playa when he does the same. I'm doing what men have been doing to us for generations and I don't feel bad for doing it." I told him.

He looked at me as if he was seeing two heads, and shook his head.

"What?" I yelled at him.

"Girl the man is married… wow… what is wrong with you women these days, don't have no shame."

"Boy, I may look and act like a woman, but oh, make no mistake she definitely thinks like a man." I said with pride.

"See that's what's wrong with women like you. All these men out here, but you want somebody else husband. What is that "act like a woman think like a man" crap anyway? Steve Harvey got ya'll women head gassed up and messed up. You may look like a woman, but you're acting like something else, and out of respect for you, I dare not say it. But if it quacks like a duck then… He said not finishing… You are a woman, so you have no business thinking like a man."

"It's not about wanting someone else's husband. If he cheats then that's on him, I don't hold any ties to his wife, he does. She can take the full-time position, as long as he's putting in work at his part-time job. Oh that's me." I giggled.

"Wow." Was all he could say, still amazed by his friend's ignorance.

"Oh, don't sound so surprised. It's always about sex with you men, which is why you go from one vagina to the next anyway. When a woman wants to do right, you want to cheat, so go ahead with all that. We put all our feelings and emotions into a relationship and you guys just dismiss our feelings like we don't exist, like our feelings don't matter." I was about to let him have it.

"You women kill me, with your overly emotional behinds. Stop it please. We have feelings too girl-- you want to talk about bad men turning good women bad, but there are women like you, he said pointing at me, that can turn a good man bad. You see, men aren't the only one's who cheat and act like a "dog", so you women say…

There are women out there can cheat even better and who can be a bigger dog." He threw at me.

"Are you calling me a dog?" I asked getting heated.

"You're missing the point." He said giving up.

"No, Dr. Phil, you had a lot to say just now, so spit it out." I urged him.

"Have you ever been cheated on?" He asked.

"No and I don't expect to be cheated on."

He rolled his eyes.

"Konnie, I know you aren't blind and you're too smart to be stupid. Stop playing yourself, please."

"What do you mean?" I said getting angrier.

"If you don't think a man will cheat on you or move on to the next then you're playing yourself. You're a beautiful woman, there is no denying it, but that's not always important. You can't go chasing after someone's husband and don't expect it to backfire. Whether he gives into you or not is not the main issue. The fact that you know he's married should make you want to send him on his way. But you don't. Then you try to justify your actions by saying that men who cheat are no good. Well, neither are the women who cheat with them." He preached.

"Boy, you must not know me. I'm the head B.I.C. Look at me, do you see all this. I look good, so I'm not worried about what you're talking about. So before you start acting like you've found Jesus or something, dismiss me with the self-righteous act. " I said turning up my nose.

"Now you sound ignorant... You don't even have enough respect for yourself. You just called yourself a female dog. How you present yourself is how a man will treat you. You think a man care about how you look? If he wants to cheat he's going to cheat no matter how good you look. You better have something to back those looks up because in the end good looks don't really get you anywhere these days. Don't get me wrong I love a beautiful woman but whenever I do decide to wife someone, I'm looking at what else they can bring to the table. I need to know if she's wifey material, if she can cook, and if she'll be a great mother to my children. After your looks have faded and that stuff between your legs is on the clearance rack then what else would you have to give?" He said turning up his nose.

Before I could answer he started talking again.

"Now, what you need to do is start respecting women and yourself, maybe if you did you wouldn't go around sleeping with their husbands." He continued.

I was getting tired of all this. He was not about to make me feel bad. I was sick and I didn't have time for him lecturing me like he never did nothing wrong in his life. Terrance has always been a straight forward kind of guy, in fact, that's what I liked most about him. He was a straight shooter, and didn't hold nobody hostage when it came to him expressing how he felt. I just didn't like being the one looking inside the barrel of the gun. Good thing, he took me by my parent's house to pick up my car, or I would have walked home. Without saying a word to him, I got up from the sofa, got my stuff and left.

Four

AFTER A FEW more days of resting, and popping medication tablets, I was back to normal. I haven't talked to Terrance since our argument at his house. I missed him terribly, but I was still angry. He really set me off and I was not going to call him and apologize. He was the one who verbally attacked me, so he's the one who needs to be apologizing. I called Dr. Reynolds office to see was the position still opened, I thanked the heavens when one of his assistant nurses told me that it was. After I submitted my resume and told her how I knew Dr. Reynolds, I was instantly told to come in for an interview.

"So… Mrs. Graham—"

"Miss Graham." I said, holding up my bare ring finger.

"Ooo…kkkayyy… I stand corrected, Miss Graham. I see you are doing better then the first day I met you." He smiled.

"Yes, thanks to you. Whatever can I do to repay you?" I sweetly replied, batting my eyes.

He chuckled, "I was just doing my job, there's no need to repay me for anything. Terrance already took care of that." He assured, taking his eyes off of me and putting back on my resume in front of him.

"There's nothing on your resume, other than the fact that you attended college." He said, looking at me.

"I don't have any work experience, but if you show me how to do something once, I guarantee you I can master it. I said it, a little too, flirtatiously, the… ummm… work duties, that is." I quickly corrected myself. Didn't want to push to soon.

He looked at me, examined my resume again, and looked at me again.

"Alright… I'm going to take a few days out of my schedule and show you the ropes. I don't have the time to train you, but if you can show me some progress in a week's top, then I will consider hiring you full time, but if not, I'll have to seek other candidates." He said sternly.

"No problem... I'm going to show you... I excel at whatever I put my mind to." I said with a smirk.

And yes, I was talking way pass my work duties.

"Well okay then... you're hired. See you tomorrow morning at 8 o'clock sharp." He replied, standing up to shake my hand, not catching my drift.

I grabbed it. He looked up at me and we both gazed in each others eyes for longer than he intended to. I could have sworn sparks were flying around us.

"See you tomorrow..." I said, breaking the stare.

"Yeah... tomorrow." He said, clearing his throat, and quickly dropping his arms to his side.

I grabbed my things and walked towards the door with a little pep in my step and a twist of my hips. I could feel his eyes on me. When I opened the door of his office, I swiftly turned around to face him. He immediately too his eyes off my behind and looked at me. I laughed inside. It figures. Men are all the same. See a woman with a nice body and don't know how to act. With his mouth he made vows to his wife, but that didn't stop those fickle eyes from roaming.

"Thanks for giving me this chance. After I show you my skills, I know you'll be glad you hired me." I smiled.

He nodded, loosening his tie.

I guess it was getting too hot for him. It's funny, because I was as cool as a cucumber.

Two Months Later

Dr. Reynolds was more than impressed with how fast I caught on to my duties as his executive assistant. Little did he know, I had my father's personal assistant give me a few tips and I did a little research on how to become the perfect executive assistant.

After taking a few notes, and keenly listening to Dr. Reynolds instructions, I managed to master the job quicker then he expected. I had to stay a little later than usual because I had to prepare for this afternoon's company meeting. His nurse assistants, partners, and a few other people who I didn't know, would be attending.

About time the meeting was over it was dark outside.

"Wow, what time is it?" I said, as I unplugged the computer that was needed to present the PowerPoint presentation.

"It's 7 o'clock." He said looking at the clock that was hanging on the wall.

"Does meetings always last 3 hours?" I asked.

"No, it usually last about 1-2 hours, but we had so many things to discuss that time just passed us by." He said, heading towards his office.

I followed behind him, so that I could put the notes on his desk. My stomach growled a little too loud.

"I… I'm so sorry. I guess my stomach is telling me how much I have neglected it today." I laughed.

"If yours wouldn't have said anything, mine would have told on me, he chuckled, would you like to grab a bite to eat?" He asked.

"I'd love to." I said.

He just didn't know how excited I was for the open invitation. This was the perfect time to express myself. I'd wasted too much time as it was. I didn't want him to think that I was some whore, so I have been waiting a little longer than I usually do to try to pursue him.

"If you don't mind, I will like to freshen up a bit. Working those few hours at the hospital, along with running back in forth to assist patients, and conducting the meeting, I've worked out a little sweat." He said, jokingly waving his hand across his nose.

"Cut it out. You don't smell, I laughed, but go ahead and freshen up."

"Thank you. While I'm doing that, you can be thinking about what you have a taste for." He said, running to his office.

Hmmmm… good idea.

Since he is known to work late hours, he had a shower built inside his bathroom. I could hear the shower blasting as I slowly tiptoed inside. The steam hit me as soon as I walked in the door. As I quietly disrobed, the moisture from the steam attacked my body. I wrapped a towel around me and opened the shower door.

"What are you doing?" He jumped, with a look of shock on his face.

"You told me to think about what I had a taste for." I said coyly.

"Yes, but what are you doing in here?" He said, trying to cover up.

"I'm joining you." I said, as I welcomed myself inside.

"This is highly inappropriate--"

His tongue must of gotten twisted because once I dropped the towel, he stopped talking and his eyes went to roaming from my head down to my little bitty toes.

"See something you like?" I asked. My tone laced with lust.

"I… I'm… married…"He gulped hard as he tried to ignore the distraction in front of him.

"Yeah, I noticed the ring on your finger." I said nonchalantly.

"I… he swallowed hard again… I love my wife."

"Why of course you do… I said gently slapping his chest. Love has nothing to do with this. I'm fine with you loving your wife." I said wrapping my arms around his neck.

The steam from the shower ignited my senses as the water from the shower tickled my spine.

"All I want… I said sliding my tongue across his lips, is a little sexual healing. Can you do that for me doc?"

"Miss Graham, please." He begged. He was having a hard time keeping his composure.

"Please… call me Konstance." I said, grabbing his manhood. He may have been acting like he had it all together, but the throbbing down yonder sent a powerful message to the folds between my thighs.

"Kon…sst…ance… please don't do this." He moaned.

"Do what?" I probed.

He closed his eyes and threw his head back as I gently massaged him. He was standing at full attention. His wife may have had his heart, but tonight I had his body. He was caught up in the moment and when I kissed his lips, he hungrily kissed me back.

Got him.

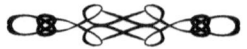

Five

"HI MR. REYNOLDS I said the next morning, as if nothing happened last night.

"Good morning, Miss Graham." He said, trying to avoid eye contact.

"Here is your cup of coffee, and don't forget you have to go check on a few of your patients at the hospital this afternoon." I sashayed over to his desk, ignoring the tension in the room.

I was used to the guilt trip married men put on the morning after. But what I never could quite understand is even in guilt, they do not mind taking a ride a second time. I knew just what it would take, to loosen Kirk up.

"Thank you for reminding me." He said. He was clearly off balance today.

"Is everything, alright?" I asked him.

"Yes. I… I'm fine." He stuttered.

"You sure are." I said, under my breath.

"I'm sorry?" He said looking at me.

"I said… are you sure that you don't need me to do anything else for you?" I quickly fixed the statement up.

"Yes, could you please file these folders for me? My desk is getting junky." He said handing me a stack of folders.

I purposely let them slide out of my hands and all the papers scattered at my feet. He apologized and tried to come across his desk to help. I stopped him and told him I would do it. I seductively bent over and picked them up making sure he saw what my mama gave me. And when I stood up I could feel him looking at me but I switched out the door with a smile on my face and I refused to look back.

"Konstance, can I see you in my office please." He commanded, ten minutes later.

I hope I didn't push so hard that I was going to get pushed right out the door. Although, my initial reason for applying for the job was to seduce Kirk, I really did enjoy working for him. I nervously went into his office and sat down.

"Yes, Doctor Reynolds, is something wrong?" I asked, feeling uneasy.

"What are you doing?" He asked me, as he walked around his desk and leaned into me.

"I…I'm sorry… I don't know what you mean." I said nervously shifting in my seat.

"You know exactly what I mean." He said accusingly.

"I've never been good with guessing games, so can you please tell me what the problem is?" I asked.

"Yes. *You.*" He pointed.

"Excuse me?" I said not sure if I was hearing him right. Something told me this will be my last day.

"That little stunt you pulled last night was unprofessional and it could have cost me my marriage. Do you realize what you have done?" He said with a look of frustration on his face.

I didn't respond. I was too busy preparing myself to hear those two words—you're fired.

"Come here." He said, interrupting my thoughts.

I looked up. The panic look in my eyes quickly changed and my lips curled up into a smile. I thought for sure that I'd read him wrong. That he was one of the men out here that was truly devoted to his wife. I thought he was going to fire me right on the spot, especially after that little performance I gave him earlier. I obediently stood up and walked towards him.

"Now what?" I asked, as I burned with a desire to kiss him right then and there.

He swiftly picked me up around my waste and placed me on his desk. Our eyes connected, my legs welcomed him in, our lips became in sync, and the rest was history.

Calgon take me away.

We exhaustingly laid on the plush carpet on the floor as we tried to catch our breath.

"Where have you been… all my life?" He said in between breaths.

"In your dreams." I said pompously.

"You're right about that… He laughed… I couldn't sleep last night, because I couldn't stop thinking about you. You're a huge distraction for me, Miss Graham." He admitted.

"Who…me?" I said with an innocent look on my face.

He looked at me and laughed, "You're something else."

"Why yes… yes I am…" I said batting my eyes.

"Have dinner with me tonight." He said, turning over on his side to face me.

"I would love that." I smiled, and then kissed his lips.

The sex was beyond anything that I have ever experienced. Out of all the men that I have bedded, he is by far the best one I've ever had. He had me wanting to take him home with me, and a man has never had the privilege of coming home with me, shoot, they didn't even know where I lived. But for this man right here… I was willing to make an exception. He already made me want to do things that I've never done before. I know… I know… I'm shocked too.

I couldn't keep from smiling at this handsome work of art in front me. This sweet chunk of white chocolate reminds me so much of Jason Statham, that if I didn't do a double take, I'd swear he was the real deal. Although his feature bared strikingly similar resemblance as Jason's, Kirk was a little taller. I guess it's true what they say… everyone has a twin somewhere in this world. Well, I was staring at Jason's twin right now.

Kirk had surprised me when he came to pick me up in a limo, welcoming me with a gorgeous smile and a dozen of red roses.

"For you." He said handing them to me.

"Why, thank you." The petals tickled my nose as I inhaled the fragrance of the flowers.

Roses was my favorite flower, but how would he have known that? My eyes widened as he escorted me to his own personal jet and revealed that we would be going to New York for dinner. I was blown away. I mean, I was used to nice things, because I was born rich, but he was scoring points, big time. More points were added under his belt when we stopped in front of one of New York's most exquisite Japanese restaurants. When the limo driver opened the door he got out and reached his hands out to me to help me out.

"This is amazing! I said flabbergasted. You sure know how to impress a girl."

I looked around the beautiful room. Japanese art was adorned on the walls; a mixture of gold, cream, and burgundy was the color theme. Classical music played in the background as people of prestige chatted with their guests. We both ordered the Kaiseki Ryori and enjoyed a bottle of Chateau Pavie.

"Interesting… you speak Japanese?" He asked.

"Yes, why do you ask?"

"Because, you could tell how you named the food on the menu so fluently." He smiled.

"I am half Korean but my father has a Japanese friend who owns a chain of Japanese restaurants throughout Japan, New York, Chicago, Detroit, Paris and Holland. I pretty much lived off of Japanese and Korean food and learn to speak the language when I was six."

"Wow. I thought you were mixed with something and I figured it had to be Korean, Japanese or Chinese. It's the eyes that give you away."

"Yeah I get that all the time." I said, taking a sip of my wine.

"You look beautiful tonight." He said, running his eyes down my black cocktail dress.

"You don't look too bad yourself." I said as I took notice of the Ermenegildo Zegna suit he was wearing.

We were having a great night and I enjoyed hearing him talk. He talked about his parents, his childhood, his children, but he failed to mention his wife. I guess he tried hard to keep her out of the equation and I didn't care any way or the other. I was just enjoying the moment. He was so easy to talk to that I found myself sharing my background with him, minus the secret parts. Those I will carry to the grave, but I wasn't so sure if my father was willing to take it to his.

"Would you like another bottle of wine?" The waiter insisted, interrupting our conversation.

"I think we've already had too much for the night. But we would take a bottle of Chateau d' Yquem to go." He said, approvingly to the waiter.

"Hmm, nice choice. I was impressed. You seem to know your wines, huh."

"Quite well actually... I own wine orchards in Julian California and in France. I love wine. I have a wine cellar at home with wine dated back to the 1600's."

"Wow. I would have never thought."

Tonight was perfect and I did not want it to end. He must have read my mind, because after dinner we checked in at the famous Herald Square Hotel. The night was still young, and we had a lot more exploring to do. If... you know what I mean.

Six

LOVE CAN BE sneaky. It can just creep up on you without you even noticing. Love can cause you to flip the script and have you tangled up in a web. I found myself challenging love and your girl was losing… big time. My relationship with Kirk was moving so fast and my heart was trying to keep up with the pace. I've never felt so happy and so in love before. I thought what my father expressed to me was the kind of love that every man had for another woman, but clearly I was wrong. Kirk was introducing me to things I've never known and feelings that I cannot managed to express.

I was diving head first in a pool of love and I didn't have any intentions of coming back up. I didn't know that loving a man could feel like this and if all went as planned, he'll no longer be my part time lover, but he'll soon be climbing the ladder to a full time position. I've grown so used to him being around that I forget that he has a home somewhere else and with somebody else. I try not to think about that fact and my goal was to help him forget. Call me what you want, but I've never really cared much about anything that didn't benefit me.

I don't see how he even makes time for her. I mean he's constantly drifting away, traveling to places like Canada, Italy, and Bermuda with me. He took me to see his wine orchards in France and in California. I learned just how much I didn't know about wine, after test tasting, and learning about the quality of each type of wine. Wine wasn't the only thing I learned about, but Kirk taught me a few things about love making and about himself that blew my mind. I have heard people say not to confuse sex with love, I don't know, but they seem to come hand-in- hand to me.

One night he surprised me by opening up to me about his wife. He told me how over the last few years he and his wife have become disconnected in many ways. He no longer felt intimately connected to her in a way that a husband is supposed to be with his wife. He said that with me he could be himself; he could connect, and share with me. He made me feel so special, like I had something more to bring to the table then what his wife could. He demonstrated to me that our relationship was more than just about sex, but about something deeper and more fulfilling.

After we made love one night, I opened up and told him how I felt about him. It was never my intentions to reveal my feelings to him, but it just came out. My plan was to keep those feeling bottled inside just in case things didn't pan out the way that I wanted them to. But he was showing me, proving to me not only by his words, but by his actions that we had something fulfilling. Although I should have known not to put so much trust in a man, let alone a married man, I did… and without me being aware of it—he'd stolen my heart and held it hostage.

Being with him feels so perfect and he's making me do and say things that I never thought I would. As of lately everything that I've said and done is a surprise. If someone would have told me that I would be in love with a man, let alone with someone else's husband a year ago, I would have laughed in their face. Now here I am sharing my bed with one for over ten months. When the "L" word escaped from my lips, I tried to suck it so far down my throat, I almost choked. Not because I didn't really love him, but I was afraid that he didn't feel the same way. When he said that he loved me too, I felt free enough to open up to more possibilities.

"I am so sick of that witch." He said full of anger, as he stormed pass me and slammed his office door.

What the…what? I said to myself, puzzled by his attitude. Good thing him and I were the only one's here. I'd never seen Kirk angry, and everyone who talks about him, have said that he has always been so calm, cool, and collected. Well, their opinions would have quickly changed, if they had been a witness to what I was seeing. I waited a few minutes before I went to his office.

"Is everything alright?" I said, cautiously walking inside his office.

"Yes, everything is fine. I'm sorry that you had to witness that.

That's not me." He said, rubbing his hands over his eyes, and exhaling exhaustedly.

"What's wrong?" I asked, coming over to massage his shoulders.

"I need this. You always seem to know just what to do. I'm so glad I have you in my life." He said, turning his chair around to face me.

I looked in his beautiful silvery blue eyes, and smiled. I wanted to be everything to him. Everything that his wife couldn't be... I knew that I can make him way happier, if he just let me.

"Tell me..." I encouraged. I sat on his lap.

"She goes and buys an $80,000 car without consulting me first. He said getting angry again. When I confronted her about it she just shrugged her shoulders and said she was tired of the one she had and wanted to get something better. She'd just purchased the car two years ago. I tell you, I'm just so sick of that woman."

"Well, baby, if you're so tired, then why don't you just divorce her?" I causally questioned, as I fixed his tie.

I really was curious to know. I was tired of him telling me how much of a bad wife she was. I wanted to know what was it that kept him still holding on, when he had me; someone who he claimed to be sooo in love with.

"I don't want to take my kids through it." He said, blowing out a deep breath.

"Your kids? You're not divorcing them you'll only be divorcing her." I tried to stay calm.

"You don't understand what I'm trying to say-- going through court about legal stuff would not only mess up my reputation but destroy my kids mentally. I wouldn't know what to do if they blamed me for everything." He said.

I didn't say anything because I didn't have anything to say. I, personally, didn't care about all that. His kids would grow to understand and I'm sure that they would be happy to see his father happy. I'm sure his wife is not pleased with all the late night "meetings", and early morning lies that he come up with after staying all night with me. And I'm sure the kids are not blind or deaf. From what he tells me he and his wife argue and fight all the time and every time he comes running home to mama. He's always telling me that she threatens to take his kids away and everything that he had if he ever tried to divorce her. Women like that disgust me. They try to use kids to hold on to a man. Why even bother trying to keep a man that doesn't want to be kept?

"You do understand don't you?" He said, kissing my lips.

"Yeah." I said letting it go.

I didn't want him to know my real feelings and he was already stressing, so I didn't want to add to it.

"Good."

He wrapped his arms around my waist and laid a kiss on me so deep and so intense that my heart skipped two beats. I almost tore the buttons off his dress shirt as I tried to take it off. Our love making was filled with hunger and a craving that sent us both over the edge. I said a silent thank you to his wife, because she was making it so easy for him to forget about her.

Seven

I'D FINALLY MADE the decision to go back to school and I was excited. Kirk had a hand in that. We were looking at the news one night and he'd ask me why I didn't pursue my dream to become a news anchor. Of course I didn't tell him the full truth, but I did tell him enough, that gave him an idea of what I was going through. He told me to put my past behind me and live for the future. He told me that if I didn't follow my dreams that life would past me by and one day I will sit back and regret it. I'd only had two semesters to complete, so I went for it. I re-enrolled at a college close to my house and walked out with a new schedule in my hand and a huge smile on my face.

I was finally taking the steps to do what I have wanted to do since I was a little girl. It felt good to finally finish something. As soon as I got to work the next day, I told Kirk the good news. The look of excitement on his face was priceless. Not only did I have a man who loved me, but I had a man that cared about my future. He promised that we'd go to any restaurant I wanted to celebrate tonight, but he had to go home so he could escort his son to his softball game. I was cool with that. I didn't mind him taking up time with his kids, as long as he ended his night with me.

It was going on 9 o' clock and there was still no sign of Kirk. I called his phone dozens of times only to get his voicemail. I didn't know whether to be angry or worried. I had a feeling that I was being stood up. Calling him wouldn't do any good. I was livid. I stomped into the kitchen and sat at my bar and sipped on my fourth glass of Diva Vodka. About time I got to the fifth glass, I was seeing double. I knew that I couldn't make it all the way to my bedroom, so I laid down on the couch and next thing I knew I was awaken by the ringing in my ear. I had a major hang over. My head was pounding and the room seemed to be spinning when I opened my eyes. I quickly shut my eyes and allowed my voicemail to take the call. However, whoever was calling me apparently didn't get the message and kept calling anyway. I reluctantly picked up the cordless phone and answered.

"Yeah?" I said sleepily.

"Do you know what time it is?" Kirk barked into the phone.

"Would you lower your voice please?" His yelling doubled the pounding in my head. He got some nerve calling my phone anyway yelling after what happened last night.

"Do you know what time it was last night?" I retorted.

"I'm so sorry about last night; Lisa wouldn't get off my back. She kept complaining about me never being home and I lost track of time." He responded.

"You could have at least called me instead of having me wait hours and hours on you. Why should you care how she feels anyway? You said you love me." I whimpered. I was really getting soft and I felt myself getting angry about the whole thing.

"I do love you Konnie." He softened.

"Well, why did you stand me up? I should come first before—"

"What do you mean? She's my wife. He interjected. I still have responsibilities. I can't be up under you every minute of every day, Konnie."

"Listen, I don't have time for this. I'm taking the day off." I said, tossing the phone on the cocktail table in front of me.

The phone rung.

"Konnie, baby, please just be patient with me." He said softly, when I finally answered the phone.

I couldn't believe him. I was more than patient and I was growing tired of waiting on him to make a decision. I was getting tired of being the other woman. I never played second to anyone, and I wasn't going to start. In the beginning I didn't care who he spent his time with, but things have changed.

"Really Kirk… I can't believe that you're saying this to me. I've been more than patient with you. I've tried to be understanding and fit into your schedule but I'm sick and tired of waiting. You told me that you were going to leave her going on two months ago." I said heatedly reminding him.

"Baby I promise I will. Please get up and come to me. He begged. I miss you and I thought about you all night. I knew I should have called you and I tried but she went to sleep around two and I couldn't call you that late at night. I'm sorry sweet pea and I'll show you how sorry I am when you get here. She can't do me like you do and you don't have to worry about a thing." He said, filling me up.

The anger in me dwindled and my heart warmed up to the words that he was feeding me. I wasn't dumb, I knew he could have been feeding me a load of crap, but as I said, my feelings had me disregarding logic. I wanted to hear him say those words to me, even if they were lies.

"I know I should be a little more patient and I will. Just hurry up and get the divorce. I'll be to work in an hour." I said tenderly.

Forget whether he was just releasing hot air, forget that he was just trying to make things right. I was about to get up and go to my man. After hanging up the phone, I stood up and had to sit right back down. All of a sudden my stomach begin to cramp and I could feel the bile in my throat rising. I closed my eyes and swallowed a few times, hoping that it would make me feel better. Ten minutes passed and I was finally able to stand up. I rushed in the bathroom and fell in front of the toilet just in time. All the content in my body came spewing out in the toilet.

I rested my head on the edge of the toilet as I tried to gain enough energy to stand up. It felt like someone was punching me in the gut, but the headache was gone and I the room was no longer spinning. I went to the sink, splashed some cold water on my face, and brushed my teeth. Just when the pain in my gut began to subside, I felt like I had to throw up again. I knew I had too much to drink and I should have called Kirk and told him that I couldn't make it, but the urgency in his voice, beckoned me to go against my better judgment. I put on a pot of coffee and popped three Tylenols in my mouth.

Once I got to work, I could barely get anything done or keep anything down. I was in the bathroom so much that one of the nurse assistants had to cover my desk the majority of the day. I have gotten drunk before and I didn't ever feel like this. I was hoping that I didn't get alcohol poisoning or anything like that. I was getting weak and my stomach was hurting me like crazy. To avoid Kirk knowing what I did last night, I took off early and went straight to the emergency room. I didn't want him to know I drink myself stupid last night. My mouth dropped and I was in a state of disbelief when the doctor came back with my blood test results. It wasn't that I had alcohol poisoning, but I was pregnant.

"Are you sure doctor?" I asked in total disbelief.

"Yes ma'am. If you think this is some kind of mistake, you can take the test again." He said looking at me for approval.

"Yes… yes… please." I said to make sure the results were accurate.

Low and behold, the test came back again as positive. I was pregnant. The doctor advised me to go to my OB/GYN or to my physician for a check up. I couldn't believe it. I was pregnant… I was pregnant with Kirk's baby! A smile came across my lips and I was filled with excitement when I thought about what I said. I was pregnant with Kirk's baby; this will definitely make it easier for him to leave his wife. On my way home I contemplated on how I was going to present the news to him. So many great things are happening to me all at once. I didn't believe in God much. I stopped believing in Him a long time ago.

When I realized that He didn't care about me. When my father first touched me, I cried out to God but He didn't care to answer my cries for help. My Grammy always taught me that if I believed in God and prayed to Him that He'll answer, but He never answered me. So, after awhile I stop calling. Pretty soon I forgot that He even existed. I don't get how people can believe in something that they can't see anyway. As far as I'm concerned, He's just as real as the tooth fairy and old Saint Nick. But based on what has been going on in my life lately, I'm beginning to find some truth in what my Grammy was trying to tell me. I have to say that I'm beginning to open up to the notion that there just may be a God up there somewhere.

I mean who else could have brought Kirk and me together? Who else could have caused a little bun to grow in this oven, when the outlet was supposed to be out? I was on birth control. I never had any intentions on getting pregnant and never actually wanted a baby. I didn't want to mess up this beautiful figure on account of no crumb snatcher. That was a risk, I wasn't willing to take. But for Kirk… I was willing to make a few exceptions. Maybe God wasn't so bad after all. I may even go to church with my Grammy this Sunday and show Him my appreciation by paying a little tithes and offering.

After doing a lot of thinking, I decided to wait to tell Kirk about the pregnancy. I didn't want him leaving his wife to be with me because I was pregnant, but because he loved me. No… I was going to wait and see how long he would take to make the decision and whenever he did, I will surprise him. It will be a new beginning for us. I was surprised to come home to a room full of pink, yellow, and white roses. He really was trying to make up for standing me up last night, how sweet. I opened the card that inside a big tall vase, filled with long steamed red roses.

I'm sorry! I know flowers does not make up for me standing you up, but after what I have planned for you tonight, I pray that you'll forget all about it. Put on the most sexiest dress in your closet, and be ready by 7.

Kirk

Eight

KIRK CERTAINLY made up for standing me up last night. He took me on his private yacht; right on the deck was a candle lit dinner waiting for us. The scenery was beautiful, the temperature was perfect, and I quickly had forgiven and forgot about what happened last night. We danced to my favorite jazz songs and when we sat down, he handed me a long red velvet envelope.

"What's this?" I asked, full of exhilaration.

"A little something to show how sorry I am."

"Awww… baby… you've done enough. You were already forgiven when I walked into my house and saw all those beautiful roses." I smiled.

"Okay then, I'll take it back tomorrow." He shrugged, reaching for the box.

"I don't think so." I said, holding the box tightly to my chest.

"Open it." He laughed.

I quickly unwrapped the gift box like a child on Christmas morning. He watched and smiled as I removed a beautiful tennis bracelet with twelve oval shaped ruby gemstones, twenty-four round diamonds and twenty-four princess cut diamonds with a white gold setting.

"This is beautiful Kirk." I gushed.

"But not as beautiful as the woman who is sitting in front of me. I love you Konnie." He said, looking deep into my eyes and touching my heart. He had me, there was no denying it. I was head over heels in love with this man.

He leaned over and placed the bracelet on my arm. I grabbed the tie that was around his neck and gently pulled him inside the yacht. The bedroom was huge and decorated tastefully. My father was never into boats because he was afraid of water. I was going to show my baby just how much I forgave him and just how much I appreciate his efforts.

I seductively pushed him on the bed and slowly gyrated to match the tempo of the music. Then I crawled on the bed like a lioness. I licked my lips, hungry for the delicious dessert in front of me.

Four Months Later

Kirk still hasn't left his wife and I still haven't told him about the pregnancy. I was beginning to show, so I knew sooner or later I would have to tell him. When he asked me why I was gaining so much weight, I lied in told him that I'd just starting eating too many fatty foods late at night. This morning I was shocked to find the doors to the office locked. I unlocked the door and turned on the lights. Kirk has never been late opening up before. Normally he is there before any of us was. I figured he must have been caught into traffic or something, so I went to my desk and turned on the computer to check my emails.

After erasing a few spam messages, I opened up a memo from Kirk telling all staff that he will not be in the office for a week and that we could consider this a vacation with pay. I wasn't mad about us having to take off, because I surely needed it. With the constant appointments and the sickness I will still enduring with this baby, I needed some time off. What really pissed me off is that Kirk couldn't find the time to call me and tell me. Now that I think about it, he didn't call me at all last night. The baby had me so exhausted that I fail to take notice to it, until now.

"Why haven't you called me, Kirk? And why didn't you tell me that you decided to take off?" I said with attitude, when I finally got him on the phone.

"Konnie, not now... I'll call you back later." He said, hanging up the phone.

I looked at my phone in disbelief. I know he didn't hang up on me. I punched his number in so hard; I thought I would break the phone.

"I said... not now... he said with clinched teeth. I'll be over tonight to talk to you. There is something I need to talk to you about." He said quickly.

"But—"

"Tonight." He confirmed, before I could say anything else, and he hung up the phone on me again.

I sat there for a minute, still in disbelief, as the dial tone played in my ear. I paced the floor pondering what it was that he had to tell me, and then it hit me…. That explained why he hasn't called me and why he was taking off. He was preparing to leave his wife and we were going to go somewhere for a perfect little get away. I was feeling good already. I couldn't wait. Tonight was the perfect time to tell him about our little bundle of joy. I smiled as I rubbed my belly. It was finally here… Kirk was finally going to do what I have been begging him to do for a long time.

I already knew where I wanted him to take me… to the place of romance—Paris. I looked around each room and tidied up a bit. While I waited on Kirk, I browsed the web for engagement rings. I know that I was thinking outside of the box, but we have been together for three years now, so there was no need for us to wait. If he doesn't propose to me tonight, then I'll go ahead and order both of our rings, and propose to him instead. I didn't mind going for what I wanted and what I wanted was to be a family with the man that I love.

I knew when I saw the five carat princess cut engagement ring from Zale's that it was the right one for me. I searched for a ring for Kirk and paid for the items with the black American Express card Kirk gave me. I even went as far as looking at wedding gowns at Vera Wang Bridal and purchased an ivory taffeta strapless mermaid gown with hand cut corsage and asymmetrical back bows. I didn't plan to waste any time. I wanted to go ahead and get married before my stomach got too big. It would be horrific for me to wobble down the isle looking like a big umpa lompa.

I was just boiling over with glee. Just when I thought I could never love a man here he comes in my life and changed the unexpected. We have a bond that no other has and I love him. My father was wrong when he said no other man could love me better then him. Kirk has proven to me that he is the one for me and I finally see happiness at the end of the tunnel. I couldn't wait to be Mrs. Kirk Reynolds. I practically ran to the door when I heard the door bell ring. I opened the door with a big smile on my face.

"Hey baby." I said hugging him, not even paying attention to the look on his face.

"May I come in?" He asked, looking over my shoulder.

"Oh, I'm sorry, of course you can." I said unblocking the doorway.

Here I am dressed seductively in Vikki's finest and he didn't even compliment me. He seemed tense and out of place. There was something definitely wrong. He sat down and immediately got back up, and then he started pacing the floor. The smile on my face disappeared and I was eager to know what was really going on. I was beginning to think him coming over here was not for what I expected. I quickly tossed the negative thought out of my head and tried to find something to distract me.

"I knew you were coming over, so I made your favorite." I said, taking the roast out of the oven.

"We need to talk, Konstance." He said.

"What's going on?" I asked, no longer smiling.

"These past three years has been the best years of my life because of you." He said, shifting his feet, not looking in my eyes.

All I could do is smile I was almost about to tear up and I knew he was going to tell me what I wanted to hear. I almost told him to hurry up and spit it out but I held my tongue and waited.

"I want you to know that I care a lot about you and I want to thank you for making me feel alive again." He held my hand and finally looked at me.

"I love you, too." I said emotionally.

"I know and that's why it's so hard for me to say what I have to say." He said painfully.

"What are you talking about?" I asked, pulling my hand out of his.

A look of confusion was all over my face. I didn't know what Kirk was about to say, but I knew it wasn't going to be good. Now I was beginning to panic. This did not sound like a proposal to me. Something was up and it only took a few more words out of his mouth to find out what that something was.

"I came over here to tell you that last night Lisa and I talked and we've decided to work on our marriage. I'm sorry." He said quietly.

I could barely breathe. My ears must have deceived me. I know I wasn't hearing what I thought I was hearing. Calm down, Konstance you're having a dream. That's what this is a dream-- a terrible dream and when I wake up I'll still be Kirk's woman. His future wife and he would call me to let me know that he was coming over so we could make love. But when I looked at him again and felt the pain in my chest I knew this couldn't be a dream. All of the happy thoughts jumped right out the window. He could not possibly be breaking up with me. After all this time I've been loyal to him, he wants to break it off with me…. No, maybe I heard wrong.

"What did you just say?" I asked, hoping that he wouldn't tell me what my heart already knew.

"I'm sorry Konstance but I love my wife and I need to work my marriage out. She doesn't deserve what I'm doing. I would like for you to come by the office and pick up your things. I don't think it'll be wise for the two of us to be working together anymore. Don't worry about finding a new job, Patrick told me that he was looking for a new assistant at his practice and I put in a word for you. He told me to tell you to come in, when you're ready. Don't worry about the salary; you will be getting paid more than what I was paying you." He continued, as if everything was okay.

I just stood there in a daze. His mouth was moving, but I couldn't hear anything coming out of it. I hadn't even felt his lips when he kissed my cheeks, and I didn't hear the door close when he walked out the door. I stood there… Frozen…. I couldn't wrap my mind around what had just happened. Kirk had left me. I'd trusted him, waited on him, and given myself away to him. How could he do this to me? What was wrong with him? This couldn't be right. We was supposed to be getting married and planning a future together.

"Oh God, the baby." I whispered to myself.

I hadn't told him about the baby. I had to see him. I had to go to him. I ran to my room and quickly put on a pair of jeans, a t-shirt, and some tennis shoes. As I ran out the door, I grabbed my cell phone and dialed his number. The call went straight to voicemail. I tried again as

I cranked up my car and headed to his house. Thirty minutes later, I parked beside his car in the front of his house. I ran up to the door and almost broke it with my fist.

"Kirk I know you're in there. Please come out and talk to me." I begged.

"Kirk open the door, I have to tell you about the ba--"

"What in the world is going on? Lisa replied, as she opened the door a little wider and turned on the porch light. Oh it's you Konstance. Is something wrong?" She replied, with a look of concern and confusion on her face. I bet she was wondering why I was banging on her door so late at night and I know I must have looked like a raging lunatic with my hair all over the place, and my face all messed up from crying.

"What are you doing here Konstance?" He said, coming to the door before I could go off on her. As far as I was concerned, she was the blame for all of this. If she would just let him go then he would be home with me.

"I need to talk to you. You left so fast that I didn't get a chance to tell you that--"

"What is going on?" Lisa asked Kirk, interrupting me.

"Lisa it's not what you think, just go in the house and let me see what she wants." He said nervously.

"Not what I think? Your assistant is standing here at my door all hysterical, wanting to talk to you at 12 o'clock in the morning because she forgot to tell you something, and it's not what I think? What I'm thinking is why would she be at my door and what exactly is it that she has to tell you that couldn't wait until morning. I take it this here, she said pointing at me and him, is not work related." She said.

She was smarter than I thought. She reminded me of the actor Jennifer Aniston, except she weighed a lot more than Jennifer. I could see why Kirk would fall for though.

"She doesn't know do she?" I asked him, knowing that he didn't.

"What is it that I don't know Kirk?"

"Nothing baby. I don't want you to make a big issue out of nothing. You know the doctor told you not to get too worked up. You have to calm down for the baby. He said to her, trying get her to go in the house, Konstance, why are you here?" He said, looking back at me.

Now I understood why she had so much weight on her. She was pregnant. He'd lied to me. He told me that he didn't sleep in the same bed with her. I was livid.

"Pregnant... ha... Kirk failed to mention that you two were expecting." I said looking at him. He wouldn't even look at me.

"Yes…we're having a little girl." She said smiled while rubbing her belly.

"Well I must say I'm suprised, considering that Kirk hasn't slept with you in over two years. I know this because he told me and besides him and I have been dating for three years now." I wiped the smile right off her face. She slapped Kirk so hard that I winced for him.

"Get the hell out of my yard or I'm going to call the police." She said glaring at me.

"Go ahead and call them. I'm sure that Kirk wouldn't dare press charges against the mother of his child. I revealed, with a look of triumph on my face. Look like we both have something to celebrate about." I smirked, putting my hand up like a gun and pulling the trigger.

"Pow!"

"Konnie. You leave my house now!" Kirk said in pure rage.

"Kirk, I want you out." She screamed as neighbors began to watch us.

"Lisa, wait." He said running towards her. She almost slammed the door in his face but he made it in the house without it hitting him.

"What are you looking at? Take your nosey behind back in the house." I said looking at this old woman that had rollers in her head.

She looked at me and shook her head and mumbled something under her breath as she walked in the house. I wasn't sure, but I could have sworn she called me a floozy. Kirk came barging out of the house minutes later.

"Kirk, I planned to tell you about the baby, ahhh…" I screamed. He yanked my arms so hard, that I thought it was going to come out of its socket.

"Why are you doing this?" He said, almost dragging me towards my car. His face was beat red.

"Stop baby, you're hurting me." I winced.

"You have no right coming here." He said loosening his grip.

"How can you do this to me, Kirk? I trusted you. I believed you when you told me that you loved me. And you got her pregnant-- wow Kirk? You're just filled with surprises and lies. You told me that you weren't even sleeping in the same bed with her. What are you doing?" I whelped in agony.

"You don't get it do you? I told you that I wanted things to work out with my wife. She isn't black mailing me to stay "I" want to stay. Now, I'm sorry that I hurt you. I'm sorry I lied. I'm sorry that things couldn't go the way you planned. But I love my wife."

"Baby I know you don't mean that. I know you love me don't be afraid of her." I said walking up to kiss him but he pushed me away.

"Leave." He said, clenching his teeth.

Before I could say another word, he opened my car door, and forced me inside. I couldn't believe what had just happened back there. He had chosen his wife over me… I felt so stupid, so used, and so broken. I was going 90 miles an hour in a 50 mile zone. The rain began to fall hard and fast, while I tried to see the road through my tears. A sharp pain ran through my chest as if someone had taken a knife and stabbed me directly in it. My phone began to ring and I quickly retrieved from the passenger seat.

"Yes, mother." I said, trying to stop the tears.

"Konnie… she said crying hysterically, your father is dead."

Next thing I knew, the car skidded out of control, I heard the horn of the semi-truck and the screeching of brakes, but I couldn't stop. The last thing I remember is the blinding headlights , then everything went black.

Nine

        I WOKE UP in a hospital. Pain shot through my body so fast that I almost lost my breath. I couldn't move.

"Konstance… baby… are you okay?" My mother cried, as she rushed to my side.

"Wha…What happened?" I said wincing in pain.

"Baby, you were in an accident. She said. Don't talk, let me get a nurse." She said pressing the button that was next to my bed.

A black lady in her mid 50's dressed in a nurse uniform immediately came in behind a nerdy looking black man, who I assumed was the doctor.

"Hello Miss Graham. I am Doctor Nelson and I will be assisting you during the duration of your time here. I must say, you were completely lucky. God was on your side for sure." He implied, as the nurse checked my vitals.

I almost laughed at his last words. God wasn't doing me any favors.

"Your vital signs are normal, you had a minor concussion, two fractured ribs and a few scrapes and bruises that will heal with time, and…" He said as the words trailed from his lips.

"And, what?" I asked.

"You lost your baby… I'm sorry." He said sorrowfully.

"No… No… NO!" I screamed as I shook my head.

I couldn't believe what I was hearing. Why was this happening to me? Why was God punishing me? What did I ever do to Him to deserve all this? I know that I have done some terrible things in my life, but so have others. The doctor quickly barked orders to the nurse. I don't know what he was telling her, but she came back with a needle filled with some clear stuff. She put it in my IV. Next thing I knew, sleepiness fell over me. I woke up to the sound of the TV and my mom whispering over the phone. My lips felt like sandpaper and my mouth was drier than the Sahara Desert.

My mom must have heard me moan because she cut whoever it was on the phone off and quickly ran to my side.

"Don't move honey; let me get you some water." She insisted, pouring some water in a cup from a brown plastic pitcher.

"I told the hospital to move you in a more private and comfortable room." She said, soothingly.

I could see the weariness in her eyes. She looked sad and lost as I watched her sit next to me. She grabbed my hand, and tears begin to fall down her face.

"Konnie, baby, I'm so sorry… she wept as her arms shook… I… I'm so sorry."

"It's okay mom. It's not your fault. I should have been paying attention to the road." I told her, assuming she was talking about the accident.

"I swear I didn't know…" She said, shaking her head.

I looked at her with a look of confusion. I had no idea what she was talking about. She must have read my mind, because she'd answered me, but her answer almost rocked me to sleep.

"Your father told me. She cried. He told me before he took his last breath. Baby, I swear I didn't know… I didn't know." She whispered, more to her self than to me.

I just laid there numb and even if I wanted to say something, I wouldn't have been able to place the words. My father had finally revealed our dirty little secret. I should have known it was coming. I could tell that what he did to me was eating him alive.

"How… How could you have not known?" I found it hard to believe that she didn't know. A mother always knows. At least, that's what I heard.

"I… I don't know… I feel so stupid… I'm so angry with him… so angry with myself. I asked myself that same question. How could I have missed it?" She choked on her tears.

"That's easy… you never cared to notice. You were so busy shopping, so busy at your fancy little country club that you didn't care to see." I barely spoke, feeling a little drowsy. The medicine had not worn off yet.

"You're right... I'm sorry... Please forgive me." She pleaded.

"It doesn't even matter. I'm used to being hurt, overlooked and abandoned. You haven't done anything to me that haven't already been done. I said coldly. Now that you know the truth, you live with it; just like I have been living with it for all these years. You married a child molester... You married a man that got so dissatisfied with you... a woman... that he had to go get it from a little girl... sadly it was his daughter. You don't care about me, you never have. I guess it's true what Grammy told me. Money is the root of all evil. You loved money more than my father, just like you loved money more than me. So go... leave... Go shopping or something." I said dismissively, as tears trickled down my face.

"Konnie... please..."

"Either you leave now or I'll have a nurse escort you out." I said closing my eyes, as my heart sunk to my knees.

She stood and looked at me for a moment and walked out the door. Just like my father the first time that he snuck into my room, just like Kirk did the other night. Everything that Kirk and I had was built on lies. He didn't love me. He just wanted to use me. Just like the other men. Just like my dad. He didn't even come by the hospital to check on me. I had the nurse who checked my vitals when I first woke up to notify him. She told me that she had and said he told her that she must have had the wrong number and to never call his house again. It was my third day in the hospital and I was losing weight like crazy. I wouldn't eat anything and if I had my way, I will just waste away until my soul just left my body. I begged for God to just take me out of my misery, but he must have enjoyed watching me suffer.

"How are you feeling today?" The same nurse came in with a smile on her face.

I don't know what she's all happy about. I didn't respond I just looked away.

"Ohhh... kay..." She said, checking my vitals, as she sung a song about loving Jesus.

"So you one of them, huh?" I looked up at her with disgust.

"Them? Who?" She stopped taking my temperature and

looked at me.

"You know… one of those Jesus lovers." I said.

She put her hands on her hips and looked at me.

"I'm so in love with Jesus, that if He came down right now and asked me to leave with Him, I'd stop everything I was doing and follow Him. So, yes, I am one of them." She said it with a sense of boldness and pride.

"Hmph… I guess He loves who He loves and dismisses the rest." I said.

She sat down and looked at me.

"Baby, there is no respect of person with God. He loves us all. He had His only Son die on the cross for every one of us."

"Whatever. Because of God, my life is in shambles."

"We all have trials in our lives, but the most of the things that occurs in our lives is because of the choices we make. That's what happens when you let Satan lead you. He's the one that's in the business of destroying temples, baby." She implied.

"My choices… so was it my choice for my father to come in my room whenever he wanted to do whatever he wanted to do to me? Was it my fault that my mother didn't care to notice because she was so into herself that she could careless about her own daughter? Tell me… was me losing my baby my choice? Was it my choice to get my heart ripped out my chest my choice because the man I loved lied to me and left me here at this hospital to bare the lost of our child alone? Please tell me…" I said getting worked up as tears threatened to come out.

"I can understand your pain and no… those are not choices that you made baby…" She said rubbing my hands.

"You know, the devil is so busy. He only comes to steal, kill and destroy, but Jesus said that He came that we might have life and live life more abundantly. His desire is for us to live not to die. I know life has been tough for you and no child should ever have to go through what you went through. But understand that God loves you and He has always been there to—"

"God loves me… I laughed. God doesn't care anything about me." I said getting tired of her feeding me lies. I was tired of people lying to me.

"Oh, dear child, but He does. He loves you so much that He spared your life on that road." She smiled.

"I would have rather died." I told her with coldness in my eyes.

"I rebuke you Satan, in the name of Jesus, loose this child." She said, putting her hand on my head.

If I wasn't so weak, I would have pushed her hands from out of mine and slapped that wig off of her head. But I was so weak I couldn't even sit up.

"Did you just call me Satan?" I said offended.

"I'm not talking to you, I'm talking to the Spirit in you child. She said pointing at me. The devil has been trying to take your soul every since you was a little girl. But I bind that Spirit in the Mighty name of Jesus. God has a plan for your life. He has work for you to do." She nodded.

"God doesn't need me… why would He need someone like me for, when He got people like you falling all over Him?" I said, pointing at her.

"He needs you more than you ever know. Before you were created in the womb of your mother, He knew you. He created you with love and anything He creates is good. Deep down inside you are still good. Underneath the scars there is a light that has been dimmed by childhood pains, unforgiveness, anger, and hurt." She said squeezing my hand.

"You don't even know me. You don't know what my life has been like." I told her.

"You right… I don't know anything about you… But I can tell you a thing or two about life. You see, we all struggle with something… We all have a story to tell. You know I worked two, sometimes three jobs, trying to put my children through college. My husband was a sorry piece of nothing. All he would do is sit in that same recliner by that raggedy TV in the living room and sip his beer. Many nights when I came home, tired, feet hurting, and just wore out, he would come in the room and just start with me about any ol' little thang. He would beat my behind from the bedroom to the kitchen. Yes, he did. My sons would look at me and I can see the question in there eyes—why you let him treat you like that mama?" She dabbed her eyes, and continued.

"I often sat back and wondered the same question. Why did I let him beat me? Why couldn't I just pick up my kids and go? I mean, I was the one working and taking care of the bills. He wasn't doing nothing but raising hell and beating the tar out of me. He called me stupid so much that I began to believe it. Maybe I was stupid. Maybe I was stupid as can be, just like he said. After all, I was allowing him to beat me. Every time I'd have the strength enough to kick him out, the stupidity in me allowed him to come right back in." She said.

"I... I'm sorry. I didn't know." I uttered.

"Please, my dear child... let me finish; because there's a message in this testimony." She said holding up her hands.

I shut my mouth and let her continue.

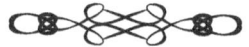

Ten

I WAS IN TEARS after she finished telling her story. She was right… There was a powerful message in her story. After hearing about how she suffered from the hands of her husband for nearly twenty years and how she almost went to prison for life after she killed him for defending herself I just couldn't imagine how she found the strength to move on. She told me about the many times she'd tried to kill herself because she felt that, that was the only way she would be able to break free from her husband. She told me about the many times she would catch him and other women in their bed. She told me about how he called her all kinds of whores and sluts when he would flip the script on her and blame her for the sexual transmitted diseases that she would get from him.

She told me about the many times he'd threatened to kill her if she ever left him. She'd even told me about her oldest son dying from AIDs, last year, that he'd contacted from his boyfriend. She then told me that her younger son just got sentenced to life in prison for killing his wife and his two children. When I asked her how she was able to stand after all of that, she told me that it was God who helped her swim through those deep valleys, guide her through the wilderness, and climb to the top of the mountain. She told me about how she hasn't always been a "Jesus lover." She revealed that at one time she blamed God. That she rejected Him and failed to believe in Him for a long time.

"You see, I didn't understand that God was making ways to bring me out, but I was the one who kept allowing the monster to come back in. God gives us free will and the ability to make choices and we can either choose His way or the hard way. Often times the hard way is what leads us right back to Jesus, licking our wounds." She laughed.

"In the process of living you will look around and noticed all the unnecessary junk that you've collected along the way. The funny thing is we can be so comfortable in living in the junk, that when it's time to start doing some spring cleaning, we find it hard to let go of the junk. It's hard to let go because we end up having a love affair with our junk. We get too imbalanced. While the other part wants to get out the other part don't know what it takes or don't want to do what it takes to get out." She said shaking her head.

I thought about Kirk and how I wasted all that time waiting for him to leave his wife. I thought about the many promises he made and the many times I'd made myself available to a man that was unavailable.

"Can I ask you something Miss Graham?"

"Sure… just call me Konnie…" I said smiling at her. Usually everyone close to me called me that, but that was something about her that made me feel like I was close to her.

"Okay, Konnie. My name is Helen. Who was that man that you had me call?"

I lowered my head, "it was the father of my child. We had been dating for over three years and he kept promising me he was going to leave his wife." I said shamefully.

"Hmph… she said looking at me closely. You cannot *date* a married man baby." She said shaking her head.

"Yeah, I guess you're right. We were sleeping with each other for three years, I corrected myself, so when he told me he was going to stay with his wife I was devastated. I went to his house, confronted him and his wife and told him I was pregnant. He didn't even care. He shoved me in my car and told me to never come to his house again. I was headed home and my mother called to tell me my father had passed away. That's why I'm laying in this hospital bed." I said looking around.

"After you told me what Kirk said, I was forced to find out the hard truth. I finally was able to see who he was and what we were." I said, as the pain in my heart began to intensify.

"So, you thought he would leave his wife once you told him about the baby?" She asked me knowingly.

I nodded my head as tears poured down my cheeks.

"See that's where you messed up at…You tried to build something with someone who had already had a foundation somewhere else." She said, pulling out a Kleenex from the counter, and handing it to me.

"I can see the need in you… the need to want to be loved… the need to want to feel love… and the need to want to be apart of something that makes you feel like somebody. What attracted you to him was not about his looks and how good the sex was, it was because he gave you validation. He told you exactly what you needed to hear, because he'd already seen the vulnerability in you. The devil knows you too baby girl. He can send people on assignments to come in confuse you into thinking that they came from God. Cause they show you a side of them that is too good to resist."

"You are so right." I said as I thought about how I met Kirk and my reasoning for wanting to be with him so bad.

"Your problem is that you are too busy running from yourself, that you don't even realize that, that same thing you running from always seem to catch up with you." She said, giving me a sip of water.

"What do you mean?" I asked, eager to know.

"You scared of what you might discover about yourself. You're trying to avoid self-awareness. You don't want to be alone with you, you've never examined who you are, never taken the time to know who you are, what you are, or how you are. And you'd given yourself to someone that you don't even know your darn self-- making promises and commitments without even considering the bigger picture." She looked at me compassionately.

"Mrs. Helen, I thought he was the perfect man. He showed me so many things and made me feel so many ways that a man never have before. I use to treat men the same way Kirk was treating me. I guess karma has its way of coming back to you." I shook my head; ignoring the part about her saying I was scared to confront me. I didn't want her to know how right she was.

"Perfect? Girl please, you can tell by his actions with you that he wasn't that perfect. You can't find a perfect mate in a married man suga. You was wrong… You and him. God ain't gon' bless no mess and the whole situation was messy. Love is not what had with that woman's husband. You may have had feelings for him, he could of possibly been your first love, even, but you were the only one loving baby." She told it like it was.

"I don't understand. He told me he loved me and he showed me all the time. I said confused. I really wanted to believe that Kirk really did love me. I was ready to marry him. You may think I'm stupider then you already think after I tell you this. I actually went online and ordered a bridal gown and our rings. I thought he was going to tell me that he was going to leave his wife and be with me." I looked away with shame in my eyes.

"I don't think you're stupid. You were just introduced to something that revealed itself as what you believed to have been love. Again, you don't even know who you are. If you was to have gotten married to that man you wouldn't have even known who the "I" is who said "I do" much less who he is that you said "I do" to. You wanted to get married but you're already taken." She said, opening her Bible.

"What do you mean? I'm not married." I told her.

"Oh yes ma'am, you're very married. You're still married to what daddy did and what mommy didn't do. You're still married to past pains, current issues, and the demons in your closet." She said, flipping through the pages in the Bible.

I just sat their stunned by the revelation. I was beginning to see things in a different perspective.

She stopped flipping, and started reading, "Love is patient, love is kind. It does not envy, it does not boast, it is not proud. It does not dishonor others, it is not self-seeking, it is not easily angered, it keeps no record of wrongs. Love does not delight in evil but rejoices with the truth. It always protects, always trusts, always hopes, and always perseveres. Do you understand what I just read to you?" She asked me, looking up from the page she was reading.

"Yes, ma'am… I realize that I have no idea what love really is." I chuckled sadly.

"Understandable. It's hard to understand love if you do not know God. For God is love and He demonstrates His love to us each and everyday, but when we refuses His love it makes it hard for us to see it and for Him to properly show us. He wants us to know Him, to know love, and He wants to be loved by us so bad." She said.

"I can't image God wanting to love me. I have done so many things that I'm not proud of. Why would he want to love me?" I said dejectedly.

"This is what makes God's love so pure and so unconditional from man's demonstration of love. No matter what we have done He still loves us. He will forgive you for every sin you committed if you ask Him. God knows I'm not perfect and I've done some things that I thought would make God turn His back on me and not look back. But God is merciful, filled with forgiveness and grace. Just ask Him and he will forgive you and cloth you with a love that you've never felt before." She smiled, as she wrapped her arms around herself as if God Himself was holding her.

"You talk as if you know." I said.

"Yes indeed. I don't speak on what I don't know. I've experienced God and I have felt Him, and tasted of Him and I know He is too good. He is too good to me, for me to give up. He is too good for me to let Him go. I can't imagine my life without Him. If it had not been for the Lord on my side, I don't know where I'd be... probably in jail or in hell one." She said holding up her hands to the sky.

"I want that kind of love." I marveled over the boldness and the sincerity in her voice when she talked about God.

"Oh baby girl, you already got it. You just have to open up to Him and receive it." She told me.

"I don't know if I know how?" I admitted.

"Oh honey that's easy... Do you believe that Jesus is the Son of God, who died on the cross for your sins?" She asked.

"That's what my Grammy told me." I responded.

"It's not about what anyone else told you or what they believe, it's going to take your own faith in God for you to receive Him. So do *you* believe in your heart that Jesus is the Messiah, who died on the cross for our sins and that He is the manifestation of God in the flesh?" She asked me.

"Yes I do." I whispered as I closed my eyes and sincerely meant it from my heart.

As I welcomed Him in a warm feeling came over. I felt a sense of peace, love, and joy all at the same time. I couldn't quite explain this kind of love. It was so different-- it was a feeling I'd never known before. I was filled with so much emotion that all I could do was cry. These were not tears of sadness or anger like before, but tears of joy.

"You feel it don't you?" She said with a toothy smile.

I just nodded my head and kept crying. After reading Psalm 51, Psalm 23, and Psalm 91, I felt like a whole new person. As if I wasn't even the same me no more. Just like Helen said, I was cleansed and now a new creature in Christ Jesus. My heart was filled with love, my mind finally had some peace, and I could feel my soul moving from it's dead place, and moving into a place of life.

Eleven

I WAS SAD because I wasn't ready to be discharged yet. I was going to really miss Helen and I wasn't sure if I was ready to go home and face everything that was left unkempt. I was surprised to see Terrance walking in the door.

"Terrance, what are you doing here?" I smiled brightly. I was glad to see my friend.

"I'm here to pick you up, what you think…" He said looking at me, and then he frowned.

"Hey what's with the frown? I don't look that bad do I?" I said, looking in the mirror. The wounds had healed nicely, but I wasn't sure about the wounds that were not seen with the naked eye.

"I'm sorry that I wasn't here for you. I'm sorry for what I said to you. I didn't mean it. I just want what's best for you." He said misty eyed.

"It's okay T. I'm sorry too and yes you did mean what you said, but you know what, I'm glad you said it. You were right and I got angry because I was too much in denial to see the truth for myself." I told him.

"Who are you?" He said looking at me closely.

"It's me… I'm just not the same ol' me that I used to be." I said winking at him.

"And you can thank God for that." I heard Helen say, as she walked in.

"Yes ma'am I can." I said smiling at her.

Terrance looked like he didn't know what was going on.

"This is my best friend Terrance that I told you about. Terrance this is Helen, my guardian angel."

"Well I'm not all that, but it's nice to match a name with a face Terrance. You take good care of her, now." She said, patting him on the back.

"I'm going to miss you." I pouted, as I hugged her tight.

"Be careful. Your ribs are not healed all the way." She said, softly touching my ribs.

"Please call me." I told her, wiping away the tears.

"You know I will and you better not hesitate to pick up that phone and call me... do you understand?" She said sternly.

"Yes, ma'am."

"Alright now, you get out of here." She shooed me away. She didn't want me to see, but I saw a tear escaped from her eyes.

I would never forget her. She helped me see things about myself that I'd never seen before. She helped me to understand God in a whole different light. It was she who helped me escape from total damnation. God loved me all along, He knew me. I realized that the other night when it dawned on me that God had sent Helen to be a messenger for me. He'd saved me twice. After a short drive home, Terrance and I finally made it to my house. I'd been in the hospital for over three weeks and I had forgotten what home looked like. My house was clean and everything was back in place.

"Your mom came by and cleaned up a bit." He revealed.

I had not spoken with my mom since the day I told her to leave the hospital. Of course, she'd tried to call, a few times but after the fourth rejection, she stopped calling. I wanted to forgive my mom so bad, but I wasn't sure how, but I knew that if I asked God, He would help me. Terrance and I talked for a long time. I told him about what happened at the hospital between my mother and I-- about what my father did to me. I told him about the conversation between Helen and I and how I surrendered my life to Christ. He stayed with me until I was able to manage on my own. I could barely feel any pain in my ribs and I felt like I was back to normal. Now I was here alone, held hostage with my own thoughts, and my mind drifted off to all the things that I was afraid to confront.

I thought back to my childhood and to the painful memories. A glimpse of my father on top of me, moving in and out of me, plagued my mind. I looked deep in his eyes, there lied lust and a deeper pain that I hadn't noticed before. The type of pain that was hidden deep inside… In his eyes I saw confusion… He didn't even know why he was on top of me. Who did he really see when he saw me? I saw shame and misery… I bet he wondered why he was doing what he was doing to his own daughter. I thought about my mom and how I yearned for her to know me, to care for me, and to nurture me properly.

I thought about the many nights I cried, wondering why she didn't love me, wondering why material things was more important than her daughter. Then I thought about Kirk and thinking of him is what hurt me the most. I thought about when we first met, how good things were, and how bad it ended. Then I thought about my child and I became overwhelmed with a feeling of lost, grief, and depression. I wasn't ready to face it. Not now… I decided to turn on some music to distract myself. I wasn't ready to face those demons. I went to my bar and grabbed a bottle of wine. I just needed to drink a glass to calm my nerves.

A funny feeling came over me, as if what I was planning on doing was wrong. I read the new testament and I told myself that drinking wine was not a sin, cause Jesus drunk it too. I failed to mention that drinking to get drunk was one though. Flashes of my father on top of me flooded my mind too, then the scene fast forwarded to where Kirk told me he didn't want to be with me anymore, then it skipped to the part where I was in the hospital and the doctor told me that I'd lost my baby. Then it skipped a scene and went to the part where my mother pleaded for forgiveness as I shunned her off after she revealed to me what my father told her.

Then the rewind button must have been pressed, because I was in the living room at Terrance house where his words sank into me like truth serum. I had finished almost half the bottle of wine by this time. I felt numb, alone, broken, and confused. I didn't want to think anymore, didn't want to see the visions, or hear the words that were terrorizing me. So I chugged down the wine that remained in the bottle and stumbled my way to the bar to get another bottle. Music has always gave me a sense of calmness. Although the wine was giving me a buzz, it wasn't erasing the pain fast enough.

Twelve

I PULLED OUT my collection of CD's and pulled out FanMail by TLC. I sipped on my wine as I bobbed my head to No Scrubs, and Diggin' On You. I was finally feeling the effects of the alcohol. Many say alcohol gives you the courage to face the truth. I don't know, but I was afraid that I was about to find out. I stumbled in my bedroom and looked into my full length mirror. The song Unpretty was playing in the background. My hair was sprawled all over my head, the eye liner and mascara that was once perfectly applied was now running down my face, and my eyes were red and puffy from crying.

I ran my hands across my body as I sung along with, T-Boz, *"I wish I could tie you up in my shoes... make you feel unpretty too...I was told I was beautiful... but what does that mean to you... look into the mirror whose inside there... I sung along as I took a swig of the bottle of champagne that was in my hand. The one with the long hair ... Same old me again today..."* I was singing out of tune and my words slurred as the alcohol was beginning to take affect *"My outsides are cool... my insides are blue..."* I couldn't move from where I was as I looked beyond the beautiful image and saw the ugliness that dwell inside of me. I wanted to move from the mirror, but my feet wouldn't follow my command.

T-Boz was punishing me with her words, but I couldn't stop looking at that reflection in the mirror, and I couldn't stop singing. *"Never insecure until I met you... now I'm being stupid... I used to be so cute to me... just a little bit skinny... why do I look to all these things... to keep you happy..."* I sung along as I thought about what my father did to me, my baby, I thought about the empty promises that Kirk made to me, and how quickly I was dismissed by the men that I loved the most. *"Maybe get rid of you ... and then I'll get back to me... If you look inside you... find out who am I too..."* I thought about what my best friend told me and the advice from nurse at the hospital kept running through my mind. I tried to shut it all out but I couldn't.

At this point, mucus was running like water out of my nose and my face was drenched with tears. I tried to stop crying but the tears kept flowing and even though the words were catching in my throat, I kept singing. I kept looking in the mirror at that image and I kept on singing. *"Be in a position to make me feel… so unpretty… I'll make you feel unpretty to…. I'll make you feel unpretty too…"* Even after the sung ended I was still singing the last words, *"I'll make you feel unpretty too."* My father was the first one to make me feel unpretty, then my mother's failure to take notice to me, to see me, to nurture me, and to be there for me made me feel unpretty, and then there was Kirk who found me worthy enough to sleep with, but not worthy enough to marry.

Yes, he made me feel unpretty. I thought about all the negative things I said to my mother, to the girls who tried to be my friends, and to Kirk's wife—I was trying to make them feel unpretty too. Anger over took me and I threw the half empty bottle of wine into the mirror. Glass shattered every where. I fell to the floor and my whole body shook as I cried. There was so much inside of me that I didn't think I had to strength to over come.

"Come unto me, all ye' that labour and are heavy laden, and I will give you rest."

I heard the voice loud in clear. It was not a loud voice, but a small still voice that flowed deep inside of my heart up to my ears. I've never heard that voice before. A calm spirit overtook me and I knew that I'd heard the voice of the Lord.

"Lord, I believe in You, but help my unbelief." I cried, not even realizing that I was quoting scripture. I didn't realize that the Holy Spirit was fighting for me.

"Let it go… Let it all go…"

There it was again. I knew what He was asking me to do. In order to move on I had to let go. So I closed my eyes, and I told God to help me to stand, give me the courage to face my fears and my troubles, and give me the strength to let go and forgive.

"Lord, I forgive my Father for what he did to me. Although I may never understand why he did it, I can't live my life holding on to the burden. He has to answer for what he did, so Lord I let it all go and place it in your hands." I cried out. It felt like a weight had just lifted off of me, so I kept going.

"I forgive my mother for not being there. Maybe she didn't know what it was to be a parent or maybe she was too consumed with herself to care. I don't know, but Lord, I open up my heart and I forgive her." I cried all the more, my mind was beginning to see clearer.

"Oh Lord, how he hurt me, but I thank him for the pain, because if it wasn't for him then I wouldn't have never known you. I know I am just as responsible for the outcome of the relationship as Kirk was. Forgive me Father for not honoring my temple; forgive me for sinning against my own body. Most of all God forgive me for sinning against You. Forgive me for fornicating. I had no right sleeping with him let alone falling in love with him. I forgive him Lord." I was crying harder now, my nose was getting stuffy.

"Lord, I forgive Kirk for not being there for me when I needed him, but then again I realized that it was you who I needed the most. Forgive me God for loving someone else more than I loved myself and more than I loved You. I forgive myself... I forgive myself for what I have done and what I failed to do. Forgive me for all the bad things I said about you. Heal my broken heart and my empty womb. Give me the strength to accept the fact that my baby is up there in heaven with You. Surely You know what's best and who knows; maybe what happened was for the best." Something inside of me was breaking. I could hear it…. I could hear the yokes being destroyed, and the shell that had capsulated itself around me cracking open.

"I give You my pain, I give You the agony, and I give You my heart Lord. Mend it Lord, revive it, and restore it. Give me a renewed and transformed mind. I want to do better, be better, and live better. Amen." I was practically in a praying position on my knees, bowing down to God and giving Him the glory.

I thought about Helen and what she said to me when I asked her about the hard part and she said:

"The hard part is self-evaluation. You have to face up to you and that can be scary. You have to face up to the good, the bad, and the ugly parts of you. Spend some time alone. Time alone enables you to observe who you are, who God is, and what is suitable for you. Don't even think about what coulda, shoulda, and woulda been, but look pass the past and walk into your future. You have to be self-aware in order to have a high level of self-esteem. Discover the you that God designed you to be, not the you that you designed for yourself."

I imagined myself at the feet of God's throne, kissing His feet. I was the Samaritan woman at the well. I was Hagar, Abraham's mistress who bared his illegitimate son. I was the lady with the issue of blood who touched the hymn of Jesus' garment and was healed. I was that sinful woman who came to the Pharisees house, with an alabaster jar filled with perfume. I kneeled at His feet and wet His feet with my tears, and then wiped them with my hair. Yes, I was the lady who almost got stoned by the crowed with the rocks in their hands. And when He asked them to cast a stone if they were without sin He noticed that no one did. I could hear Him telling me "I don't condemn you… GO… from now own, sin no more."

When I got up off the floor I walked in liberty, love, joy, peace, and real happiness. I swept up the pieces of glass off the floor. I couldn't predict my future. I may be at my lowest point right now, but God is lifting me up. I know I may stumble as I'm walking towards my destiny, but i thank God for what's in front of me. It's going to be a long journey and I know I still have a lot to deal with and a long way to go. But at least I want be walking alone this time around. I can get through this because the same power that raised Jesus from the grave is built on the inside of me, so I have power. I'm not just a conqueror, but I'm more than a conqueror in Christ Jesus. I cut off the stereo and after I took a hot, soothing bath, I looked in the mirror and no longer saw the ugly monster that I'd help create. I was beginning to see the beauty inside. A beauty that I'd never really known… I smiled to at the reflection in the mirror. And whispered… *"You're so pretty"*.

Broken Scattered Pieces

Chapter One

WHAT IT'S LIKE to be in love? To be loved? To understand it's true meaning? Can mankind ever conquer it, ever be sensible enough to meet its expectations? All my life love has been foreign to me. I never knew what it was, because I never experienced it. I've never known what it meant, because it was never defined for me. I never knew what it looked liked, because know one has ever showed me. I never knew what it felt like because nobody has ever taken the time to touch my heart, just my body. I stopped wondering whether loved would ever know me.

Happiness abandoned me and left me with sadness a long time ago. I stop trusting when the one who I expected to guard me and shield me, left me uncovered and available for anyone to do anything they desired to do to me. When I was a little girl, I had hopes, I had dreams, and I had an idea of who I was, what I wanted to be, and who I wanted to become. I remember my grandmother gave me this gorgeous antique bisque porcelain doll. Its delicate features with a matte finish, gave it a realistic skin-like texture.

Her skin was painted like a sandy brown, much like my skin tone, with flushed cheeks. She had slick, short, dark brown curly hair, with a silk pink ribbon tied in her hair like a bow. Her eyes were round, dark brown, and intriguing. She wore a pink and beige striped dress with ruffles. My grandmother said I reminded her of the doll when she picked it out in Germany on her trip. She said I was created with the most expensive materials and that although the skin was tough, it was also fragile. She saw so much in me that reminded her of the doll. I didn't play with her, because I was scared that I would break her.

So I just sat her on my night table beside my bed and talk with her, looked at her, and visualized her as a reflection of me. I called her Princess Anyla because she reminded me of royalty, class, beauty, and poise. I wanted to be her, I often times looked in the mirror and wished that I was her. I just didn't realize back then how much I'd really had become her. My mom was fifteen years old when she gave birth to me. She never spoke of my father and I stopped asking when she told me that I didn't need to know. She dated many men until "uncle" Earl became my step father. He seemed quite promising and likeable when I first met him.

He would bring me candy every time he came over. He promised my mother butterflies and rainbows, but in the end she would find herself chasing after a pot of gold that would never be at the end of the rainbow. He went from having a job at the post office to becoming jobless when he came to work drunk. Drinking was always his issue but it had gotten worse soon after. He would come in the house drunk, she would ridicule him, put him out for a few days, and welcome him back in after realizing that she still loved him, whatever that means.

It wasn't that he was the one bamming down the front door. It would be my mom who would go out looking for him, begging him to come back. She was so busy chasing after him, that she didn't have time to take care of me. To busy wallowing around in misery and worrying about her next fix to notice or care when Earl would come in my room and touch me. It started out with him wanting me to touch his private area, then he wanted me to kiss it, then he wanted me to kiss him. He would put his slimy tongue in my mouth and I would almost gag. Then it got to the point where he no longer asked me, but demanded me to.

When I wouldn't he would get mad and beat me something awful. He told me that if I ever told anyone that he would kill me and my mother. So, even when he took things to another level, I never told. I was eleven years old when he decided to take what rightfully belonged to me. I didn't quite understand sex back then, but I remembered what it felt like. It felt like somebody was ripping my insides open in between my legs. Blood had drowned the sheets, and although I dared not cry on the outside, my inner most parts cried out like the pouring rain.

One night my mother came in high and it was clear that she'd just got finished shooting up heroin. Things had begun to turn for the worst. The once beautiful, honey-tanned, long-haired, model-shaped woman with the doey-eyed brown eyes had metamorphosed into someone I didn't even recognize. Her hair was no longer long, but short and matted to her head. Her skin was no longer flawless, but a dark brown color. She had sores, and needle holes every where. Her skin was sunken and she looked skeletal, and when I looked into her eyes, I saw coldness, bitterness, and sadness.

She was not the strong woman I remember, no... this woman looked like she'd been tossed by the waves of life, and she'd looked blown away by a strong wind against a house made of straw. I stood in the corner staring at her with a look of fear and disgust on my face. She was scratching the scabs on her arms, rocking back and forth, and talking to herself. She looked at me in smiled, but that smiled quickly turned into a frown. Her eyes were glassy and her mouth was twitching. I know it sounds strange, but I was relieved to see Earl when he came crashing in the door. Too much for relief because he could barely hold himself up. He was drunk as all get out. My mother jumped up like a jack rabbit and ran to him.

"Earl, do you have 20 dollars?" She begged.

"Get away from me. He said, pushing her to the floor. You been out there doing that dope, haven't you."

"Ain't nobody been on nothing. Why you always coming in her accusing somebody? You the one drunk." She said, getting up off the floor.

"If I want to have me a drink or two then I can." He snarled at her.

"I don't care about all that. I just need twenty dollars." She said looking at him with pleading eyes.

"I told you, I'm not giving you no money....Gone head on now." He said waving his hand.

"Please Earl." She said falling on her knees, grabbing his ankle.

"Woman, get off me." He said unable to shake her off.

He saw me in the corner and smiled. All I noticed was his brown decaying teeth. I almost vomited.

"Well… I guess I can give you twenty dollars." He said with a sinister smile. He didn't take his eyes off of me. I stood there shaking.

"Really… she said excitedly. Thank you baby." She grinned, wrapping her arms from around his leg.

"But I want something in return." He informed her, as he licked his lips.

"Okay baby." She said seductively, removing her clothes, like I wasn't in the room.

"Naw… I don't want none of that. He said as if she'd lost her mind. I want some of that." He said pointing at me.

I stood there mortified. I didn't know what he meant, but something just didn't feel right. Deep in the pit of my gut I knew that something he wanted wasn't anything good. It was like looking in the eyes of the devil, and I was stuck in hell.

"Why would you want that little girl, when you have all this woman right in front of you?" She grinned with teeth just as atrocious as his.

"Either you give me what I want or you want get what you want." He said, as he pulled the twenty dollars out.

She looked from me to him to the twenty dollars that he was holding in his hand.

"Baby." She said, reaching out to me with a seemingly pleasant smile on her face, but I knew better.

I just stood there. Afraid of what was going to happen.

"Baby, please do this for your mommy, you love your mommy don't you?" She smiled, still trying to get me to come where she was.

I didn't say anything to her; I just stood there in shock. I couldn't believe that my mother was willing to sell her child for a twenty dollar fix.

"You don't have to ask her nothing. You her mammy, you just tell her." He said with forced.

"Desiree, go in your room and get undressed." Her voice was not forceful.

I didn't budge. I couldn't even if I wanted to. My heart was pounding like crazy, everything that I had eaten for dinner felt like it wanted to come up. I couldn't really recollect what was going on around me.

"Go, Desiree." She said with forced, pushing me into my room.

I can still remember the stench of his breath and the smell of alcohol that reeked from his pores. I still remember the lust in his eyes when he instructed me to take off my clothes and lay in the bed. I can still remember the fear and the lump in my throat as I slowly took my Barbie panties, and my matching Barbie pajamas off. I remember his pop beer belly and the nappy looking hair on his chest. His skin reminded me of a black seal. I felt sick to my stomach as he climbed on top of me, forced himself inside of me, and forced me to say dirty things to him.

That night that my mother sold me to her husband wasn't the first time and it wouldn't be the last time. Every time she didn't have the money to get her drugs, she would offer me up and he didn't reject the offer. I started fighting and resisting, hoping that would help, but it only made things worse. I stop trying. I had no fight left in me and I begin to think that there was nothing left to fight for. I use to always cry after he finished but after a while the tears stop falling. At one point I could remember the pain, the humiliation, the fear, and the hope that somebody would come rescue me. But I'd become numb, no longer feeling, and no longing hoping for my rescuer.

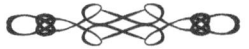

Chapter Two

THIS NIGHT WAS different from the nights before. Yes, it was the same scenario. My mother would come begging for more money and Earl would come in my room, expecting me to assume the position. But this time, I felt different. Something inside of me changed. I couldn't quite explain it, but I knew I couldn't keep letting this happen to me. I was now 17 years old and I was still being controlled by my mother's addiction and Earl. If I didn't have the courage to fight back, then things would continue to be as they are. I was tired of my mother pimping me out and Earl tricking me out. I vowed to myself that next time I was either going to come out alive or die trying to defend myself from the hands of this devil.

Yes, Earl was the devil. He came in this house like an angel of light, but his mission was to kill, steal, and destroy. He killed my dreams, stole the essence that I possessed, and destroyed my life. My grandmother had taught me about prayer and I went to church with her a lot when I was little, but I stopped after I turned thirteen. I would pray every night that God will take me far away from my mother, from Earl, from Earth. I used to beg Him to let me come to heaven with Him. Every time Earl would come in my room, I would pray that God will somehow stop Him. But my prayers were never answered. I assumed that God must have had more important things to do. One night Earl slithered into my bed after having a fight with my mother.

"Lord… I know you may be too busy, but please answer me, just this once. I promise I will never bother you again." I silently prayed.

I could feel Earl's hands rubbing on my butt.

"My grandmother said that I could always pray to You if I am scared and if I need You to protect me."

Then he turned me over and touched my breasts.

"Well Lord, this is one of those times." I was crying out now, silently of course.

He got out of the bed and started pulling off his clothes.

"I need You to help me Lord. I need You to come and protect me." I said, as a tear escaped from my eyes.

He was back in the bed rubbing on my body and pressing his dry lips on mine.

"Lord, please hear my cry. If You can't come, please allow one of Your angels to come down from heaven and get this man off of me." I pleaded.

He began taking off my clothes until I felt the cold air brush across my body, making my nipple involuntarily erect. He opened my legs and I felt his tongue down there. It felt so funny. Without thinking, I snapped my legs shut and almost crushed his skull.

"You little—"

I felt a sharp sting assault my cheek. He slapped me so hard my ears begin to ring. I was so taken aback, that I'd forgotten all about my little chat with God. He pried my legs open and forced himself inside of me, this time without a condom. I did not want to get pregnant, especially not by him. Since God wasn't going to rescue me, I guess I had to try to be my own savior.

"Please . . . not tonight. I said, looking up at him. Why don't you go get some from your wife?"

"Maybe I don't want your mother, maybe I want what's already in front of me. Your mother ain't got nothing I want. She out there smoking that dope and letting all them men run in and out of her." He slurred.

"But you— He said, pointing in my face. You fresh and best of all, I'm the only one who had you." He smirked.

I didn't know what I was going to do and how I was going to convince this man not to touch me but I had to come up with something. I know begging him not to would only increase his desire to do it. So, I used my head and decided to play along.

"Wait a minute daddy, let me go freshen up for you and put on something nice." I said licking my lips.

"Now, that's what I'm talking about. Go get right for me baby." He said getting excited.

I could see his little Vienna sausage pocking out of his boxers. I walked into the bathroom and turned on the sink so he could think I was washing up. I walked in the kitchen and got a butcher knife from the kitchen and carefully stuffed it in the back of my panties. I made my way back into the room and closed the door. To keep him distracted, I turned on the radio, loud enough so that my mother couldn't hear.

"Strip for me baby." He breathed loudly, as he stroked his disgusting little penis.

I almost vomited right where I stood but I knew I had to do what he asked if I wanted my plan to work. I slowly moved my hips to the music and peeled off my nightie in a seductive way.

"Now you know I was just playing. I know you didn't really think that I wanted to see that sloppy looking body of yours. Look at you... You trying to make me lose my appetite. He laughed. You too fat to be trying to do all that. I'm surprise you can dance for that long without needing some oxygen." He joked.

I stopped dancing. I was used to him and my mother reminding me of how fat I was. I wasn't always fat. I started eating a whole lot after he raped me the first time. Yeah, I was depressed, but I mostly ate anything that I could think of just to gain weight. I figured if I got too fat, that he would find me unattractive and stop having sex with me. But that didn't work. One day he said, "You need to stop eating so much. If you get too fat ain't no man gone won't you." That was music to my ears. But the music abruptly stopped when he said, "your weight ain't got nothing to do with what's in between your legs though."

We lived in a small country town called Tifton, Georgia. It was one of those hot and humid nights. The fan was on but it wasn't blowing out any air. I wanted to smack that smirk right off his ugly face. I couldn't wait to plunge this knife in him so deep that it pierces through his filthy soul. When I finally got the nerve to get in the bed with him, he didn't waste any time touching my breasts again. I was so nervous that I didn't know if I would be able to do it but I held my demeanor and concentrated on getting the knife that I slickly slid from my pants and sat by the bed when he took off his boxers. While he roughly pounded his flesh inside in me, I cautiously wrapped my hand around the handle of the knife but as I was about to lift it up he flipped me over on my stomach. The knife fell from my hand with a loud thud. My breath caught in my throat and I almost liked to have had a bowel movement.

Chapter Three

HE WAS SO engrossed in what he was doing that he didn't even hear the knife slide under the bed. I finally let the oxygen escape from my lungs. My mind was running rapidly, trying to figure out how I was going to get the knife. It would be hard trying to get it from under the bed because I didn't know how far it was. Then I had an idea and I begin to lift up my waist. As he was having his way with me, I moved closer and closer towards the end of the bed.

"Yeeaaahhh. Got you running from it... Good ain't it..." He growled, in a heavy breath.

I was now close enough off the bed and I moved my hands around hoping that I could feel the knife. After a few minutes of probing, I grabbed the handle of the knife and right when he was about to ejaculate, I plunged the knife into his heart. The light from the moon glowed into the room was bright enough for me to see the shocked look on his face. He grabbed at his chest. He fell to the floor, his arm knocking over Princess Anyla off the table. I tried to catch her, but she smashed into the floor.

The fragments scattered all over the floor. The once, beautifully crafted doll, now had cracks and bruises that seemed irreparable. I cried out in agony as I looked down and saw her broken in pieces. Then I looked over at Earl, and saw the pool of blood around him. He was holding the handle of the knife in his hand, but he must have been too weak to pull it out.

"You little fat trick." He spat, as blood begin to trickle down his chin.

"You will never ever hurt anyone again. I hope the devil have a blast tormenting you." I trembled.

I was scared out of my mind and I was beginning to panic. I didn't know what to do and I was afraid to tell my mother. So I went to my closet and started gathering everything I could fit in my backpack.

"Where do you think you going?" He grabbed my ankle.

He'd manage to slide all the way to my closet. There was a trail of blood following behind him. I took my free leg and kicked him in the nose. I heard him yelp in pain. Minutes later I heard wheezing, as if he was trying to catch his breath. I turned around and looked at him in horror as he tried to reach out to me. I just stood their horrified by all the blood. And the smell of poop invaded my nose. I realized that he'd defecated on himself. I almost gagged from the scent. Just when I was about to pull out the knife, I heard my mother room door open.

I moved as quickly as I could to the window, pushed it up, threw my back pack out, and hurried out the window. As soon as I placed both feet on the ground I ran as fast as I could. I stopped at a nearby service station and called my grandfather to come and pick me up. My grandfather was horrified by the way I was looking. I was sweating, I had on a pair of jeans, a raggedy shirt, and Earl's blood was on my hands.

"What happened to you?" My grandmother cried out, as she rushed over to hug me.

I couldn't speak. I just shook my head from side to side and miserably cried out. I didn't know what to say. I didn't know what state Earl was in, but based on how he looked, I knew it wasn't pretty.

"Honey, she said she's stabbed Earl for trying to rape her." He told her for me.

On the way over there, all I could say over and over was that I stabbed him and he was trying to rape me. My grandmother called my mother, but hung up the phone after realizing that our phone was disconnected. Then she called the police and had an ambulance go to my house. I was so scared. I didn't know whether I was going to go to jail, but in all honesty, I didn't care. I did what I did and I would have rather been in jail. I knew it had to be a lot better then the prison I'd live in for so many years. After my grandparents and I spoke to the police, I was taken to the hospital to be examined. I thought my next destination would be to the county jail.

But after the police lady heard my story, I could tell she believed me. She took down my statement, while her partner took some pictures of me and collected samples. She told me to try to get some rest, and she would talk to me in the morning. I was so thankful that she was willing to do that for me. All I wanted to do was go home and take a shower and scrub my skin in some scowling hot water, hoping that it would clean all the grime away. I felt different when I finally was able to speak up and speak out about what Earl did to me. I thought I would be relieved but I felt dirty, exposed, and I was sure that everyone thought I was bad.

I bet they think it's my fault since I allowed him to do it for so long. The next morning I found out that Earl was dead. My mother called hysterical, cursing through the phone, calling me everything but the child of God, before my grandmother hung up on her, I heard her saying that the police was on the way to lock me up. My grandmother told me to change my clothes and not to worry. No more than ten minutes later, we heard sirens outside. There was a loud knock at the door. My grandfather opened the door and the two officers who spoke to us last night was at the door with a look of disdain on their faces.

"I'm sorry, Mr. and Mrs. Davis, but we have to arrest your granddaughter." They said, as the man who took my picture, pulled out his handcuffs.

I walked down stairs, prepared for whatever came after this.

"Is all that necessary?" My grandmother asked, looking at the handcuffs.

"It's okay. She doesn't need to be handcuffed." The lady officer said to her partner as she escorted me to their car.

"Don't you worry Desiree, we're right behind you." I heard my grandfather yell out.

Sure enough, they were right behind me. Since I was not 18 yet, officers were not allowed to question me without the presence of my guardian. While my grandmother waited, my picture was taken and I was being fingerprinted. My grandfather had called my uncle, who was a lawyer to come defend me. After I was put in an interrogation room, my grandfather told me not to say a word until my uncle got there. My uncle was able to convince the judge to set a bond for me. I wasn't aware of how the judicial system worked, but all I know is that I was glad to be out of the holding cell they had me in and in a comfortable surrounding.

I knew everything wasn't over. I was being charged with manslaughter. During my trial my mother testified against me, telling them that I should pay for what I did and she hoped I rot in jail. But after a perfectly good defense from my dear uncle, and testimonies from my grandmother and a few other close friends of my mother, the truth was out and the jury found me not guilty of all charges. My mother was not pleased; she yelled out to the judge that I should be locked away. It wasn't her lack of love and support for me that surprised me, I couldn't miss what she never gave in the first place, but what startled me is how much hate she had in her eyes when she looked at me.

Come to think of it... I should have noticed it long time ago. When she wouldn't sit at the table with me and help me with my homework, when I had to go find me something to eat because she wouldn't fix it. I had to learn how to do my own hair and pair up my own clothes. She never cared if I went to school or not. Come to think of it... she never cared about me at all. I never understood why she didn't love me.

Chapter Four

IT HAS BEEN TEN years, since that day, and I continue to carry that nightmare with me. I rolled over and looked at the stranger in my bed. I knew his name, but that's all I knew. Let's just say what my mother predicted of me was true. I guess she really did know her daughter. I guess it's true what people say—the apple doesn't fall too far from the tree. Many men have come into my front door and I watched them leave. Sometimes when I think that I've found the perfect guy, they would leave just like the rest. Somehow or another, I stopped worrying about whether they would stay or not. I knew there would be some who would leave before daybreak and skip breakfast.

Sleeping with all these men is something I disdain, in all truth, I don't even like sex. I never did. But I have sex because I know that's what men like and that's what they expected from me. Sex is the only thing that seems to make the men want me and I wanted to be wanted and to feel wanted, even if it was for one night. I always required having sex in the dark. I didn't want the men to see my body and I closed my eyes so that I couldn't see their eyes. See, their eyes would reveal to me what I already knew. I saw Earl in their eyes. Filled with lust, pleasure, and gratification... Nothing much has really changed about me.

I still have the sandy brown complexion, I still have doey, round, dark brown eyes like my mother, and I'm fatter than I was when I was younger. I have upgraded from a size 14 in juniors to a size 20 in women's. I guess it would be fine if I was tall, but I was short, 5'1. My hair is long and thick like my mother's use to be, but I had it cut in a short bob. Every one at my job told me I reminded them of that actor Monique. They would always say, "You're a pretty big-boned girl, just like Monique." What exactly was big-boned? I never knew skeletons had big bones. It's not the bones that are big, it's the fatty tissues that stick to the bones, and the layers of flesh over the bones that determines the size you are.

They saw it as a compliment; I took it as an insult. I was nothing like Monique. Monique was strong, dignified, and classy. Monique was brave and she was proud of who she was and what size she was. I was… well… I was… everything my mother said I would be. I don't look in the mirror much, scared of what I might see... Scared of who I might be… Princess Anyla shattered into pieces a long time ago. So, here lays beside me, "the man of the hour". I knew that eventually he would wake up, put on his clothes, and promise me he'd call me later. I didn't expect the call no more than I expected to see him again. I knew what happened next, I was already prepared.

I met John at the gym. A few of my co-workers invited me to go with them, so I went. I got a seven-day membership that the gym offered. I figured the treadmill would be easier, since I could control my pace. There stood beside me John. He was tall, dark, and handsome. His skin was the color of milk chocolate; he was toned from his chest down to his ankles. He was running at top speed, perspiration covered his face. He took off his shirt and I almost lost my balance. He was ripped, with his eight-pack.

"Are you okay?" He asked, noticing my slip.

"I'm okay, thanks." I said embarrassed.

He ran a few more minutes, slowed down his pace to match mine, and we just struck up a conversation. He was so friendly. We talked about sports, the news, and whatever else that came to mind. Talking to him made it easy for me to walk those five miles. My legs were sore and my thighs were on fire. I took a shower in the locker room and I was surprised to see him waiting on me. What surprised me more is when he asked if we could go out for drinks. I dismissed my co-workers and caught a ride with my new friend.

He was refreshing…. He wasn't like the guys that I was used to. He seemed interested in me. I don't know how much alcohol I had consumed but I was feeling really good. We sat in my living room and talked some more. Next thing you know, his hands were riding up my legs. I knew what was going to go down. I wasn't crazy. As soon as he asked me if he could come in, I knew what was up. But this time, I was really looking forward to our night together. He didn't rush, but he took his time with me.

I usually don't like for a man to start caressing me until the lights were out, but the way he looked at my body made me feel comfortable. He didn't look with disgust, but he looked with satisfaction. I motion for him to follow me to my bedroom. He was gentle with me and very attentive in what he was doing. He wasn't only interested in pleasing himself, but me as well. He had me wrapped all up into what he was doing to me. I guess this what it was like to be made love to. But I guess it's hard to make love to someone you just met.

So I'd just say we had soft, sweet, passionate sex. I hoped that what we had last night would open up for more possibilities, but when I noticed the wedding band on the floor beside his pants I already knew what time it was. He wasn't so different from the other guys; he just had a different technique. So I just dealt with him just like I did all the rest. And just like the others, he woke up, took a shower (I guess so his wife wouldn't find out), put on his clothes, and promised me he'd call. As soon as the front door closed, I knew that was the end of our rundaevoo.

Chapter Five

TODAY WAS NOT MY DAY. I was still caught up in my feelings after being up all night tussling with the decisions I have made with my life and what I have allowed to define my life. I needed to make some changes. Furthering my education was the biggest accomplishment that I ever made. I may have agreed with my mother on other things, but not when it came to my education. I wanted her to see that although my body may not be much to look at, my mind was sharp enough to succeed. I could agree with her about my promiscuity, but I fought hard to prove that I wasn't as dumb as she wanted me to be.

I am still going to school to obtain a Bachelor's degree in Criminal Justice, with hopes of becoming a cop. I wanted to work in the special victims unit to help catch rapists. You can just about imagine where my inspiration came from. Right now I am a correctional officer at a prison facility in Chester, Georgia. A lot of the correctional officers treat inmates like their caged animals. After working as a guard for over 5 years, I'm still amazed at how another human being, can treat another human being like trash. Yes, I understand that these men are "criminals", but they are still human and they still deserve to be treated right, no matter what they did.

I don't focus on treating others the way I would want to be treated, because I haven't been treating myself right. So, I try to treat others the way that I wish that I treated myself, and the way I hope someone would treat me. Last night I browsed on Facebook and read Iyanla Vanzant latest status. After watching her show Fix My Life I have become a major fan. I wanted to send her message to fix my life, but I was too embarrassed to do it. Anyway, her status is what made me think about my life in a different light.

Her status made so much sense to me, she said, "The only relationship we can have in this life is the relationship we have with ourselves. We cannot love anybody more than we love ourselves. We cannot treat anyone any better than we treat ourselves. When you forget you, give up on you, or devalue yourself, anyone coming into your life has a universal responsibility to follow your lead." Normally, I would be that nice officer that every inmate respected. I would be the one that would not write them up, and give them a little freedom. But today was another kind of day. I didn't feel like being bothered and I wasn't in the mood to be trying to chastise no grown behind men.

So far I was having a good day, today was quiet and slow, just the way I wanted it. As I was about to go on break, Jane, the prison nurse, paged me asking if I could escort a prisoner back to his cell. My stomach was growling and you know how big people are about their food. When I asked her if someone else could do it since I was on my lunch break she stated that they were low on staff today.

"Where's the inmate and where is his cell located?" I asked the nurse, clearly showing my aggravation.

"Dewayne Thomas... He is going to J-3." She responded.

"Fine." I said.

"Thank you." She said apologetically.

"No problem."

I didn't pay much attention to the inmate I was transmitting, I was hungry and I was ready to eat. The sooner he gets to his cell, the better.

"Let's go Thomas."

We were almost half way to his cell, when he stopped and looked at me.

"Excuse me, but you need to keep walking." I said pulling him along, still not looking at him.

"Hold up, hold up, you ain't got to be man handling me like that. You just too pretty to be acting like that, I'm sorry I didn't catch your name?" He said.

"That's because I didn't throw it and if you don't start walking then I'll have to write you up." I threatened.

"Why you got to be like that, ma?" He said but kept walking. I didn't answer him until we reached his cell.

"First of all I'm not your ma. I don't recall giving birth to you. You address me by Officer Davis... You got that..." I told him, as I rolled my neck with much attitude.

"Well, excuse me Officer." He said holding up his arms, so I could take the cuffs off his wrist.

"Thank you."

"I was just giving a compliment to a pretty lady. You seem like you are having a bad day so I was just trying to cheer you up. I know my position here but I don't have to be treated like an animal." He frowned.

I'd finally looked up at him. He had a handsome face. He was clean cut, with a nice smile, and the sexist lips I'd ever seen. Lord forgive me... because I'm having impure thoughts about those lips. Just a shame... All that goodness locked away from the world. I softened up... Not because of his gorgeous face or his alluring lips, but because my conscious was tugging at me. I had no right taking my frustrations out on other people.

"It is not my intentions to treat you like an animal. And if I came at you the wrong way, I am sorry. Yes, I am having a bad day but it's nothing you need to be concerned about." I finished, while locking the cell door.

"Nice meeting you and I am sorry you're having a bad day but things will get better." He spoke up as I was walking away.

I didn't even respond because I was too busy trying to get to my food. I've seen many good looking inmates at the prison, so I was wondering why Dewayne was locked in my head, and constantly on my mind. After our little interaction, I couldn't get him off my mind. There was something about him, but I couldn't call it. The man was in prison for Christ sakes, there's nothing he could do for me, and there's nothing that I could really do for him. There are 99 reasons why being interested in Dewayne would be a no-no. But 1 main and most important reason is that I'm not willing to sacrifice my job for anybody. It don't matter how fine he is.

Even though these reasons was justifiable, deep down, he perked up my curiosity and crazy as it is or crazy as I must be, I wanted to get to know more about him. When I got to work the next morning, I logged into the inmate database and started researching Mr. Dewayne Thomas. He was convicted of having a possession of a fire arm. According to his record, he only had a year left until his release date. Then I strolled down to view his picture. I was so engrossed in that picture that I didn't realize my colleague Jessica was behind me. She was in charge of processing and I was in her seat.

"What's up?" She asked, looking at me and then at the computer screen.

"Nothing... just looking up some information on this inmate for his probation officer." I lied.

"Oh, looks like he'll be getting out soon. He's cute too." She responded, looking at his picture.

"Yeah, he does look good." I said, not liking how she was looking at him.

Then I wondered why I even cared, it wasn't like he was my man.

"Let me give you your seat, so I can let you do your job." I said, logging out, mostly because I didn't want her looking at him.

"Yes, thanks."

I checked the log to see what floor I would be on today and I was kind of disappointed that it wasn't J-3. They had me doing all kind of stuff today, that wasn't even in my job description. By the end of the day, I was beyond tired. My feet and the lower part of my back were killing me. I couldn't wait to get home and soak in the tub. However my body said otherwise; as soon as I got home I crashed out on the couch. The next morning, my stomach was cramping like crazy. When I went to the rest room to go urinate, I almost fainted from the burning sensation. A white substance was in my panties, and I knew it was time for me to go to the doctor. I knew I couldn't go to work feeling like this. When I finally got myself together, I called the prison and let my boss know that I was sick and wasn't coming in today. After ending the call with her, I decided to call my doctor and schedule an emergency appointment. When I finally was able to see the doctor, she asked me a series of questions, insisted that I take a pregnancy test, just to be sure and told me that she'll be back in about 15 minutes with my results. I prayed to God that I wasn't pregnant because Lord knows I was not ready to be nobody's mother. I've slept with so many men that I wouldn't even know who the father was anyway. I could just have the stomach flu or something. I was almost done browsing through a magazine when my doctor finally came back in the room. She looked at my chart and glanced down at my chart.

"Desiree… she said looking at me, you have Chlamydia. If you are unaware of what that is—"

"I know exactly what it is." I intermitted.

"Yes, ma'am… It is required for us to inform you to bring this attention to anyone you have slept with in the past few weeks so that they can come get treated if they have contracted it. I will be writing you a prescription and in a few days you should be back to normal." She said, scribbling on a pad.

I had no idea which partner gave me the disease and even if I wanted to call them, I couldn't. I'd tossed their number as soon as our night was over. I shamefully took the prescription, waited until Wal-mart pharmacy filled it, and popped one of the pills in my mouth, and chased it down with water as soon as I got in my car. The doctor was right. After a few days, my symptoms were clear and the sexual transmitted disease was gone. I always used a condom, but I guess they don't protect you from getting diseases. I'm just grateful that I didn't contact something worse.

I suddenly thought about what could have been and I laid in my bed and cried. Even when I didn't deserve it, God obviously had liked me enough to grant me a little bit of mercy. I silently thanked Him. I was getting tired of my lifestyle and the way it made me feel. At that moment, when the men is holding me while we are having sex, it makes me feel special, but when it's all over, I feel nothing. The loneliness lingers, and the hole in my heart never gets filled. I'm counting my blessings and I vowed that this come around,

I'm going to start caring about me and loving me. But it's easier said then done for someone who didn't even know what love meant.

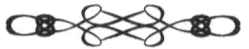

Chapter Six

AFTER TAKING A few more days off of work, I was finally scheduled to J-3. I usually would be excited, since I get to see Dewayne but I've been feeling a little gloomy lately. If I could have taken another sick day I would have, but I needed to get back to work. I did have some time to myself to think about a lot of things and I have made up in my mind that I was going to stop selling myself short and try to get back the life that was taken from me a long time ago. I caught up on a lot of my school work. I had one more class to complete, before I graduated. I was so excited. But that didn't erase everything else that was less exciting in my life.

I was tired of all the men. I was tired of each and every one of them leaving without saying goodbye. But most of all I was tired of the way I felt afterwards. My plan was to ignore Dewayne and just do my job when I got on that floor. It was time for inspection, so another officer and I started checking each cellt to check for anything that wasn't supposed to be there. It surprised me how many cell phones we catch inmates with on a regular basis. It doesn't take a rocket science to know that officers are bringing cell phones in the facility. Inmates will never admit it, but I know that the guards probably sell those phones for triple the amount of the original price.

It's a shame… I can understand why inmates are tempted to get one, but one would think that they'd try to stay away from things that would get them in trouble. Breaking the rules is still wrong, no matter what their intentions are. I admit that I have looked over a few inmates who I caught with cell phones, but during shake down, I have to follow the rules. Each inmate was required to stand by their door until inspection was completed. I was right next to Dewayne but tried to take the cell next to him until the other officer jumped in front of me and began inspecting, so I didn't have a choice. After going through his things, I gave him permission to come in.

"Find anything?" He asked me.

"Excuse me?" I looked back at him with a serious expression on my face.

"Just asked you if you found anything." He shrugged.

"If I found something that you weren't supposed to have then you would be in the hole by now. In besides, you are to remain quiet while inspection, you know that." I told him.

I was waiting for him to say something else. When he didn't, I walked in front of the officer who was helping me with the inspection so that she could close the cell. It was time for me to escort the mates to church service. Usually I don't listen to the services that they have but today I needed a little church in me. I sat next to the preacher and her topic for today was, "Love Thy Self". She said that in order to understand the meaning of love, one must seek God, because He is love.

"It is God, who is the creator of love, who is love that will show you, teach you, and help you understand what love is and how to walk in love. To know love is to know how to walk in love and spread that love to someone else. It's hard to love God, love yourself, and love others without knowing what love means." She teached.

"Can somebody share with me their opinion on what love means to them? Can you love someone without respecting them?" She asked, looking around.

Dewayne raised his hand and I was waiting to hear what his response would be.

"I find it impossible to love someone but not respect them." He responded.

"Why not?"

"It's like this. If a man is cheating on a woman, beating on her, cursing her out, sexing her and then downgrading her, then there's no love in that. When you love a woman, you respect her mind, her body and her spirit. You can't love who you don't respect and you can't expect anybody to respect you if they don't love you."

186

He said simply.

"Okay, very good..." She spoke, moving on to the next question.

What he said really hit home. I'd let all them men disrespect my body because I did not understand the essence of what love meant. Then I thought about how much I disrespected myself without realizing it. When I looked up at him, I was shocked to see him looking at me. I felt exposed, as if he knew what I was thinking. He looked into my eyes and smiled. I almost melted in my seat. I better stay as far away from this man as possible before I go against the job policy. Before Dewayne walked into his cell, he handed me a folded up piece of paper.

"What is this?" I said waving it in the air.

"What it look like?"

"Look . . ." I said about to lay him out.

"Stop, before you get off the chain, he laughed, it's a letter. I want you to read it and if you don't respond to it by tomorrow then I won't bother you again." He said.

"You know I don't suppose to accept letters from inmates." I told him.

"I know... but just read it." He insisted. I nodded my head, took the letter and put it in my pocket.

I didn't know whether to read the letter or throw it in the garbage. My mind was telling me to just trash it, but something in me screamed read it. I couldn't even concentrate the rest of my day at work. I was too interested in what was in that letter. Now, I'm pacing the floor in my bedroom, nervously looking at the folded piece of paper lying in the middle of my bed. "So what if I read it, it's not like it's going to change anything." I said to myself, trying to calm my nerves. Before I got to crazy, I quickly sat on the bed and picked up the letter. What does he possibly have to say to me, that he couldn't tell me face to face, he always running his mouth any other time? I carefully opened the paper, as if it would easily tear and read:

Desiree,

I know you wondering how I know your first name... I asked Officer Clayton what your real name was. Please don't be mad at her. But anyways, I know you ain't the type of woman that's with all the small talk so I'm going to just cut to the chase before I lose my nerve. Every since I met you in the nurse's station, I haven't been able to get you off my mind. You're a firecracker but I'm digging it though. I'm digging you. I know what you may be thinking, but not all prison men are interested in commissary. I'm not that kind of guy.

I noticed a tear slipped from your eye at service to day, and I wanted to know what that was all about. I know you don't know me and I know you're not eager to find a friend in me. I know you like me, I can tell by your body language when I smiled at you. But I understand that you don't want to jeopardize your job, and I wouldn't want you to do that on account of me. My intentions are not to complicate your life but there's something about you that makes me want to know more about you. I know under that tough demeanor you try to carry, there is a softer side of you. I just want to know that softer side.

I want to know what makes you smile, your dislikes, your dreams and all of that good stuff. If you feel like I'm wasting your time, then don't write back but if you think I'm worth your time then hit me back. I promise I won't do or say anything that can cause you to lose your job but make my day and bring joy into my heart by responding.

Dewayne

He had to watching me hard to notice that tear. I really didn't know how to respond or if I wanted to respond, but I grabbed a pen and paper and just began to write. Of course I wouldn't be putting my name on it or his.

D,

I don't know what to make of this letter and to be honest I don't know if I could trust you. Why should I, when I don't even know you? What is your motive? I know what you're thinking, since I'm fat, it means I can't get a man and if I can't get a man I could easily be persuaded by one. Don't come at me with the games because I don't have time for jailhouse lies. I'm trying to get my life together and I don't need you coming into it and making it worse than it already is. Now, I'm only writing you to speak my mind since I've given you the chance to speak yours. You are an inmate at a prison in which I work and I am an officer. Let's not mix business with pleasure.

DD

I re-read what I'd written and placed it in a blank envelope. I don't know what Dewayne got up his sleeve but I'm not going to fall victim to his games. I was scheduled again to be in unit J-3 for the rest of the month and I didn't know how to feel about it. I didn't know whether I could face seeing Dewayne every day after the letter I had read. Luckily, one of the officers downstairs told me to give the inmates their mail so that allowed me to sneak my letter to him. I opened each letter to see whether anything illegal was in them and once I was satisfied I allowed the inmates to come pick up their mail. When it was time for Dewayne to get his mail, I quickly shoved it in his hand and called another inmate.

He looked at me some kind of way but I ignored him. When I walked down the hall, I finally relaxed and blew the air that I was holding in. My mind was going in full speed and I was curious to know what Dewayne response was to my letter. He said he would leave me alone if I didn't respond but I did respond but not the way that he wanted. Will that letter make him back off? Did I really want that? It was almost time for me to go home but I had to go do a head count before I left. When I walked past Dewayne, he grabbed my arm. I looked at him like he'd lost his mind. He quickly apologized and handed me another folded piece of paper.

If the other inmates weren't focused on watching TV, I would have never taken the letter.

DD,

My intentions are not to hurt you and I was only telling you how I felt. I know what they say about prison men trying to talk to women who they think are desperate enough to talk to them. I promise you... I don't feel that way about you. I don't want to play games; I'm too grown to be playing games with anybody. I don't have to lie to you about anything. If I was in it just for what you could give me, then I would have got at you a long time ago. I've seen you around. I'll be going home soon and I would love to get to know you better outside these walls. I'm not trying to cake you, have sex with you, or use you. I just want to know who you are.

Regardless of your weight, you are a beautiful woman and plus I love a woman with some meat on their bones. When I'm giving you all my love, I'll have a lot to hold on to.

I couldn't help but laugh at that.

I'm not talking about sex... I'm cool with just holding you. You shouldn't be ashamed about what you look like, because understand that what one person may not like another one will. I like every inch of you, from your short silky hair to your soft looking thighs. I know you don't know me and you got a right not to trust me but give me a chance. I don't need your money because I have my own and I'm not pressing for letters to make my time easier because like I said, I'll be touching down real soon. Take a chance on me, I promise, you will not regret it.

D

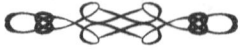

Chapter Seven

DEWAYNE AND I have been secretly writing each other back and forth for the past eleven months. There was something about his soft brown eyes that made me want to believe in him, to trust him and give him a chance. He seems to be sincere in what he has been saying so far, so I decided to take a chance on him. I've never had a man interested in getting to know me other than sexually. He could be like the rest of the others or he could be exactly what I hoped he would be. I didn't have anything to lose.

So far, he has been everything that I hoped for and more. He had me feeling, like a million bucks and I loved it. I guess this is the way love feels like. It feels like I'm standing on a cloud, drifting slowly from the earth until I reach heaven. We don't spend much time together, because we want to keep our relationship a secret. We don't talk on the phone at all, and we only converse through letters. I did manage to sneak one of his tee-shirts. I wore it be bed every night. Just the smell of his scent makes me feel closer to him. Even though his situation is wrong, being with him feels so right.

I love these new feelings that have taken over me and I hope that they last forever. I'm falling in love with him and I hoped that at the end of this journey that he would be there at the end of it to catch my fall. One day, I was escorting him to the nurse's station. The nurse had not gotten there yet, so we had time to talk.

"Baby, I can't wait until I get home." He said, looking at me.

"I know, I can't wait either." I said, counting down the days.

"I know when I do get out I'm going to make you my wife. You been holding me down ever since you agreed to be my woman and I appreciate it." He said, making me smile.

"Awww, you going to marry me for real, you sure you're ready to make that step?" I asked feeling a little doubtful.

"Stop playing with me girl. You already know what it is. I love you." He assured me.

"I want to believe that." I said softly.

Finally, things seem to be falling into place for me. I've finally graduated and Dewayne and I were so excited when I got accepted at the Special Victims unit in Atlanta. I was so thrilled when he told me that he would follow me there. Dewayne talked me into going to visit my mother after I told him about her. He told me that I would never have closure if I didn't face my fears and let my mother know what was in my heart. I was a little nervous about it, so he said that he would break the rules just this time to call me. He used one of the inmates' cell phone and stayed on the phone with me until I ranged the door bell. I didn't know what to say to her when she opened the door. I haven't seen her since that day in court. I didn't know what to expect.

"What the hell are you doing here?" She said with venom, as she looked in my face.

"Mom, I was just—"

"You were just what?" She interrupted.

I looked at her from head to toe and noticed just how bad AIDs can affect a person. She looked far worse then she looked when she was on drugs. I just wanted to take her in my arms and hold her… everything that she ever did to me didn't matter at that moment; she was my mother.

"Grandmother told me about your condition and I was just coming over to check on you." I said almost in tears.

Even though my mother took a man side over mine and hated my guts, I still loved her with all my heart. I don't know… I guess a child's love for their mother runs deep.

"Yeah, you probably come over here to laugh in my face." She insisted, with a sarcastic laugh.

"That's not why I am here, whether you believe it or not, I love you and I just wanted to see if you needed anything." I said softly.

"I don't want you here and I don't need your sympathy."

She responded.

"Mom—"

"There's isn't anything you could ever do for me. You took away everything I needed. You're just like your father, think you can do things to me and I'm supposed to let it go. Get your fat ass off my porch; I can't stand to look at you. Why don't you go do what you do best, but then again you've probably ran through the whole city. Yeah, I heard about you, the streets are talking." She said, turning her nose up at me, as if she smelled something foul.

I thought by now I would be used to her downgrading me, but I guess I have forgotten since Dewayne's been in my life. I was getting sick of her crap and I was so tired of her talking to me like I'm not her daughter, but her enemy. This is the same woman who carried me in her womb for nine months. If she didn't want me, why didn't she just give me up or better yet get an abortion? I wanted to curse her out so bad, but that would mean that I would stoop down to her level and I vowed that I would never be like her, but if I wanted to move on and live, I had to get a few things off my chest. It's long overdue.

"What have I ever done to you? Why do you hate me so much, mom? All I've ever tried to do was please you and when your good for nothing husband had sex with me you put it all on me. Did you forget all the times you pimp me out for your habit? You took everything from me. YOU are the one who stole from me!" I said jabbing my finger where my heart was at.

"All I ever wanted was your love and I went from man to man trying to seek it but never could grasp hold of it. You are looking down on me when you should be looking down at yourself. Look at you....You're dying and still mean as a snake. You know what the problem is; you blame me for your own failure. You are your own failure and even if you don't love me, I'll forever love you. I'm better than this and I'm better than you. Have a nice life mom, and may God have mercy on your soul." I said as tears fell from my eyes, I'd forgotten Dewayne was on the phone.

At that moment a big weight had lifted from my heart and I felt so good. For so long, I held on to so many things as and dealt with so many devilish things that she did to me. Those demons will no longer taunt me anymore. I am sick and tired of running and its time that I start challenging my demons.

"Awh... save the drama honey... You will never be anything but a fat, worthless, whore. I don't need your prayers, keep them for yourself. I've never loved you and I should have thrown you in the garbage like I wanted to. You fat, dumb tramp... Don't you ever come to my house again." She screamed before slamming the door.

Who was I fooling, thinking that she would be different and be woman enough to make amends with me I wanted her to apologize and tell me she loved me, but instead she just told me to stay out of her life. I think throwing me in the trash, would have been the best thing she could have ever done for me. All my life she'd made me feel like garbage. I stopped looking in the mirror, because I felt like trash. Maybe I would have been better off if she did follow her first mind. She didn't want me in her life, then fine... I'm doing just fine without her. I got what I came here for. She wanted me out of her life, fine, I'm gone.

I'm walking away; away from her house and her life forever. I'm putting the past behind me and I'm not going to allow the past pain to hurt me or control who I am any longer. See, I noticed that my mother could never love me the way a mother is supposed to love her daughter, so I'm not going to try anymore. I've freed myself from the hold she had on me but I have enough love in my heart for the both of us. Even after all she said I will never hate her. She will always be my mother, nothing can change that and she will always be loved by me. I'm learning the art of loving, and I believe in loving from a distance.

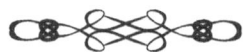

Chapter Eight

DEWAYNE HELPED me get over what happened between my mother and me. He had three days left before his release date and I was so happy. I've finally let go of my past and decided to accept love into my life because I finally realized that I deserve to be loved and give love a chance. Dewayne has been my motivation and I love him a lot. I'd already started preparing for my move to Atlanta and I couldn't wait for the fresh start. Things were going great in my life. I was super excited when Dewayne told me that he would be able to get released a day earlier then he was supposed to. He didn't tell me what time to pick him up, so I decided to be there, so that when he got out I could take him shopping. I was so nervous. I couldn't wait to see my baby. After I waited two hours, he still hadn't walked out the gate. I called the prison to find out what time he would be released.

"Hello. I am Dewayne Thomas's sister and I was calling to find out what time he was going to be released today?" I couldn't tell them who I was. I haven't resigned yet.

I heard her clicking on computer keys in the background.

"Yes… He was released an hour ago." She told me.

"Okay, thank you so much." I said hanging up the phone. I sat there, not knowing how to feel. All kind of thoughts begin to enter my head. Why didn't he call me? I was beginning to think the worse when my cell phone rung.

"Dewayne, where are you?" I questioned, relieved to hear his voice.

"Chill out, I went to the mall." He said.

"Mall? How did you get there? And why didn't you call me and tell me that you were already released." I said throwing him questions.

"My brother picked me up. I'm sorry I didn't call you, but I wanted to get you something special before I saw you. You can meet me here at the mall." He said, apologizing again.

"Okay." I said excited, wondering what he got me.

I spotted him by Foot Locker, leaning on the wall. He looked so good and I still continue to ask myself, why he chose me when he could have had anybody else. When he noticed me coming, a wide smile spread across his face and he walked up to me and put his arms around my waist. If I could, I would have stayed right there, in that same spot, wrapped into his arms. I couldn't believe that this day had finally come. We can now be together. My baby was finally free.

"What's good, baby?" He said.

"Don't try to change the subject. I'm still mad at you. I wanted to be the one to pick you up." I pouted.

"Awwh, I'm so sorry baby." He said kissing my lips.

"You forgive me?"

"I guess." I responded.

I'd already met most of his family, so his brother had already knew who I was. We finished shopping and I noticed a gift bag that was dangling from his finger. I was simmering in anticipation. They transferred his stuff from his brother's trunk into my trunk. Him and I headed home to make magic. It is so amazing how Dewayne makes me feel. I would have never thought in a million years that I would have fallen in love with somebody from prison. But it was not about his past, I was focused on what lies ahead in our future.

"I'm stronger, stronger, strongerrrr . . ." Mary J. was ringing in my ears… It was my phone ringing.

"DD, your phone." He said, handing it to me.

"Oh, thank you."

"Hello." I answered.

When I tried to listen to the news that was given to me I could barely concentrate. I almost dropped the phone from my ear. Here I was feeling pain shoot through my heart and I didn't even understand why. I felt so much sorrow. I couldn't stop the tears from falling.

"What's wrong, baby?" I heard Dewayne ask me more than once.

I couldn't answer him and I couldn't respond to my grandmother who was on the other end of the phone.

"Desiree, did you hear what I said? Your mother died last night." She spoke through the phone.

"Yes, I heard you." I finally managed to speak up.

She told me to come over and make funeral arrangements with her and all that stuff but I didn't even know if I was up for all that. I kept thinking about my last conversation my mother and I had. How could a woman, who was once so sweet, allow evil to overtake her? I bet if she could, she would band me from her funeral. I still couldn't understand why she didn't love me. I prayed for her soul... I prayed that God will show her mercy, inspite of who she was. I'm so glad that Dewayne was home, because I couldn't have gotten through all this without him. Everything around me has been changing for the better. Just months ago, I was giving myself away to the man that was worthy of me.

I told Dewayne about my life and he still said he loved me. After all the men I've slept with, he still wanted to be with me... I can't help but thank God for giving me a love that feels so right, so pure and so forgiving. I haven't stepped foot in a church in years and when I heard the preacher preach at my mother's funeral I began to miss the atmosphere. My grandmother had me in church every Sunday but when I got old enough, church was far from my mind. I guess what the Bible say is true, "train up your child in the way that they should go and when their older they will not depart from it." I didn't depart from a lot of things but in the end mistakes taught me a lesson and now I'm wise enough to know not to do those things again.

It came as a shock to me, when my grandmother told me to come to the reading of my mother's will. I didn't even know she had a will and when my grandmother told me she had insurance that surprised me too. Dewayne waited outside as I sat down in a chair and waited for the lawyer to speak. I didn't even know why I was there; I know she wouldn't leave me a dime. But I continued to sit there and allow the lawyer to speak.

Chapter Nine

"*I, JOSEPHINA ROSELLE DAVIS-PRUIT, being of sound, mind, and body, leave my entire interest in the real property which was my residence at the time of death, valuable jewels, life insurance policy of five-hundred thousand dollars, the remaining balance in my bank account at Decatur's First Bank in Decatur Georgia, in the amount of five thousand dollars to my daughter Desiree Giselle Davis.*" The lawyer read as she smiled up at me.

I nearly fell out of my chair, when that woman said my name. I couldn't believe that my mother would leave me all of her possessions. I thought she hated my guts. Five hundred and five thousand dollars belong to me and it was given to me by a woman that I thought cursed the ground that I walked on. I didn't understand and I had to ask the woman to repeat what she said.

"Your mother left you her whole estate and she also told me to give you this letter." My grandmother said.

"You knew about this?" I asked my grandmother, a little hurt that she didn't tell me.

"Yes I did. I figured since you and your mother was so… distant, that you wouldn't be interested in knowing. I'm sorry. It was never my intentions to keep anything from you." She told me.

"I know mama…" I said, hugging her.

My mother's handwriting was always beautiful and everyone told her she should write cards for other people. When I got in the car, I cried my heart out. I was so happy but shocked at the same time, I told Dewayne the good news but left out the full amount of money that was left to me. I have learned that you can never let anyone know all your business. All he knows is that my mother left me a house and five thousand dollars that was held in her account. I plan to take the deed from the house and give it to my grandmother. She could sell it or keep it I didn't care. I was moving and I thought it was fair that my grandmother should have something.

Dewayne was still happy for me and told me not to question why things are the way that they were but to accept the blessings that's given to me. Every since we've been going to church, he seem to be more engrossed in his Christianity and I am proud of him. When I opened the door to my mother's house, it brought back so many memories, memories of pain and lost. I looked at the recliner in front of the television and envisioned my mother sitting me between her legs and braiding my hair. She stop doing that when I was eight, but those moments was my most memorable moments because those where the only time she act like a real mother.

I went into each room of the house and inhaled my mother's scent. When I reached my room, I hesitated for a long time before I opened the door. To my surprise everything was left the way I left it, except the blood. I walked in my closet, the clothes that I left was still there. Tears caught in my throat when I saw Princess Anyla. She was no longer lying on the floor, with pieces of her shattered on the floor. She was sitting where she always sat. Right next to my bed on the side table... My mother had her put back together. The cracks were still visible, but she looked beautiful. Just like I remembered... I grabbed her and held her in my arms. I sat on my bed, closed my eyes, and pulled out the letter out of my purse, with my mother's beautiful handwriting and read:

Dear Desiree,

I know it comes as a shock that I am writing to you. If you are reading this letter it means that I have passed on and that you got the news from my will. I know I wasn't much of a mother but I wanted to make it right in the end. When you left my house, I thought about what you said. I cried and cried all night, asking God to forgive me for all that I had done to you. I know this asking too much, but please forgive me for what I did to you. On my porch you asked me why I didn't love you, well one night a man that I adored and thought would be my shield, my protector, did some unspeakable things to me.

I ended up pregnant but your grandmother told me that I was going to keep you and raise you since I went out there and made you, but the truth is, you were created in mother's house and in my bedroom. Your grandfather raped me time and time again but I never let mother know because I knew it would break her heart. That's a secret that I kept to myself and had hidden from the world until now. So every time I looked at you, I saw him and I couldn't bare the sight of you. I tried to love you and I wanted to so badly but I couldn't. I made you feel low because I was feeling low myself. I allowed that man to come into your room and do the things that my father had done to me.

I wanted someone to feel my pain and you were the only one there that I could take it out on. I am so sorry and I know now that my stupidity caused you to look for love in other place. I'm sorry I couldn't be a better mother. No matter what you do, when you have children, love them, support them, and guide them into the right direction. Be a better mother than me.

I Love You,
Mommy

Chapter Ten

ALL I EVER wanted was for her to say she loved me. I couldn't believe that my grandfather was my father and as much as that sickened me, my heart couldn't hate the man that took care of me until the day he died. I'd finally gotten the closure that I needed to move on with my life. After I left the house, I went to my mother's grave. My mother had given her life to God. I was overwhelmed with emotions. I stood there for hours as tears slid down my cheeks. Calmness fell over me and I felt the need to pray. I dropped to my knees, closed my eyes and confessed all my sins to God. I asked Him to mend the brokenness that dwelled inside of me, heal my soul from all the hurt that I'd suffered.

To complete me where I was broken, to strengthen me where I was weak. To forgive me for never seeing how precious I was and to forgive me for never realizing how merciful He had been. At that moment, I felt a feeling of warmness surround me. I felt at peace and I knew then that God had me under His wings. Holding me, protecting me and shielding me from everything I allowed to come in hinder me. In returned I embraced Him back, accepted Him and allowed Him to do whatever he needed to do to get me where He wanted me. I left all the baggage, the waste, that had been holding me down, right there, at my mother's grave.

"I love you too, mommy. I forgive you for all that you did to me and in some way I understand. I promise you, I will be the best mother I can be and I thank you for not giving me up or worse having an abortion." I kissed the top of her gravestone and walked to the car.

"Are you alright?" Dewayne asked me, wiping away my tears.

I blew out a huge breath that I must have been holding in forever. "Yes, I am." I said really meaning it.

"I got something to show you and don't ask me what it is." He said.

"What is it?" I asked, laughing.

"Real funny, let me drive and put this blind fold around your eyes." He handed it to me.

"Now you're talking crazy, you aren't about to take me nowhere and kill me. I watch horror movies." I said pushing the blind fold away.

He laughed.

"Girl, I could never hurt you. I love you. Just trust in me and I promise you won't regret it." He vowed, with a serious look on his face.

I allowed him to place the blind fold on my eyes and we were headed to a destination that I didn't know. Ten minutes later we came to a complete stop, he opened my door and led the way. I felt grass under my feet and he seemed to sit me down on a warm cloth. When he took the blind fold off, my heart almost jumped out my chest. There surrounding me was, a picnic set up with candles, roses, wine and exotic fruit. I tried to speak but he told me to be quiet. The sun began to go down and we kissed as the sun began to set. It was so romantic, I thought I was dreaming. As the sun began to take its resting place and the moon began to start its shift, he lit the candles.

"Dewayne, what is this about?"

He bends down on one knee and pulled out the small bag that I saw him place in his pocket at the mall. I had forgotten all about that and he pulled out a black velvet box.

"From the moment I first saw you, I knew you was something special. You have made me the happiest man on the planet and I couldn't imagine my life without you. Like I promised, I would never hurt you and will continue to be here for you. You make me happy and blessed to be alive. In the past I didn't know what I was going to do with my life but you came in and changed my whole world around. I want to be the first person you see in the morning and the last one you see at night. You have been through so much in your life, so let me take the pain away. With God's help I know we both can make it. Please accept me as your husband I will spend the rest of my life pleasing you." He said as a tear slid from his eyes.

"Oh my God, oh my God, I can't believe this is happening. Dewayne . . . I, oh my goodness." I said ecstatic.

"Woman my knees getting dingy." He said as we both laughed.

"Of course I will. Yes." I said and he jumped up and we kissed what felt like for an eternity.

I was sitting on top of the world and didn't ever want to come down. I can finally say I'm happy. I can finally say I know what love is. To feel loved. To be loved. To know what love does. I was finally free from all the hurt and the pain from my childhood. Pieces and pieces of me are slowly reattaching and now I feel complete. Love had truly been good to me and as I accepted his ring, I thanked God for throwing me down, yet another blessing. Now I had someone in my life that loved me for me. I didn't have to wonder if he'd stay the next morning and I could finally serve someone my grandmother's homemade buttermilk biscuits in the morning.

Chapter Eleven

THERE I STOOD, in front of my mirror. I ran my hand over the wedding gown. I'd lost over 105 pounds and I looked and felt great. It was hard work, but Dewayne worked out with me and pushed me every step of the way. I hated him then, but I thank him for it now. Losing the weight has nothing to do with the love that I now felt for myself. It was all Jesus… He reminded me of who I was and exactly whose I was. He gave me, me back. I looked at Princess Anyla and I thought about her falling to the floor that night. I always wished that I was her and I now realized that she was a symbolism of me.

God made me beautiful, but I was knocked down by insults from my mother, abuse from my stepfather, damaged by my own self-perception, by low self-esteem, and the lack of self-actualization, that caused that once beautifully crafted image to be shattered in pieces until I was unidentifiable. I wasn't able to see who I was, but because of God He has mended the shattered pieces that took away my self-identity. I wouldn't have ever thought that Princess Anyla would ever be able to be put back together, but she was. Those broken pieces that was hard to assemble… has been molded, re-shaped, and rebuild by the hands of God. God has recreated me and has designed me to be the woman He intended for me to be.

I may look the same, but I'm not the same old me. For old things have passed away— the past pains, the drama, the shame, the blame, and the unforgivenes and all things have become new… I am a new creation— a new porcelain doll in Christ Jesus. I may have some cracks, much like Princess Anyla, but that's alright. Those cracks reminds me of what I went through and what God did. It is those cracks that remind me of how strong I am. That I may not be perfect on the outside, but I have something priceless on the inside. In I know after this day, I will never be the same. I stood in facing the man of my dreams. We vowed in front of all our family and friends in the church, in front of the pastor, and in front of God that we would love, honor, and respect each other for the rest of our lives.

I planned on being the best wife that I could be. I'd entrusted Dewayne with my heart long time ago, now I have trusted God to be the head of my life, my family, and my marriage. I don't know what life holds in store for me, but I couldn't wait to live it. I was headed to Atlanta to pursue my career and Dewayne had just got accepted at the most prestigious law school in Atlanta. He said that he wanted to be a public defender and help people just like him. I was so proud of him— so proud of us. We were now living in alignment with God and I knew with God on our side there is nothing we can't do. I was finally able to look into a mirror and feel good about me. I loved who I was, who I'd become, and who God has prepared me to be. I was so lost, but now I'm found. Thanks be to God…. Thanks be to God.

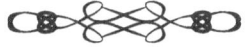

"In My Fathers House"

One   I WILL NEVER understand how a person can transform from one personality to another. I was living with Dr. Jekyll and Mr. Hyde… My father could be the most loving, caring, kind, and humbled individual that you could ever meet, but when he drinks his poison—alcohol, he can be one of the most evil people you wished you never met.

"Woman… why do you insist on testing me? You like making me angry… you like seeing the worst in me." My father yelled at my mother.

"No." My mom said shaking her head in fear.

"You're a liar… he snarled. You like making me mad and you like disrespecting me." He slurred, turning beet red.

"Jonah, please." She begged.

"Jonah, please." He mimicked, twisting his face.

"I come home expecting a decent meal and all I come home to is cold food." He said pointing at the plate on the kitchen counter.

"Please Jonah, don't act this way, Danielle is in the room sleeping. Please."

"Never mind all of that. She can wake up and get it too. Why the hell should I have to come home to cold food?" He said, refocusing his attention on the food.

My mother no longer had the sparkle in her big blue eyes, the sparkled dimmed down years ago. She's been going through this with him since I could remember and I always wondered if she was ever going to be tired. There was nothing wrong with the food, because I saw the steam rise from the plate. I heard the beep of the microwave minutes before my father stepped in the door. My father or my mother didn't notice me hiding around the corner. As I looked around the room I noticed he'd broken all the dinnerware.

"You act like you're slow or something; I don't know why I married you. You act so stupid. You aren't good for anything at all." He slurred, tossing the hot plate of food at her.

I covered my mouth fearing the worst, as my mother screamed from the hot food that had landed on her chest. As she fell to the floor and begged my father for mercy, my heart broke in two. Even though he has done some horrible things to the both of us I still couldn't bare the pain that he was causing.

"Yeah, you don't have anything to say now. See, you want me to act this way. All I try to do is do right and take care of my family, but its people like *you* that ruin it. You're just a selfish and ungrateful piece of nothing. I took you out of that raggedy trailer you shared with your mother and now you want to act like you can't listen to me. God said you should become submissive to your husband and do as he says. You disobedient and you should be punished for your sins. I don't feel any honor by you fixing me this cold ass food, so now I've made you wear it." He laughed like he'd told the funniest joke ever.

He picked up one of her legs and dragged her over the floor. My mother tried to kick as hard as she could but my father was too strong for her. Painful screams from my mother began to fill the whole house as the broken glass began to pierce through her skin. I hurriedly, ran to my room so that my father couldn't see me. Moments later I heard my parent's bedroom slam and through the wall I could hear my father having sex with her as my mother pleaded for him to stop. All I could do was cover my head with my pillow and cry until I fell fast asleep.

Sunday Morning

Going to church was the happiest times of my life. This was the time my family seemed perfect in the eyes of everyone around us. This was the time my father showed the perfect side of him. He was blameless, righteous, and respected. When he talked people listened and when he spoke something in someone's life they believed him. I watched my mother carefully pick out her clothes, choosing something that would cover up the cuts and bruises that my father inflicted on her. He would never hit her in the face that would reveal too much. She winced in pain as she put on her pants suit. I walked in her bedroom and put on her shoes for her.

"You look so beautiful." She said smiling down at me, looking at my dress.

"Thank you. You look pretty too."

"Oh, I don't know about that." She said, touching the cut on the side of her stomach.

My mother was indeed a beautiful woman and I looked so much like her except my eyes. She had the most gorgeous blue eyes that I have ever seen, that sparkled every time she smiled. When we had our own personal sleepover together, she would let me comb through her long soft honey blond hair. Those personal times that my mother and I spend together are my happiest times as well. My mother was the sweetest person that a person could ever meet, which is why I didn't understand what she did that made my father so angry.

My father always left home before we did, so that he could get to church before everyone else did. I could tell my father must have apologized to my mother and doctored on the wombs that he had caused, because she had a huge gauze on her chest where he'd burned her with the food and band aids all over her legs and back where she'd been cut. That's how my father operated the morning after his drunken spell. When he'd fall down from his drunkenness he would then realize what he'd done and cry his way back into my mother's good graces. He always apologized and promised to never hurt us again but when that alcohol take over those promises are quickly forgotten.

"Mom, you are the most gorgeous woman I know, both inside and out and I don't know why you let him hit you but I know God will make a way." I told her, as I held her hand.

She squeezed my hand as a tear slid down her cheek. I could see the pain and her eyes and I held her as she cried and released all her feelings.

"You know something, Danielle; you are so smart. Promise me that no matter what, you will never allow a man to hurt you in any way. Do you promise?"

"I promise. Now you have to promise me something…" I said

looking at her.

"Anything." She said smiling.

"Promise me that you will never leave me no matter what." I said looking at her.

"Why would you ask me to promise you something like that? I'm not going anywhere." She said reassuring me.

I couldn't be so sure because my father doesn't realize the force he uses when he hits us. I don't want her to end up dead from the hands of my father. I couldn't bear losing my mother and I wouldn't want to lose my father either. I didn't answer my mother's question; I just needed her to promise me that before it gets too bad she'd leave.

"Come on, sweetheart, we can't be late for church." She said, rushing to her vanity to fix her makeup.

She never did promise me.

Two WHEN WE STEPPED into the church, praise and worship had just ended and now it was time for the Word. Up to the pulpit walked a well dressed, well groomed, nice looking man. When he preached he stirred up emotions inside everyone who was listening. His preaching was powerful, boastful, and authoritative like he knew what he was talking about. When he teached everyone listened and understood. He never preached about prosperity and God sending us riches from up above.

He preached about the sinfulness in the world and about the trials and tribulations that we face today that will one day be brought to a halt when Jesus comes back. My light brown eyes were just like his but his skin was tanned but my mother and I was a little paler. He stood at 5'9, weighing at least 200, he wasn't all that muscular but his body wasn't bad looking. His head was bald and he wore a goatee and his face was so clear without a hair out of place. I could see how my mother could fall in love with a man like him. He has a way of talking that if he told you pigs could fly you would say "how high?" But I was told that even the devil knows the Bible and just because you can preach don't make you a preacher… it just means you're a man who can preach.

"How many of you believe that the Lord is good?" He spoke into the microphone.

"Amen!" The congregation yelled in agreement.

"I don't hear nobody, I said, how many of you know that the Lord is good?" He repeated.

"Amen!" They yelled even louder.

"Let's bow our head and give honor unto God." He told everyone.

"Lord, we come to You as humbled as we know how, asking You for guidance, love and support. Lord, we come unto You imperfect and ask that You forgive us and clean us from our sins. We ask that You walk with us through our journey and guide us to our destiny.

Lord we pray for the world. We pray that those who are in need of You follow You and those who are in need of love seek You. Lord I pray that the message that You have laid on my heart be of comfort to Your people. Lord we give You all the honor, all the glory and all the praise. Amen." He lifted up his head and look towards the congregation.

"Folks, the topic for today is titled, "The Battle Is Not Yours"..." He said, opening up his Bible.

"We all have weaknesses where God has to come in and strengthen us. We all make decisions that often times aren't the right ones, but that's why we serve a God who we can go to in our times of trouble. In our times of weakness... When we don't know what we should do or where to turn, the Lord will be our guide." He paused for a moment, while the congregation shouted their Hallelujah's in Amen's.

"When our flesh tries to intervene, we get on our knees and pray for the strength to fight. Everyday there is a battle, life is a battle, whether we are fighting the enemy to stay righteous before the Lord or whether we fighting drugs, alcohol, and all that other stuff people fight when they are out there in the world sinning. You see, nobody is perfect and everyone has fallen short. I just thank God for His loving kindness and His ability to forgive us when we make mistakes. God knows, I've sinned because I am not perfect. I thank God for His forgiveness and a family that stands beside me even when I don't make all the right choices." He preached, as he glanced at me and my mother.

I looked over at my mother and noticed the fake smile plastered on her face. Nobody knew the pain she had to face when my father pounded on her until he was tired. Nobody knew the countless nights that we weren't able to sleep, because we were afraid of what he might do when he walked in the door. Nobody knew how frightened we were in our own home. Nobody knew how scared I was for our lives.

"Turn to your Bible to Deuteronomy chapter eight verses thirty and thirty-one." He said putting on his reading glasses.

"Deuteronomy chapter eight verses thirty and thirty-one." He repeated, as he waited on everyone to find the page.

When everyone said amen, he asked us all to stand up and read it together out loud.

"The Lord, your God, who is going before you, will fight for you, as He did for you in Egypt, before your very eyes, and in the desert. There you saw how the Lord your God carried you, as a father carries His son, all the way you went until you reach this place." We all said in unity.

My father took off his glasses and closed his Bible.

"You see, the Bible states that the Lord will carry you and not only carry you but fight for you. He want us all to understand that even though times may be rough and when our burdens are too hard to bare or when we seem to be in the fight of our lives, He will be there to fight for us and carry us through it all. God loves us so much that He not only took the time to preciously craft us from His own hands but He allowed His son to come down and die for us. If that ain't love I don't know what is… Saints. How many of you, will be willing to lay down your life for someone? I don't know many who would." He said walking down from the pulpit.

"Preach, preacher." An old woman with a huge white hat shouted.

"God is a just God, a merciful God, a God of power and strength. He will not let us down. He said that as long as we continue to follow Him, He would keep us. God has never made a promise He couldn't keep. How many of you know that, if it had not been for the Lord that was on my side . . . ya'll don't hear me now." He said shaking his head, wiping the sweat from his brow.

"Hey God! You better preach," said another woman jumping up out of her seat and raising her hands towards the sky.

"If it had not been for the Lord, I could have been dead a long time ago. You ought to praise God, for simply waking you up this morning. For putting life into your body, for giving you the strength to get out of bed, for blessing you enough so that you have food on your table, clothes on your back and a place to lay your head. From the time of Abraham, He promised that His children would live abundantly." He said getting into it now.

"Thank you, Jesus, hallelujah God," shouted a number of people.

"If it had not been for the Lord . . . ." My father said, in a preaching tone.

"Understand that it does not matter what you use to do or what you did on yesterday but today God has forgiven you for all the sins you committed. God is not a God that holds grudges, for He said that if you ask Him for forgiveness He will forget about them. So, if God is able to forgive and forget about your sins, you should be able to forgive others and yourself. The Lord knows that I am imperfect and I stand here at this alter in repentance and I'm asking God to forgive me of my yesterdays and create in me a clean heart. You see, even the preacher needs prayer and I pray your strength in the Lord and I ask that you pray for me in return. So everyone learn to forgive your enemies and those who persecute you because your battle is not yours alone, but it is God's."

"Amen." Another said in the back of the church.

Yes, the preacher in the pulpit was my father and after he preached another hour before he ended the sermon by telling all of us to read Psalm 51, which is my favorite psalm by the way, aloud, the service ended.

"That husband of yours can surely preach," Sister Annie Mae said, as she hugged my mother.

Sister Annie Mae has been a member of this church since before I was born. I was told that when my great grandfather first opened the doors of this church she was one of the first members to join. Our church was mixed race, mostly blacks, but they didn't seem to mind having a white pastor.

"Yeah, he's something else, isn't he?" My mother responded, not too enthused.

"Yes, he is. You know he remind me so much of his great grandfather. You know even his father was a preaching man, God rest his soul. I remember when the doors of this church first opened. There were only about twenty members at the time, now we barely have enough chairs to seat everyone. God is surely a blessing, I tell you. Pretty soon we'll have to get a bigger church." She babbled.

My mother was so kind that she was willing to listen to anyone but I wasn't all that patient. I was ready to go.

"You're right; the church is beginning to be quite small. I'm going to talk to Jonah about us considering expanding the church." My mother said.

"Well, Dinah, I have to get going so that I could take my turkey wings out of the oven." She said motioning towards the door.

After we all hugged one another and wished each other well, we were off to eat Sunday dinner at a restaurant. When he decides not to drink on Saturday night, my mom cooks a nice southern dinner, but since that doesn't happen a lot we mostly eat out. The next few days had been going well since my father's last episode. As I was coming home from school, I overheard my mother telling my father that he should consider expanding the church. Surprisingly, he'd agreed and said that he'd already had that in mind. As I was walking into his study he put a huge piece of paper on the desk.

"This is the blueprint of how the new building is going to look." He smiled.

The building was huge. I was impressed by the floor plan that was laid out. My mother seemed happy again and my father seemed to be doing better as well. The weekend was drawing near and I really did not know what to expect. So, I came up with an idea that I hope the church will consider.

"Hey, you guys." I said walking into my parent's room.

They were both in their bed reading the Bible. My father was preparing himself for Sunday's service and my mother find reading the Bible comforting.

"Hey sweet pea, what's up?" My father said removing his glasses, while my mother moved over so that I could lie in the middle. This was Mr. Hyde.

"I was just wondering if we could go to Disney World this Saturday and spend some time together. We haven't did anything fun in a while and I was hoping that we could have some fun as a family." I said looking at my father.

"Disney World, that's in Florida, honey and besides you have school in the morning." He said.

"Well, I was hoping that we leave in the morning so that we could make it home in time for service on Sunday. Daddy tomorrow is Friday and I have never missed a day of school so it shouldn't be a problem to miss one day." I pleaded.

"Well, what do you think, honey?" He asked my mother.

"Certainly, I think it would be a great idea." My mother said looking at my father.

I could sense her fear of him and I felt sorry for her. I know she felt like if she didn't agree with him then he would act out but that was only when he was drunk.

"Well, looks like we'll be going to Disney World." He smiled at the both of us. Then he tickled me until I couldn't take it no more.

"How would you like to bake some chocolate chip cookies with your mother, huh?" My mother suggested, gently tugging on my ponytail.

"Yay, cookies," I said excitedly.

Both my parents laughed at me as I nearly tripped trying to get to the kitchen. While my mother put the chocolate chips in the oven she stopped in looked at me.

"I know what you were doing, and I thank you." She said looking at me.

"You're welcome." I said, already knowing what she was referring to. I was trying to find a way to keep daddy from going out to drink.

Three

IT'S BEEN SO long since I'd had so much fun. I was bone tired from riding all those rides and my stomach hurt from all the cotton candy. Usually, my parents wouldn't let me eat so many sweets but I knew they wanted me to have a good time. After Disney World daddy took us to this seafood restaurant where I was able to eat as many crab legs as I wanted. I just wanted to stay in Florida forever. I didn't know when I was going to be able to have this much fun again. Most of the time we stayed sheltered in the house until new wounds that my mother would heal. My mother didn't work because my father wouldn't allow it. He said that it is a man's job to provide for his family and it was her job to raise me and take care of the house. I just thought it was his way of trying to stay in control of her. My father and my mother met after college, she was going to school to be a doctor and he was going to Harvard majoring in business. After she graduated with honors, she quickly accepted the offer for Princeton on a scholarship and lived on campus.

They'd met during a Kenny G concert in Chicago. My mother told me that during that time, their love was beautiful. She thought he was the perfect man for her. He would pay her way to come see him as much as he could and after he graduated he'd asked her to marry him. They were completely opposite, my mother have always been sweet and quiet. My father was wild and rebellious but he made sure his studies came first. My father lived in a middle-class neighborhood in Chattanooga Tennessee with a preacher for a father and a school teacher for a mother.

On the other hand, my mother was raised in a trailer in Kansas with a mother who spent her government checks on her many boyfriends. My father was always telling my mother that he took her from poverty but the truth is they both went to school on campus and he did not know much about my mother's situation until after they got married. I guess he was just saying those things to hurt her. Anyway, after almost completing three years in medicine my mother had to drop out because she was pregnant with me. My father was offered a position for a prestigious company in San Francisco and he took it.

Those times were perfect for me, my father was doing something he truly loved and my mother was happy as well. There wasn't anything that I didn't have. I lived like a princess and we may not have lived in a mansion but it was like royalty. Things began to change when I was around eight years old. I can remember during my eighth birthday my father came in the house in a drunken spell. I had never seen him like that before, he held my mother as he told her that his parents where killed in a plane crash. He had a hard time getting over their deaths and during the reading of his parents will, his father gave him the church and asked him to come back home and preach.

Always, following his father's demands, we moved to Tennessee where he was ordained as the pastor of Mount Zion Temple. His drinking got worse and worse through the years but he didn't result into hitting on us until I was around ten years old. My mother told me he blamed himself for his father's death because the night of his death he'd had a heated argument with his father. Instead of going to seek help he turned to alcohol. No matter how many times my mother begged him to seek counseling he refused and told her that she the one who needed counseling. I guess after so many times of trying, she quit talking about his alcohol habit altogether.

Another Saturday Night

"Dinah!" my father yelled as he was coming through the door.

It was almost two in the morning and we both knew where he'd been. Just when I thought everything was going good, he just had to go and drink again. My father couldn't even handle liquor well and for the life of me I couldn't understand why alcohol. A lot of people think that heroin and cocaine is the worst drugs to get on. But what some people don't know is that alcohol is used more than any other substance and even though heroin is highly addictive, the health hazard is surprisingly low as well as its contribution to death.

I just hope my father get it together before it's too late. I could hear my mother coming out of their bedroom and I crept up behind her without her seeing me.

"Jonah, what's wrong, everyone is sleeping?" She whispered.

"You know I don't care about all that, wake your ass up and warm my dinner." He yelled louder than before.

She opened the refrigerator to get his plate and slammed it closed. I could tell that she was angry. Then she opened the microwave set the time and slammed the microwave door even harder.

"Keep slamming doors if you want to. You got an attitude or something?" He asked walking up to her.

"Huh?" He yelled in her face, causing her to jump.

"No, I'm just sleepy is all." She responded, fearing for the worse.

"Sleepy? You don't have a job, so what you got to be tired for? All you do is sit around the house and look crazy all day. Then you want to come in here slamming stuff, like you pay a mortgage." He said pointing at the microwave.

"I'm sorry Jonah." My mother trembled.

"Every time I look around you're sorry. You're the most sorriest woman I ever met." He complained, staggering back to the table.

My mother must of sense my presence because she looked up at me. I looked in her eyes and I could tell that she was pleading for me to go back in the room but I wasn't going anywhere.

"While you looking around like you don't have anything to do, you could at least fix me something to drink." He taunted my mother.

She opened the refrigerator again and fixed him some lemonade and sat it beside him.

"I don't want no lemonade; did I ask you for some lemonade?" He said throwing the glass against the wall.

My mother and I both jumped. She just looked at him. The microwave beeped letting her know that his food was ready. She got the food out of the microwave and sat it beside him.

"Bring me my bottle of Jack Daniels out of the cabinet, Dinah." He said eating a forkful of his food.

"Now I know why I kept you for so long, you may not be good for nothing else, but you sure can cook." He grumbled as he ate his food.

"Jonah, why don't you drink a glass of water? I don't think it's a good idea for you to be drinking so much at one time." She told him.

"You don't think, because I didn't ask you to think. You think you can sit up here and tell me what's good for me." He said through clinched teeth. Then he suddenly pushed the plate of food off the table. He looked down at the food as if he was dissecting it.

"Get on your knees and eat it." He told my mother with an icy look.

"Jonah, please." She said looking back at me.

"What you looking back there for? I told you to get down here and eat. I'm going to treat you like the female dog that you are." He said not leaving his seat.

My mother looked at me one last time, begging me to go back the bed with her eyes. Tears fell down my face and I felt so helpless. Without warning, my father got up and slammed her head in the food.

"What you keep looking back for? I told you to get down there and eat it." He said leaning over her.

"Ugh." My mother wept in pain. I thought he'd broken her back or something because she laid still for quite some time.

"So you're just going to lay there." He said leaning down over her and then he slapped the spit out of her. My mother eyes flew open as she held her stinging cheek.

"Yeah, wake up." He said standing up.

My mother must have taken too long to get up because he kicked her in her stomach.

"Jesus!" She said, barely getting the words out.

"Don't be calling Jesus now. He ain't got anything to do with this." He said kicking her again, this time blood spilled from her mouth.

Four

I COULDN'T TAKE IT anymore. If I didn't do something, he was going to kill her. I crept in my mother's room and picked up the bat that my father used to play baseball. He coached a bunch of troubled teenage boys, trying to keep them out of the streets. My hands were trembling as I walked back in the kitchen. My father was still hovering over my mother, watching her cry out in pain, as if he was enjoying it. That made me angry, so I ran as fast as I could towards him and swung the bat across his back with all my might.

"Uggghhh . . ." He screamed as he turned to me.

"You little—." He yelled barely walking towards me.

I swung the bat at him again but this time he caught it with his right hand. He pulled the bat out of my hand.

"So you want to put your hands on grown folks, huh, he spat at me, well I'm about to teach you about putting your hands on me." He said.

Before I knew what was coming, he hit me right cross my right arm with the bat. Pain shot through my arm so quick I didn't know what to do. I wanted to cry out but I couldn't. He hit me again on my left thigh, causing me to stumble on the floor.

"Turnover; I want to hit you on your natural behind." He said turning me over on my stomach.

Before he could hit me again with the bat, the door bell rung, he looked towards the door and back at me.

"Don't you breathed a word; as a matter of fact don't breathe at all." He said walking towards the door.

He opened the door and two police officers stood at the door.

"How can I help you officers?" He said trying to sound normal.

"Hey Pastor, neighbors said they heard a lot of commotion over here so we're here to see if everything alright." One of the officers said.

"Everything is fine officers; I messed around and dropped my food on my feet and it was so hot I yelled a little too loud." He told them.

"Okay, sir." The officer responded.

"Where are your wife and kid?" The other office spoke up, not too convinced by his story.

"Oh, they are asleep." He answered.

"They didn't wake up when they heard you scream?" He asked, trying to look over my father's shoulder.

"No, they sleep real hard." He told them, blocking the entrance so the officer couldn't see inside the house.

"Well, we're sorry to disturb you and get that feet treated okay." The first officer said walking off the porch.

"Thanks officers." He smiled and waved them goodbye.

He didn't even look at me and my mother twice as we laid on the floor in agony. He sat back at the table, drinking his Jack Daniels as if he didn't have a care in the world. The next morning I woke up on the floor. My father wasn't there, I figured he'd went to church service this morning. I looked towards the dining room and saw my mother lying on the floor. She wasn't moving and I was scared that my father really had done it this time. I was in a lot of pain but I built up enough strength to crawl over to my mother. My arms and legs felt as if they were broke and I could barely lift them up. I kissed my mother's cheek and cleaned up the blood from her lips with my shirt. She stirred and winced from the pain.

"Mom, are you okay?" I asked, as she opened her eyes.

"I'll be fine, did he hurt you?" She asked me.

"When I saw him kicking you, I went into your room and got his bat. When I hit him, he snatched the bat from me and hit me on my arm and my leg. He was going to hit me again but the police came." I told her.

"The police? Did they arrest your father?" She asked in a concerned tone. She didn't want anyone knowing what happened between these walls and feared that he being arrested will destroy his image.

"No mother, he gave them some kind of excuse for the noise and they left. I think he's at church." I told her looking around the room.

"Thank God, she said blowing out a huge breath; heaven knows we don't want your father going to jail." She said lifting herself off the floor.

When she stood up, she instantly fell back to the floor. I tried my best to help her get into bed. My arm and leg was killing me. After I finally got her into bed, I laid beside her. She wouldn't let me call the police or call the hospital. Daddy had a doctor on call that normally came to treat us to prevent us from going to the hospital. He knew that the hospital would ask to many questions.

Five   MY MOTHER AND I was finally able to move around after that night of torture that my father took us through. I missed almost two weeks of school and the doctor advised my mother to stay in bed for a week. I wondered why the doctor never asked us questions during his emergency house visits. But of course, my father had a hand in that too. My father came in the house one afternoon all happy, telling us to get dressed because he was taking us shopping. I guess he thought that would make up for what he did.

He tries to fix everything with material things, instead of him just loving us enough to stop. If alcohol made him react like that to those that he claims to love, then he needs to quit drinking. He swore time and time again on a stack of Bible's that he would never hit us again, but time and time again he broke his promises to God and to us. A week had passed and he was doing great. He wasn't drinking, he was reading his Bible, and he was being nice to me and mom. Sadly, I wasn't holding my breath, I was still waiting to see if Dr. Jekyll would show his ugly face.

Church Service

As always, we made it in time enough for my father's preaching. My mother is a great singer and is always singing around the house, but for some reason, she always skipped praise and worship. When we walked towards the front to sit in the first pew, I noticed a woman giving us a icy stare. I'd never seen her at church before but by the way she looked at us it seems as though she knew us. I paid it no attention; I just figured she was having a bad day. As my father stepped up to the pulpit, he looked over the audience and seemed pleased by the crowd. This church was getting bigger; it seemed like every Sunday there were new people.

He began to tell the members about his idea to open up a new church and he set a date. Everyone clapped their hands and praised God. See, most of the money that was put into the building was my father's money. Not that the members didn't give, but a lot of money was to be put in the new church and the money saved from the offering and tithes was not enough. My father made some good investments before he came back to Tennessee and thanks to those good investments he really don't have to work another day in his life. He broke us in with prayer and asked us all to stand.

"Today's message is "Can't Hold Me Back". Everyone open your Bible's to Luke chapter eighteen versus thirty-five. When everyone have it say, Amen." He said putting on his glasses. When everyone had it, he asked us all to stand so that we could read it aloud.

"As Jesus approached Jericho, a blind man was sitting by the roadside begging. When he heard the crowd going by, he asked what was happening. They told him, "Jesus of Nazareth is passing by." He called out, "Jesus, Son of David, have mercy on me!" those who led the way rebuked him and told him to be quiet, but he shouted all the more, "Son of David, have mercy on me!" Jesus stopped and ordered the man to be brought to him. When he came near, Jesus asked him, "What do you want me to do for you?" "Lord I want to see," he replied. Jesus said to him, "Receive your sight; your faith has healed you." Immediately he received his sight and followed Jesus, praising God. When all the people saw it, they also praised God." We all said as we sat down.

"God is awesome, isn't He?" He spoke.

"Yeah," everyone shouted.

"There was this blind man and I'm sure he was poor because the Bible said he was sitting on the roadside begging. He heard a commotion and there was Jesus passing by with a crowd of people. And this man had so much faith in Jesus he knew he would be healed if only he could get Jesus' attention. So he cried, Jesus! Lord, I need you, pleeeaaasssee." My father paused for emphasis.

"Glory," the lady beside me said.

"You see the crowd tried to hold him back from receiving his blessing, they wanted him to stay as he was. Broken and stuck in his past, but the man refused to listen to them. This man wanted his blessing, he wanted his breakthrough. They were trying to hold him back, but how many of you know that even though he was rebuked by many and ignored by those around him, he still had the faith to call on Jesus, he refused to let them hold him back from his healing. He said even louder than before, Jesus! Have mercy on me! Jesus hears him, He stops and the man was brought to him. Now this blind man, poor, unworthy, with a crowd that was trying to keep him in his past of darkness had enough faith to keep calling on Jesus. He was determined to get his sight, determined to get out of his past and nobody could hold him back. He cried, Jesus, please, I need you, please, don't go by without healing me. So, Jesus asked the man, "What do you want me to do for you?" And his reply was, "Lord, I want to see." The Lord healed this man because he had faith and he immediately received his sight and praised God."

My father was a preaching man and I hope he had enough faith to ask God to heal him.

"How many of you, who had people surrounded by you that tried to keep you in your past, keep you from receiving what God has for you, keeping you from receiving your healing and your breakthrough? But you wanted out so bad, that you said I refused to let you hold me back. Jesus! I know I'm not worthy but I know you and I know you can heal me. Please, Jesus! Please don't pass me by. Lord, I'm in my mess, Lord I'm unclean, Lord I'm so broken, but I know you can heal me. Jesus!" My father shouted through the microphone.

There were so many members jumping up, praising God and there was one lady who jumped up dancing and jumping, calling out to God.

"If you are allowing someone to hinder you from your breakthrough, tell them, "You can't hold me back, I know the Lord and I know He's able to heal me. I will not let you keep me from receiving my blessings from God. You will not stand in front of what my God has for me. You may want to still be stuck in here but I know the Lord, has something better for me. I want out! I'm coming out! I'm coming out! You can't hold me back!" My father continued as people stood up and cried out to God.

Service lasted a little longer since my father prayed over a lot of people and gave them a chance to get themselves together. My mother stood talking to one of the members of the church but I knew she was getting restless because she told me to find my father and tell him to come on. I finally found my father in his study, with the woman who gave me the mean look when I walked into the church. My father looked at her angrily and held her roughly around her wrists. He didn't seem too happy to see this visitor.

"I told you never to set foot in my church, around my family." He shouted to her.

"Jonah, you're hurting me." She winced.

"Don't ever come here again." He shouted, but looked over at me and released the grip he had on the woman's arms.

"What is it, Danielle?" He shouted making me jump.

"Mommy said, to come on." I said barely getting it out.

I kept looking at the woman and she had tears in her eyes. I was curious to know who this woman was and why was she in the study with my father. I have never seen her before but she knew my family. The woman walked past me and out the door. I looked at my father as he tried to get his self together.

"Daddy, who was that woman?" I asked.

"Nobody and you better not tell your mother what you saw, do you hear me?" He demanded.

"Yes, sir," I said.

Something didn't feel right and there was something about that woman that rubbed me the wrong way. I knew something was up and I hope it wouldn't tear my family apart. But as the Bible say, "What's done in the dark, will come to the light."

Six   "MOMMY, WERE ARE you?" I coughed. I was trying to see if I could see my mom through all the smoke. The house was on fire and I could hear my mother screaming out to me but I couldn't see her through the smoke. I walked in my parent's bedroom and fire was all around my mother. I tried to reach out to her but, but the flames rose higher. All of a sudden the fire caught on to my mom's clothes and I heard her scream in agony.

"Danielle." I heard a voice behind me and I looked back and it was my father with the reddest eyes I'd ever seen.

"Danielle." He called out to me as he drew closer.

"Danielle." I began to hear his voice louder.

"Danielle, wake up," my mother said waking me up from my sleep. Oh, thank God, it was only a dream. It was the scariest dream I'd ever had.

"You were having a nightmare. Are you okay?" She asked wiping the sweat from my face. My body was soaked from all the sweat.

"Yes." I said trying to gulp in some air.

"Let me go get you some water and then I'll help you change your clothes and these covers off your bed." She said.

"Yes, ma'am." I responded.

After we changed all the covers, I took a warm bath and put on some clothes.

"Do you mind telling me what had you so scared?" She asked me as soon as I was finished. She sat beside my bed and I sat beside her.

"There was this huge fire and I heard you screaming for me. When I found you in your bedroom there was fire all around you. When I tried to reach out to you the fire rose and the fire caught on to your clothes and you were screaming. There was smoke everywhere mommy and you were burning. Then behind me was daddy with the reddest eyes, I'd ever saw. He was trying to come close to me but you woke me up." I told her through tears.

"Awww, sweetie, it was only a dream." She said hugging me.

"But it felt so real." I wasn't convinced that I should just dismiss it.

"Sometimes dreams could feel that way but as you can see the house is fine and so am I." She said, turning around with her arms wide showing me that she was fine.

I could clearly see that she was fine, but I couldn't shake the strange feeling that gnawed at me.

"Mom…" I said, sitting up in the bed, and crossed my legs.

"Huh?" She said sitting next to me.

"Daddy said that a wife is supposed to obey her husband."

"Yes… that's what the Bible says. Wives are supposed to submit to their husband. The husband is head over the wife." She said.

"Yes, but God is the head of us all." I told her.

"Yes, I suppose that is true." She said, looking at me, wondering where all of this was coming from.

"I know that the Bible says that the wives are supposed to be subjective to their husbands, but I was reading Ephesians chapter five and it says that husbands are supposed to love their wives, just as Christ also loved the church and that they also are to love their own wives as their own bodies."

"Yes, it does." She marveled.

"So, Dad must not love himself very much." I told her.

"Well, why do you say that?" She asked me.

"Because, he beats on you and hurt you. Wouldn't that mean he is hurting himself when he hurt you?"

"How old are you again?" She joked, but a tear fell from her eyes.

I took her hand in mines. "Mom, daddy does not like us because he does not like himself. He hurt himself with all that alcohol, but he hurts us with his fist. The Bible says, that a husband who understands that his wife is apart of him, his own flesh, then he will treat his wife like he treats himself… And that's just what daddy is doing… He is treating you… his flesh… and me… his seed… like he treat his self."

"You got all of that out of that scripture?" She said looking at me amazed.

"Don't you?" I asked her with a confused look on my face. I know she's read that scripture before.

"Yes I have, but I guess I got so caught up in trying to honor your father, that I tend to forget the part where it says he has to honor me too." She said squeezing my hand.

"I just asked God to help me understand and he did." I told her.

"You have the wisdom of Solomon, the heart of David and the tenacity of Peter my dear daughter. God is going to use you... He's already using you." She said looking at me in admiration.

I smiled at her. God was my only friend. My father would not allow me to befriend anyone at my school nor did he allow my mother to have any friends either. He said he didn't want people all up in our business but I already knew he didn't want people to know his other side. There was only one person that I could confide in and even my father couldn't keep Him away. When I needed to release what I was feeling, I would always go to my secret place and talk to God. He was the only one that my father could never take away from me, not even if he tried. People ask how you can love something or someone you cannot see or something you cannot touch. But some people don't understand that when you love God, you can feel when He loves you back.

When you need to be held, you can feel Him holding you. It is hard to explain and all I could tell a person is to seek God and they'll understand. My mother said I was wiser than some adults. I never quite understood what she was saying. In my mind all sixteen year olds thought like me. I read the Bible a lot and talked to God not only through prayer but I talk to Him like I'm talking to a normal person, and He talks back to me. I prayed for my mother and father daily hoping that my father has the mind to let go of the alcohol and my mother have the strength to leave if it gets worse. Since my father hit me with that bat, I have been very distant with him. Honestly, I am afraid of him. He doesn't realize how much he is affecting himself and his family.

My mind instantly flashback to the woman I saw at the church. She seems angry when she looked at me and my mother but in my father's study she seemed vulnerable and hurt. My father told me not to say anything to my mother and out of fear, I didn't dare say a word, but I did tell God about it. I know God could keep secrets, because He always keeps mine. As I sit in my secret spot and pray out to God I felt his warmth surround me and I knew He heard me. Who else can save me from the hands of my father, besides him? Everyone has so much respect for my father that even if I did say something, nobody would believe me. They loved their beloved pastor and they wouldn't believe that he was capable of harming anyone. But I wondered if they read the scripture that warned the Saints to beware of wolves in sheep clothing…

Seven   AS I WAS preparing myself for the second service, I had a funny feeling. I wasn't sure why, but I had a feeling I would find out sooner or later. Usually, when I have feelings like this, something bad always happened. It was first Sunday and so communion was about to be prepared. I love when we have communion because I enjoy the grape juice that we have. I usually took three of the little cups when the tray was passed to me. My mother would always look at me disapprovingly and I would always give her the sweetest smile that I could muster up. My mother was in the study with my father after the first service and I walked in and caught them kissing.

"Oooh, what are you two doing?" I said as if they were in trouble.

"Nothing," my father said innocently.

"It didn't look like nothing to me, but what do I know, I'm just a kid." I said shrugging my shoulders, smiling at the both of them.

They both laughed at me. My father told me to come where they were and we all hugged each other. I wished we could freeze time and stay in that moment forever. My father was finally beginning to come through and now I know God heard my prayers. Silently, I thanked God for saving my family. When it was time for the last service, my mother and I sat in our normal seats in the pews and song a long with the praise and worship team. I was amazed, because my mother actually enjoyed herself. Her smile lit up the room, and I know it was all because of Dad's new transition. After praise and worship my father began to preach about the transfiguration of Jesus.

In between his preaching he stopped abruptly and looked towards the entrance of the church. Both, me and my mother's eyes followed his and there stood the woman that I saw in the study. That bad feeling that I was feeling earlier began to resurface. There was something going on with my father in this woman. The woman eyes were puffy and red as if she'd been crying. She just looked at my father as if she was trying to burn a whole through his soul. My father didn't say a word he just tried to regain his composure and started preaching again.

"Yeah, you're good about ignoring me aren't you, Jonah?" She said causing the whole congregation to look at her.

My father tried not to pay her any attention and once again tried to finish were he left off, but everyone was focused on this woman.

"Yeah, you full of it, preaching God's word but not living by it yourself. Don't listen to this man, he is a hypocrite." She yelled over the congregation, over talking my father.

"Woman, have you lost your mind? How dare you come into my church and disrespect me like that. Now, I warned you to never show your face here again." He said getting angry.

"Jonah, who is this woman?" My mother said.

"Oh, you didn't tell her about your other life, Jonah?" The woman asked, looking at me and my mother.

"Vanessa, shut up and get out of my church before I throw you out." My father said with fire in his eyes.

"I'm not going anywhere; I'm tired of playing second with them, when you have a son that you barely even see." She said letting the cat out of the bag.

Everyone in the church began to mumble and when I looked at my mother she just stared at my father.

"You leave, right now, before I—" He screamed.

"Before you do what, hit me? You wouldn't do that in front of all these "saved" people would you? No, that would reveal the true you, won't it." She went on.

My mother was still looking at my father. I felt so sorry for her. There was nothing I could do and I was just as hurt as she was. My father swiftly walked from the pulpit, grabbed the woman and tossed her out the door.

"Church the service is dismissed today." He said walking into his study without looking up at anyone.

My mother snapped back into reality and walked out of the church. Everyone was asking her was she alright and being the woman that she is she apologized to them and ended the service properly. When we got home, she went into her room and closed the door. I left her alone as I went into my bedroom and prayed out to God. I was hurting so bad and needed to talk to my friend.

"God, I prayed and begged for You to keep my family together but it's all a mess. What did I do? Are You mad at me? I'm following all Your commandments, reading my Bible and praying. What else do I need to do? Lord, I don't understand, please… help me understand." I said as tears fell from my eyes.

I could hear my mother crying her heart out to God. I walked in the room and held her as we cried out to God together.

"I know from the moment I saw that woman that something wasn't right." My mother began.

"What do you mean, mom?" I asked.

"I saw the woman in the back of the church last Sunday, looking at us in a weird way. I didn't pay it any attention but when I saw her come out your father's study. I knew something was not right." She said, shaking her head.

She never indicated that she knew. I know she had to see me going in the study. I felt bad for not telling her.

"Mom, daddy told me not to tell you she was in his study, I'm sorry." I began to cry.

"It's okay sweetheart, I know your father and I understand why you kept it from me. I am not mad at you. Stop crying because everything will be alright." She said holding me tight.

There she was again, acting like there was a solution to the problem but I'm afraid she can't cover this up with makeup or with long sleeve shirts and pants. The woman said what she said in front of the whole church and the way the church gossip, I'm sure all of Tennessee knows by now.

"When I asked your father who that woman was, he said she was just someone who wanted to join the church. When I asked why she was in his study, he simply said that she didn't feel comfortable talking in front of the members of the church and preferred to speak to him in private. I figured that was a logical explanation and stupid, gullible me, believed him." She said mostly to herself than to me.

"Mom you're not stupid." I said wiping her tears with the back of my sleeve.

"I should of known better, I should of followed my gut and questioned him some more." She said getting angry with herself.

"Mom, did you hear what the woman said?" I asked her, as the ladies words assaulted my memory.

"Yes. I don't know who she is, but I need to talk to her. I need to find out what is going on." She said, as she jumped up and ran to her room.

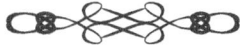

Eight

SHE WAS LOOKING all through my father's things. She went to the bedroom and started searching but obviously she didn't find what she was looking for. Then she ran to his study. We were forbidden to go in his study, but I guess my mother was so angry that she didn't care about all of that. She started looking for information in his computer, searching for anything that would tell her about the woman. Nothing… She looked in his safe, in his desk, and all in his files, but she still couldn't find nothing. Just when she was about to give up, she tried to open the bottom drawer of his desk, but it was locked. She told me to her help search for the key. We looked everywhere, we couldn't find the key. She started paying close attention to the desk, she looked underneath it and there she found it, taped under the desk. When she opened the drawer, both of our mouths dropped. There was dozens of pictures of the woman we saw at the church. Dozens of pictures of her and my father kissing, smiling into the camera, holding hands, family pictures of them with a little boy that looked just like my father.

"How could he do this to me, to us?" She stood, looking at the pictures.

As she began to dig deeper she found out the little boy name was Joshua and he was five years old. Then there was a will that included my mother, me and Joshua but not his mother. Then there were life insurance policies on all of us including Vanessa.

"Who in the world is this man? Lord, who is this man?" My mother looking up at the ceiling. She was furious and her hands were shaking uncontrollably.

"Mom, please calm down." I said, trying to keep it together but inside I was confused, hurt and even angry. She kept looking through the pictures, until she came across one that nearly blew both of us away.

"This can't be…How could this be?" My mother said in complete shock.

"Oh my God," I said, covering my mouth.

There stood my father and Vanessa smiling like two loved birds cutting cake together. They were at their wedding. Vanessa was pregnant, must have been pregnant with the little boy. She wore a cream gown and he wore a black suit. There was nothing I could say to make this right. I knew this was real. That it wasn't some sick joke or one of my dreams.

"How could he? How could he be married to me but to someone else? After all these years, how could he do this to me?" My mother said mostly to herself.

We heard a noise at the door and when we looked up, there stood my father. Without a second thought my mother rushed at him. I was in surprised because I didn't know my mother had it in her. She has never raised her voice at my father, let alone her hands.

"You lying, cheating, son of –" She said, throwing hits at him.

"Let me explain." My father said blocking the punches my mother was laying on him. I was surprised that he was letting her hit him. He wasn't angry, he looked sorry.

"Explain? Explain what? Not only do you have another child, but you have another wife. Another wife... Jonah, what have you done? What have I ever done to you to make you do me like this? I followed the same guidelines in the Bible in Proverbs 31, like you instructed me to. I submitted my life to you and never was unfaithful to you. I allowed you to beat on me as if I was your personal punching bag. I forgave you time and time again because I loved you. I tried to understand you, I tried to understand your behavior... But all you've told me was lies.... Just all lies...." My mother said storming out of the room.

"Dinah?" My father yelled, running after her.

My mother slammed the door to her room and locked it behind her. I could hear her slamming things against the wall and crying. I could feel her pain and I felt like he'd cheated me too.

"Danielle, you must understand, I love you and your mother and I will never intentionally hurt you." He said looking at me.

I didn't respond to him and as tears fell from my eyes I tried hard not to hate him. I know God said never to hate but He allowed this to happen, so I'm done with it all. How could He love me and allow this to happen to me? He said He'd never leave me or forsaken me, so why do I feel forsaken? I looked at my father with venom in my eyes and spat in his face. He didn't even hit me, he just walked out the door. I stared at the back of his car, as he drove out of the parking lot.

Three Hours Later

My mother was still packing when I feel asleep. She'd told us that we were moving out. After packing up my things in my room, I was tired. I was awaken by a loud commotion in my parents room.

"Stay away from me you hypocrite. How could you preach to all those people and be such an abomination to God?" My mother yelled.

"Don't you ever talk to me that way again; I am still your husband." My father warned.

"Husband . . . you're a bigamist. You're married to another woman; you have another family that I didn't even know about. No, you're not my husband; you and I should have been over a long time ago." I heard my mother respond.

"It's not in you to leave me, you have nothing. If it wasn't for me you would be on the streets. Go ahead, leave." My father said taunting her.

"You're pathetic. Look at you, drunk, and you call yourself a man of God." She said as I heard her walking towards my room.

"Danielle, put on some clothes and let's go." She told me.

When I walked out the room, my father was sitting in his normal spot drinking a glass of Jack Daniels. His eyes were fire red and he scared me, then that feeling swelled up inside of me again and I was scared.

"You like spitting in my face, huh." My father said looking at me.

My mother was in her room getting a few things.

"Stay away from me, Jonah." I said, addressing him by his first name. I didn't have respect for him anymore and as far as I was concerned he was no father of mines. He stood from the table and quickly walked towards me, liquor bottle in hand.

Smack.

My right cheek stung from the slap.

Smack.

He slapped me again, this time I fell to the floor.

"You think you're grown, now." My father spat at me.

He lifted me up by my hair and slammed me against the wall. My mother must have heard my scream because she quickly ran into the room.

"You leave my child alone." She said running towards my father.

Before she could hit him, he punched her in the head so hard; I thought he'd cracked her skull. She fell to the floor like a sack of potatoes. Then he looked at the bottle in his hands and poured the remaining alcohol all over my mother.

"She thinks she can disrespect me and then threaten to leave me. She must have lost her mind. She is my wife and before she goes anywhere, she'll die first." My father said looking at me. Before I knew it he pulled a match from his pocket and lit it.

"No!" I yelled as I tried to run over to my mother but before I could he dropped the match on her. As the fire began to consume her I ran out the house screaming.

"Call the police! My mother is on fire!" I yelled to the next door neighbor, who'd heard my scream.

Ten minutes later the police was there arresting my father and my mother was rushed to the hospital.

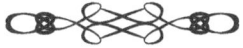

Nine

WHAT MY FATHER DID TO MY MOTHER was all over the news, everyone knew what happened, and my father was finally exposed. My seemingly perfect family, was now blemished and what my mother tried to keep a secret was finally revealed. Almost sixty-five percent of her body was burned. Her hair was gone, her whole lower body was burned and so was one-third of her face. The doctor said that through surgery they could reconstruct her face back to normal but couldn't do anything for her lower body. My mother has always been beautiful and to see her like this tore me apart. When she finally woke up from the coma she was in, she couldn't stop crying after she saw her face.

She refused to look in a mirror and when she thought about it she cried for hours. I wish it was something I could do for her but I knew I couldn't. Vanessa came to the hospital and told my mother about her and my father. She told us that in the beginning she never knew about us and didn't find out until she saw us all on television at a charity event with the mayor. She said when she confronted my father he admitted it but he said he had to stay in the marriage to keep up his image. He promised her in time he'd get up the nerve to tell us the truth, but the truth never came, and she kept on waiting.

"Vanessa, didn't it seem awkward for him to be gone so much? I mean, I know you said you knew about us after seeing us on television, but before then. Did you ever wonder why he was never at home with you at night?" My mother asked.

"Yeah I did, I talked to him about that but he said he was still working for the company in New York and he had to fly out there all the time. After a year, he told me that he had moved to Tennessee because his father left him a church. He would come over to my house on Saturday and I would have to kick him out by the end of the night because he'd start drinking." She said.

So instead of at the bar he would be at her house, now everything was beginning to make sense. Five years ago, my father was gone days at a time and we wondered what was going on. He told us he was trying to get up with some old business friend to help build the church. We'd forgotten all about it and when he showed us the blueprint I guess all of it began to make sense.

"So, what made you finally decide that you were tired of being his part-time "family"?" My mother asked her.

"I've been married to Jonah for five years and out of those years he's barely spent time with me. I found out about you three years into the marriage. I was already wrapped up in him. I believed him when he told me that he was leaving you. Joshua was three years old and I wasn't willing to raise him by myself. I know it sounds selfish, but I wanted Jonah to leave you so he could be with me. He is my husband."

"No, honey, he is *my* husband. My mom corrected her, I was married to him first and we've never divorced. So you see, you both are just two people, committing adultery."

"Like I said, I didn't know he was married at first." She said.

"Five years is not nearly as long as seventeen years. I can't blame you. You didn't know that you were sinning, and even when you did find out, you still remained in your sin. But I can't fault you; you have to own up to your sins to God, but Jonah… that's another story." She said trying to get comfortable.

Vanessa just looked at her and really felt sorry for what had happened, she felt like she was the blame.

"Did he ever hit you?" My mother asked looking at her.

"Yes, when he got drunk he would but will stop when Joshua walked into the room, then he would leave." She said, clearing her throat.

"Wow, he had enough respect not to hit you in front of your child, but he didn't have a problem beating on my mother in front of me, not to mention beating on me." I said with envy.

"I'm sorry." She said sincerely.

"No, you don't have to be sorry, but Jonah should be." My mother said, bitterly.

"Not fully, when she found out he was already married she should of left him alone. It's her fault that she accepted his ways and when she got tired she wanted to ruin our family because she knew he wasn't going to be a family with her." I said still angry.

"Danielle, watch it." My mother warned.

I walked out of the room. I knew if I would have stayed there, I would have defied my mother. I went to the first floor of the hospital, in the back there was a lounging area, and no one was able to see you unless they turned the corner. This is where I would come to do my homework, think and find peace, whenever I came to visit my mother. My grandmother was staying at our new apartment with me until my mother got out of the hospital. I was angry with God at first, but after I talked to Him I realized that although things didn't happen the way that I wanted it to, that what occurred, happened for a reason.

The dream I had was not a dream, but a premonition of what was about to happen. God had told me what was going to happen to warn my mother, but she didn't listen. I apologized to Him for being angry with Him. I sat there in the lounge chair, seething. But God was speaking to me, telling me to pray for my enemies, love unconditionally, and to forgive. I closed my eyes, and let the Spirit within me speak what I couldn't say. I opened up my heart to Him and allowed Him to fill it up with that familiar warmth that I knew all too well. I prayed for my father, I prayed for my mother I prayed for Vanessa and her son, and I prayed for myself.

Apart of me felt that it was my fault because I was not able to help my mother. But the Lord reassured me that I was not to blame. When I went back in the hospital room, I apologized to my mother and to Vanessa. Vanessa then apologized to me. The first time I met my brother, I did not know how to respond to him. I tried not to be jealous because now I was not the only child. Instead of despising him I chose to embrace him. After getting to know him a little more, I really started liking him, and apart of me was glad to have a sibling.

I couldn't blame an innocent child for destroying something that my father destroyed a long time ago. I wanted to blame somebody else, but it was my father who broke up our home and I had to blame him. My father tried calling the hospital but I told the hospital to not accept any of his calls. After he called and harassed the doctors and staff they were forced to block his calls and reported him to the police station in which he was incarcerated. Then the letters began to come in the mail and I forwarded the letters back to him without even reading them.

My mother was healing— physically, mentally, and emotionally. She was praying more than she use to, reading her Bible with me, and we had created a bond that was stronger than ever. My mom was happy. Her eyes sparkled again and when I looked at her, I know longer saw her as weak, but she was strong, courageous, and yes… virtuous. She stayed with my father because she was loyal to her husband, committed to her vows, and dedicated to her marriage. That is not weak, but that is a level of strength that many women did not possess. When I first went back to school, I expected everyone to look at me funny and ridicule me because of the actions of my father.

Instead, people embraced me, and I was now opening up to people. I had friends now and I finally felt like a kid. Since my father been in jail, I have been having the time of my life. For years, I have tried to hide my sorrow and now I don't have to. I don't have to pretend to be the perfect daughter of a preacher because even the preacher, was far from perfect. I looked over at my mother, as she slept. I imagined that this was the most peace that she'd had in a long time. Even with the scars and the bandages, she was, to me, the most beautiful woman alive.

3 Months Later

My mother had undergone surgery and it went successful. I was amazed at how they were able to make her face look like it was before. The first night my mom came home to our new apartment, she twirled around the room and singed praises to God. She looked in the mirror in her bedroom and she smiled at herself.

"This is the body of a warrior." She said, rubbing her hands over the scars on her chest.

"It sure is baby." My grandmother said, as she held her from behind and looked in the mirror with her.

From that moment on, she would look in the mirror every day and say, "I love you girl." It took her some time to reach this place and I know God was working His magic. He was, after all, a miracle worker. He was performing miracles on the inside of both of us, holding us when we felt like giving up, wiping our tears, mending our broken hearts, healing our wounds. Members from the church was coming over, checking on us and bringing us meals. It felt good to know that there were people that really cared. My mother didn't know how to react to them at first, because she wasn't used to interacting with people like that.

I could see the freedom that she was feeling. She was finally able to embrace who she was and she was no longer held hostage to the demands of my father. My mother allowed my brother to come over and bond with me and even Vanessa would sit and chat with us for a while. There was no spite or jealousy but understanding and similarity between them. They'd both been through about the same; one longer than the other but still their lives was not so different. In fact, my mother had found a friend in Vanessa.

Ten   MY MOTHER DECIDED to drop all charges against my father… She said that if she'd pressed charges it only meant that she was seeking for revenge and that didn't justify anything. She said God is the revenger, who will fight all her battles. She said it is not her to judge the outcome of someone's life but that she will allow God to judge and punish him for what he has done. She said putting him in prison did not help the situation, but it was would be one more father who was taken from their kids. I didn't quite understand it, but it wasn't for me to understand everything. Vanessa divorced my father. The assistant pastor was preaching in the absence of my father. Pastor Timothy Luke was not only the assistant pastor, but my father's best friend. My father was so secretive, that even Tim was unaware of his second family, his drinking habit, and the domestic violence. His topic this Sunday was, "Restoring the Repentant Heart".

"As Christian's we are expected to be perfect, to have everything in place, but people tend to forget the human in us. We do fall short, we do have weaknesses, and we do have our imperfections." He began.

"As preachers and teachers of the faith, we are required to present ourselves a certain way. I am not excusing or approving of anyone's sins, but I am saying, we have to give each other a break. We have to learn to love each other beyond our mistakes. Once apon a time, we all were caught up in our sins, but God didn't give up on us and we must not give up on each other. We are all apart of one body. We are all children of the Most High God." He said, pointing his finger up towards the heavens.

"Amen." We all said in unision.

"One of the most quoted scriptures that are thrown to everyone is Matthew 7:1, "Judge not, lest ye be judged." This scripture has been taken out of context for years to come. We are taught not to correct anyone when they are wrong, not to speak up for anything that is right, because we are afraid of rebuke from others. This verse only refers to those who are hypocritically judging; those who are sinning or committing the same sin that they are trying to rebuke. Turn to 1 Corinthian 6:1-4." He said, slipping on his glasses.

"Does any one of you, when he has a case against his neighbor, dare to go to law before the unrighteous and not before the saints? Or do you not know that the saints will judge the world? If the world is judged by you, are you not competent to constitute the smallest law courts? Do you not know that we will judge angels? How much more matters of this life." We all recited.

"Did you hear that last part? The Saints of God will judge the angels, so how is it that we cannot judge, or should I say, correct people when they are wrong? We must speak the truth, but we must speak it in love." He just looked at the congregation and smiled.

"Turn to Galatians 6:1 and I will read, you just follow along… Brothers, if anyone is caught in any transgression, you who are spiritual should restore him in a spirit of gentleness I'm going to flip to verse 32… Forgive each other, just as God forgave you because of what Christ has done." He said closing the Bible.

"So not only do we have permission to judge the angels, but we also have permission to help restore those who are caught up in sin. People these days, confuse correction for condemning, and restoration for damnation. But it's not so much as the people fault, because some of us "Saints" present ourselves to others like we are holier than thou… Oh… don't nobody want to say nothing now. I must be stepping on a few toes." He said backing back.

"Amen." Some of the members shouted.

"We want to act like we've been saved all of our lives. We forget that God saved a wretch like us and when we were lost, there was somebody out there that helped us find the Savior. Love covers a multitude of sin. It is that same love that allows us to embrace people, to forgive people, and to help others, even those who you expect not to make a mistake. Let's not kick others when they are down, or turn our nose at those who are weaker than us. We are all weak in some area." He said, looking out in the crowd, as if he was looking for someone.

"That's true." My mother spoke up.

"We have to make ourselves available so that those with a repentant heart can be restored. Jesus came for the sick not for those who were already healed. The church of God is not only for the Saints to come together, but it is designed to bring healing to those who are sick. It is a place established for everyone. For those... who are... wounded, scared, damaged, and in need of a place to run to when they need help." He continued.

"For those who are looking for a Savior that can save them from the snares of the enemy... A place where they can find love... peace... hope... joy... and freedom. Saint's of God... The house of God is that place. That place where people should be able to come and be embraced and be loved... A place... where... they can find Jesus right there at the altar." He said pointing in front of him at the altar.

"Don't be the reason why people reject coming to God. Don't be the reason why people are afraid of coming to the House of God because they don't want to be around a bunch of self-righteous, gossipers." He uttered.

"Now, I have talked to God concerning our pastor and I am required to follow the instructions that He has given to me." He said, looking at me and my mother.

"Just because we stand in the pulpit with our fancy robes, does not mean that we don't have flaws, Saints. Even pastors get weak. We need to be prayed for too. Yesss...the devil troubles us on every side. Our pastor, who is like a brother to me, has done some unspeakable things, but we must forgive him and let him know that we are here for him. As Children of God, we ought to act love like God. Let us come together in love and embrace the man of God." He said, holding his hands out towards the isle.

My father came out of the back pew and slowly walked up to the pulpit. Tears were streaming down his face everyone cheered him on. Once he stood up at the podium, he embraced Pastor Luke and looked at me and my mother. He looked different... When he stood at the podium, I know longer saw the strong man with the bold voice. No... I saw a man who was broken and trying to correct the wrongs in his life.

"Thank you so much." He said, wiping his tears, as he waited for the congregation to stop clapping.

He glanced over at me and my mother and smiled. My mother walked out the church, causing everyone to whisper. I quickly followed behind her and so did Vanessa.

"I know this is hard for you... shoot... it's hard for me too, but you have to forgive him." Vanessa said encouraging her.

My mom just looked at her as a tear slid down her cheek. "I know what I'm supposed to do and yes I've forgiven him but I will never forget what he did." She responded.

"And you are not supposed to; all you can do is live day by day by being the best Christian you can be. Nobody said it was going to be easy and you have come a long ways. You're stronger now and God has renewed you into the woman you've always wanted to be. If you really have forgiven him like you say, then go back in there and face him. Listen to what he has to say." She said holding my mother's hand.

"I can't believe you are saying this out of all people." My mom laughed.

"I know right. She laughed with her. But God forgave me, so it's only right that I forgive him."

"Yeah, you're right." She said, grabbing my hand and walking back in the church.

Some looked at us with sympathy and some smiled because they were happy that we came back.

"Bless you, Dinah." Pastor Luke said.

My mom just nodded her head, gave a weak smile and sat back in her regular seat.

"Lord, help me say the right things." He said closing his eyes.

"Just say what's in your heart Pastor." A lady yelled from

her pew.

"Picture a little boy who tried to do everything right. Everything to please his Father, because his Father was always seen as good, just, and right in the eyes of everyone who knew him. So the little boy adhered to the desires of his Father, without embracing his own. He walked into the calling in which his Father told him to walk in, without fully understanding what that calling was. That little boy was me. I loved my Father, respected him so much that anything he wanted me to do I did. I went to college for business. I wanted to start my own record label and be the next Berry Gordy. Not Christian music either, because although I was raised with two wonderful, saved, and Holy Ghost filled parents, I wasn't like them. So, when my Father told me to preach at his church before he died, I thought it was my duty to carry own the tradition. I was trying so hard to be like my Father. I read the word so many times until I memorized it in my mind. But there is a difference between knowing the word and living it."

"Amen." Someone spoke up.

"You can know the Word and not live it and you can put on a good sermon, but that doesn't mean the message comes from God. I didn't come into this church because I was called by the Father on high, I came this church because I was called by my Father on this earth. And I was mad at my Father because he forced me to take on a position that I was not fit to take. He didn't consider the fact that I wasn't devoted to the ministry before he ordained me to minister. Frustrated because I put my dreams aside just to fulfill his. And I took out all that pint up frustration out on my family. But it wasn't about my Father entirely... The problem was, was that I prayed for something that didn't work out for me. I asked God to do something that He didn't do. Then I had to sit up and look at other people succeed and flourish in the very thing that I wanted to do. I didn't see success in standing in a pulpit. I thought by now I would be further than that. That I could do the music and preach the gospel at the same time. That way I can fulfill the dream of my daddy and my dream all at the same time. But it hasn't worked out the way I planned. I thought that I could prove who I am and I became frustrated because everything had changed and what I envisioned for myself didn't happen. So not only was I angry with my daddy, but I was angry with myself and God."

"Jesus," Mother Esther said who was shaking her head, as tears ran down her cheeks.

"I couldn't be happy so they couldn't. I couldn't be who I wanted to be, so they couldn't I couldn't pick and choose the job, the friends, and the future I wanted so I was selfish enough to snatch theirs away. I followed the desires of the flesh and now I have another family that I created that has now been broken and torn." He said, looking at Joshua and Vanessa.

"I was angry with myself so I beat myself up and started beating up on those who I loved. So, as I was hitting my wife I was hitting me. Just because she was the closest thing I could hit without feeling the pain. The Bible says, that I must love my wife as I love myself. But I didn't love me, so I couldn't love her. I beat her, I beat my daughter, because I didn't like myself. Too angry over what didn't work out for me, angry over allowing my Father to choose a path for me, angry cause I didn't have it in me to say no, because saying no would disappoint him, and the frustration was driving me crazy. Unresolved frustration leads to failure. I failed at being a husband, failed at being a father, failed at being a preacher, and I almost failed at being me. Have anyone ever lost themselves just to find themselves? Have anyone ever lost, just to gain so much?" He asked, eyes filled with sorrow.

"I know I have." Murmured a man, beside me.

"But I have learned so much along the way. I didn't know the plan that God had for my life. I thought that I was supposed to be discovering talented R&B artists and be successful. Never fully realizing the success that God has already given me. The level of success is not in the money you make and how famous you are at making it, but to touch a life, reach a shattered soul, and to be used by God. Life was given to me so that I can live life serving God. And I give thanks to my Father, because although he may have given me the title too early, God is equipping me for the title right now. I had to go through a dark place so that I could see the light. Even though I messed up,

God was willing to give me another chance at getting this right. Now I am not a preacher who just preach, but I am a sheep of God that is being used to give a life-altering message to His people. I have accepted the Lord as my Lord and Savior and I have a long ways to go, but with your help and your prayers I know I can make it." He said, looking out at the congregation in tears.

"It's okay Pastor. We will pray your strength in the Lord. It is your transparency of imperfection that will allow the people of God to receive you all the more. Even Jonah had fallen, only to fall to his knees before he could really got the message. He was caught up, and had fallen into the belly of a whale until the Lord trusted him to carry out what he was set out to do. Now you've been in the pit of the whale, heard the Lord's voice, He has picked you up, now do what He has commanded you to do." Pastor Luke encouraged him, while patting him on the back.

"I am so humbled and so grateful that I have a church family like you guys. I thought for sure I'd be tossed in the lions den soaked in meat juice." He joked. Everyone laughed.

"We love you Pastor." Sister Annie Mae yelled out to him.

"I love y'all too." He smiled.

"First, I would like to ask that not only the members of this church for forgiveness but my family. I have made some inexcusable mistakes over the past years and there's no way I can take the things I did back. I've taken the time to seek God whole-heartedly and He has forgiven me for what I have done. But the most important thing is that I have been able to forgive myself. Dinah, you have been that virtuous wife and no matter what I did or said to you when I was drunk, you still forgave me." He said looking at her.

My mother moved uncomfortably in her seat, but she did not take her eyes off of him.

"I know I haven't been the best husband and father over the past few years but I'm determined to make a change. I have failed my parents, the church and I've failed you. You have always been the light of my life and understand that there was nothing you did that caused me to act in such a way. My own ways was of my own and when you tried to help me I pushed you out. I'm so sorry, Dinah and Danielle for the hell I've taken you through. I know it's going to take you two sometime and I'm going to do whatever I can to get back and your good graces. I love you, both." He said as tears quickly fell from his eyes.

"To Vanessa and Joshua… I am so sorry for bringing you into this mess. I know I hurt the both you. Vanessa I'm so sorry…" He said breaking down.

My heart went out to him and I thought about all the good times we had. When he would push me in the swings at the park, toss me up in the air until I'd had enough, tickle me until I begged for mercy and all the times he was there for me when I thought a monster was in my closet. I missed those times and I believed that he has changed. If God can forgive and forget, then so can I. At that moment, I walked up to him and hugged him.

"I forgive you, daddy. No matter what you are my father and I can't change that. I love you and I'm happy you're back to the old you." I said, kissing his cheek.

"Thank you sweet pea," he said as he hugged me.

The whole congregation was in tears.

When I turned around my mother was behind me, smiling. I moved out of the way and allowed her to hug my father. Following behind my mother was Joshua and Vanessa.

"Let's embrace this family and we pray that God keep them and heal their family. What God put together, no man shall tear apart. They will prosper and with faith their relationship will be stronger than ever. People we must forgive this man of God and help him get back to the place where God wants him to be." I could hear Pastor Luke said.

After we all cried together, prayed together, and rejoiced in the Lord together, my father had a talk with us—my mom and I and Vanessa and little Joshua.

"My father's death took a toll on me, I felt guilty for the way I treated him and before I could apologized he died. I thought alcohol would take it all away, but it destroyed me. Dinah, I must admit that

I cannot keep it all together, but with your help and with God's help I know I can make it. I will go to counseling and alcohol programs to help me as well. If you want a divorce I understand but if not I will fight until my last breath to make our marriage work." He cried.

My mother looked at Vanessa for approval.

"Oh girl, please don't make your decision on account of me. Like you told me, he was your husband first. If God has told you to take your husband back who am I to block it? I've already done enough. If you're looking for my blessing then you have it. All I ask is that we can remain friends and that Joshua will be welcomed into your family." She said.

"Yes, always." My mom said to her.

"Then carry on." She said waving her hands towards them.

We all laughed.

"Jonah… it took me some time to forgive you. It took even longer for me to find restoration. Thanks to God I have joy and I'm truly happy. I forgave you months ago, but I must admit that it will take some time to trust you. This will be your last chance to make things right. I warn you Jonah… Don't you ever put your hands on me again or Danielle. And if I smell a hint of alcohol on your breath I will sign those divorce papers so quick it'll make your head spin. I'm not your dog… I'm not your punching bag, but I am your wife. You are to treat me as your wife. I am NOT the woman that I used to be. I will not tolerate your foolishness. Do you understand?" She said boastfully.

"Yes…Dinah…I do…" He said as if he was a little puppy being chastised.

"Then I accept you." She said.

"I love you so much." He said hugging her.

"I love you Danielle and Joshua." He said hugging us too.

He looked at Vanessa and Vanessa gave him a hug. We all continued our conversation off at our apartment, while Vanessa and mom served dinner. My father stayed true to his word. He never put a liquor bottle to his mouth again. After we terminated our therapy sessions with the family therapist, my father was finally able to go back and pastor. Vanessa and Joshua still came over. She and my mother came together and opened up a shelter for battered women. My father proposed to my mother again and she accepted. They stood in front of the church and made vows to each other again. I could see the love in their eyes.

That spark that put our family back together... I have the slightest idea about how a marriage is supposed to be, but if I had to guess I believe that this is what it's all about. Having the courage to overcome hardship, pain, test, and trials in order to embrace change, gain wisdom, and come together in laughter, love, and forgiveness... This is what love is all about. This is what Jesus demonstrates everyday... We may fall short, let Him down, and even disappoint Him when we make bad decisions. But no matter what we do, we could never do anything that will make Him hate us. When He loves He loves for real... sacrificially and unconditionally. I was amazed... My parents survived inspite of the broken pieces.

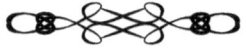

www.ingramcontent.com/pod-product-compliance
Lightning Source LLC
Chambersburg PA
CBHW070049260626
47160CB00004B/1150